The Night Clock

Paul
Meloy

First published 2015 by Solaris
an imprint of Rebellion Publishing Ltd,
Riverside House, Osney Mead,
Oxford, OX2 0ES, UK

www.solarisbooks.com

UK ISBN: 978 1 78108 375 8
US ISBN: 978 1 78108 376 5

Designed & typeset by Rebellion Publishing

Printed and bound by
CPI Group (UK) Ltd, Croydon, CR0 4YY

There are weapons down there, weapons with *minds*,
The armaments, darling, of the compartments of Hell.
They *clamber*, these weapons, my dearest, they *climb*,
At the awful sound of the Night Clock's chime.

I PULL LES out of the pub. He doesn't complain. He's a good old boy. He just raises his eyebrows and resists me long enough to put his pint down on the table nearest the door. I've grabbed Les because he'll know; Les knows most things and he's the one I call on when I come here. We go outside onto the street. It's a winding road through the village. You can see the hills climbing away behind the terraced cottages across the road. They begin to rise at the end of the long, narrow gardens and small allotments and roll gently into the distance, verdant and rugged. There's another pub directly opposite ours. It's called The Night Clock. It's set back from the road and has benches out front. We don't go there. Things come out from it and we have to fight them. We think the cellar is a compartment of Hell. So Les and I step outside and it's bright blue sky and soft, warm summer air. Les looks up and shields his eyes with his hand. He squints, it's so bright. He's wearing brown corduroy trousers and a blue pullover the colour of the sky. I need to know something. It's urgent but I don't really know what it is, or how to articulate my need, but as usual, Les gets it. "Ah, yes," he says. "That's Mercury." I look up and now I can see it, too. It's been there all along, a pale and spectral disc. It's about a third the diameter of the moon and is hanging over the village like a pallid eye just opened and already closing. As I watch it seems to drift across the sky like it wants to set behind the pitched roof of our pub. But this isn't what I needed to know. It's chilling and wonderful but not what I needed Les for.

EARLIER I'M SITTING alone at one of the wooden benches in front of the pub we don't go into. Behind me the honeysuckle growing over the porch is rotting, a blackening swag of compost, and the windows either side of the door are screens showing the bright reflection of the sky dulled like the silver at the back of an ancient mirror. I'm kicking my feet in the dust and thinking. Across the road I can hear voices from our pub, THe Dog WitH itS EyeS SHut, but this makes me feel lonely and I get up off the bench and walk onto the path. There's something in the sky. I look up and see, moving with an unusual flickering, stop-frame jerkiness, a flying creature circling above me. It is quite large and has wings webbed like a bat and full of holes. Its legs and arms are thin like twigs and its head is odd, insect-like. It drops lower through the blue sky and makes a sound like a jackdaw; a metallic clattering that fills me with sudden, profound disgust.

THE SKY WAS white, featureless, and cold. I was sitting by the window in a carriage on a train. The tracks ran straight, past low fences at the ends of long back gardens. And then the train had stopped, and I was walking along a verge towards a space of grass. It was snowing; the snow had lain deep very fast. At the end of one of the long, bare gardens a little girl played with a pile of cogs. She was small, aged about three, and was wearing a grey flat cap. She looked up at me as I stood there, my hands in my pockets, tears in my eyes. She didn't smile and her expression remained serious as she played in the snow at the end of this garden with those cogs in her cold hands. But somehow I felt her love for me, her good will, and I wanted so much to hold her.

* * *

HE AWAKENS FROM these dreams in the small hours of every morning, at twenty past three exactly, and he's weeping and he feels so tired. And he knows this place is real and he needs to find its equivalent in the waking world and all he can hear is the Night Clock, ticking, and ticking.

What is the Night Clock?

I see a wooden tower that leans back against a dark and restive sky. Clouds reel away in an unending stream behind it. I see a painted clock face; grey, peeling, and painted hands at five past three. The tower is empty; there are no workings, no cogs or wheels; no pendulum sways the seconds away.

Yet still, the Night Clock ticks.

1

LEWIS WATCHED BARRY Cook stumble across the lawn with the green loop of a hosepipe caught around his ankle. He stopped, looked up. Lewis froze as Barry's eyes, redblack as blood blisters, fixed on the kitchen window; his tongue lolled, redblack too, behind his teeth. His left arm reached out, fingers clawed, and made a feeble grabbing motion toward the window. His right arm was gone; just a stump remained, congealed and tattered, torn off at the shoulder. Through the glass, Lewis could just make out a low, miserable moaning sound. Barry looked down at the hosepipe snagging his ankle.

Barry reached down, fingers still making that reflexive grabbing motion, and tried to unhook the hosepipe. The task was beyond him; he toppled forward and cracked his forehead against the marble birdbath.

"Someone should put that poor sod out of his misery," Dawn, Lewis's mother, said as she joined Lewis at the window. She shook her head as Barry began levering himself up, using his one arm to push himself to his knees, his chin resting on the rim of the birdbath. He had sustained a gaping, bloodless gash to his brow. His expression was one of stunned incomprehension, that of someone perhaps fallen victim to fierce and unanticipated incontinence.

Barry regained his feet. The fall had dislodged the hosepipe and Barry used this new freedom of movement to gather enough momentum to propel him up the garden towards the house. He reeled across the patio and thudded against the back door. Dawn gasped, pushed past Lewis and tried to fumble the bolt across but Barry was already pushing his way into the kitchen. The side of his face and his butchered shoulder pressed against the frame, one unlit crimson eye glaring through the gap, the final incredulity of his own astonishing death still embossed in its expression. His mouth opened and he uttered a choked, throaty shout.

Dawn leant against the door. "Go away, Barry!" she hissed. Barry's expression didn't change but at the mention of his name he doubled his efforts to get in. He was feeble but the kitchen tiles were slippery, Dawn was small, and she was wearing socks. Gradually, Barry managed to shove the door wide enough to squeeze his upper body and one leg through. Dawn staggered backwards and sprawled across the large wooden table that stood in the middle of the kitchen. Lewis ran to his mum and they stood together, their backs to the cooker, while Barry uttered more insensate cries, flailed one arm about, and gawped around the kitchen with those awful congested eyes.

As Dawn and Lewis began edging away from the cooker, keeping the kitchen table between them and Barry, trying to get across the room to the door to the hall, Barry made up his mind what he wanted. He lunged for the cooker.

Dawn and Lewis dodged away and made it to the hall. They heard a clatter and they both turned. Barry was at the stove. He was standing with his belly up against the oven door, leaning over the large saucepan of beef chilli Dawn had been stirring. He cocked his head and seemed for a moment to be responding to some kind of internal stimuli, perhaps just the aroma of the chilli and nothing more than that—a trace memory of chemical detection still functioning in his poor decomposing head; then he raised his left arm and thrust his hand into the pan. Dawn and Lewis cringed against each other as Barry scooped up palmfuls of steaming chilli and shoved them into his mouth. He choked, unable to swallow and a wad of mince flew against the tiles and slid down behind the grill. He plunged his hand into the pan again, and forced in another mouthful. This time he turned and displayed his sauce-smeared jaw to Dawn and Lewis. His mouth was jammed wide with a dense bolas of mince and kidney beans. His left arm was red up to the elbow; drops of sauce flew from the ends of his fingers. Barry staggered back against the cooker and clawed at his face. His eyes bulged.

The kitchen door banged open and a man came in carrying a pitchfork. He squared his shoulders and took the pitchfork in both hands. "Come on, Barry. Time to go," he said and walked across the kitchen.

Barry shambled backwards, clattering into the cooker. His arm came up and he waved it in the man's direction. The man advanced. Barry's eyes continued to bulge but Dawn thought for a second she could see something new in his expression; fear perhaps? Barry's last *knowing* thought?

Barry tried to bolt but the man came up behind him and thrust the pitchfork through the middle of his back. Barry's mouth flew wider still and the wad of chilli was ejected onto the draining board. He made an awful cackling, throat-filled rattle as the tines of the pitchfork punched through his chest. The man braced himself and leaned down on the handle. Barry went up on his toes. The man moved to his right. Barry sagged a little then swung to his left. He looked at Dawn as he was pushed past the door to the hall and Dawn could see resignation on his face, even if it was partially masked behind chilli sauce. Despite his condition, and in some primal way, Barry Cook knew his future.

Dawn and Lewis edged out of the hall and went to the door. They held hands and watched as the man propelled Barry down the garden, across the lane and into the field opposite. Two men were walking towards the middle of the field. They stood together and waited for the man with the pitchfork to reach them. They were carrying jerry cans. They looked grainy and insubstantial in the overcast early-morning light, like an image on a hand-cranked camera. The man drove Barry across the field, both of them stumbling amidst the dark, blocky chunks of turned earth until they reached the others.

The man stopped in front of the others. Barry hung from the tines of the pitchfork, his head down, arm limp by his side. One of the men approached and appeared to speak to him. Barry opened his mouth and tried to flail him away. Dawn heard his rasping shout, borne across to her on that sodden wind, and it was that as much as the sight of the cans of liquid being poured over him, and one of the men returning to strike the light, that made Dawn turn away from Barry, set ablaze up there on the hillside.

2

ACROSS THE FLOOR of the play area, she pushes the wheeled wedge of the VTech baby walker. It looks like she's been left to play in a frame of a cartoon the colours are so bright and unusual. The walker has a voice. It sings in an accent that is surprisingly highborn, like a throwback to *Watch with Mother*.

She runs in her socks, tiptoe, delicate.

A father in Matalan clothes with a blue chin ponders his son engulfed in the ball pit, nourished by the new adolescence of divorce; the sulks, the drink, the *self*. She's sitting on the floor playing with a drum. The carpet tiles are a hideous stormy blue, a laboratory colour concocted to suggest good cheer by scientists with antisocial personalities. She looks like a chimney thrown into relief against a thundercloud.

One of the children is jocose with Down's syndrome. He plays in eternal delight, with hands displaying the form and dexterity of a drunken labourer, with a heap of stacking blocks. He seems a happy refutation of evolution.

She's on the plastic slide; she waves. Leftley waves back. She's trying to avoid the unwanted attention of a three-year-old called Olly who keeps approaching her with an open and mystified expression.

Now she's horned in on another girl's playtime with her mother on a dwarfish pine rocking horse. There's an unspoken obligation to be inclusive, but who wants the bother of someone else's kid? Her narrow sidelong glances over at Leftley sitting there in his chair with his book indicate a wish for him to entertain his own kid. He smiles and takes a sip of his coffee.

He watches her play at a low table with some kind of tortured abacus attached to it. She plays sweetly with the other children.

Leftley finishes his coffee, closes his book—it's *A Confederacy of Dunces* by John Kennedy Toole, his favourite book—and puts it on the table next to a cold bowl of chips he had bought for his daughter half an hour earlier. There's a sachet of vinegar and some salt and pepper. He was going to share with her, putting some chips on a serviette before dousing his own, but she was too busy playing and he didn't really feel that hungry.

She's waving again.

He doesn't wave back this time.

Instead, he reaches into the sports bag at the side of his chair.

He stands, a gun in his hand, walks towards the play area, and starts shooting.

NEIL GOLLICK WAS happy with his limitations. Said limitations were externally imposed and so boundaried him with a municipal comfort. He patrolled his roads and alleyways, overpasses and balconies, with easy confidence. He wore the rustling, high-visibility coat, the waterproof trousers, and the slash-peaked cap with authority, and with the buoyancy of an astronaut riding within the complex, life-sustaining casing of his space suit. He had everything he needed on his belt and in his many capacious inner and outer pockets.

Gollick was a bit of a cock. Everyone that knew him, worked with him or had the misfortune to run afoul of him on the streets of the estate, thought as much. A small dog had once nipped a tiny turd off on a verge while its owner, an elderly lady, kyphotic and bandy, had been chatting to a friend at the bus stop and had not noticed her pet trembling at the end of its leash. But Gollick had noticed and had presented the old girl with a ticket, a fine. Forty quid.

He'd laughed as he'd watched her attempt to right the wrong, plucking at the soggy mess with a fragile leaf of Kleenex, watching it cake her fingers. She needn't have bothered.

Police Community Support Officer Gollick was the guardian of minor civic misdemeanours. His powers were boundaried by a strict code of professional conduct and if you give a fool a set of rules you can be sure he will apply them without an iota of flexibility. Why is this? The more menial the job the more rigidly those employed to execute it enforce their regulations. Have you ever sat blocked in your car while a dustcart shudders like a docking ferry in the middle of the road and watched as its malodorous operatives stroll its flanks dreaming only of what might come later, after work; beers, footie, *gash*?

Gollick marched through the long, cold shadows of the overpasses with an assured step. Eastern Europeans passed him; Gollick could tell them by their big hard faces, round-headed with complexions like dusty grey stone, small fierce eyes, ex-army physiques and terrible strength in their hands. The girls had great bodies but faces like a witness description.

Gollick emerged onto a wide expanse of concrete. Behind him rose one of the blocks of flats that stood in a row across the middle of the estate. Their balconies were painted in faded toy box colours, an attempt to make them appear optimistic, welcoming, but all that they achieved was a dissipated and domineering aspect; they were full of filth, with atriums of blasted charcoal caused by arson and faulty wiring, piss-puddled nodes and walls tigered with forensic stripes of blood and bile.

How could there be authentic *cheer* here? Gollick hated it, but appreciated that it needed to exist, with its perplexing and demoralising warrens, inbuilt structural rot, gutters, alleys and stairwells choked with domestic and human waste, in the same way ghettoes and shanties were an unavoidable feature of society in other parts of the world. Gollick continued his patrol. His heavy boots strode across the fractured pavement, across constellations of chewing gum grey and imperishable with age, his coat and trousers crackling like a crisp packet. He eyed the buildings, the low utilitarian blocks of housing, the lockups and the garages with both vigilance and proprietorial licence. His mind was clear of distraction, indeed clear of most things. Gollick was on his rounds and the estate was a safer place for having his visible and reassuring presence.

Gollick crossed the main road that ran through the estate and approached the shopping parade. Two shops remained open: a Ladbrokes and Balv's, the general store. Everything else was boarded up. The parade was sheltered beneath a concrete walkway. At the end of the walkway was the estate pub, the Snowcat. It had reinforced glass windows and the edges of its flat roof were tinselled with rolls of razor wire. There was an old bench outside and a plank table. The table held at least six wide metal ashtrays each containing a pile of cigarette butts built up with the care and complexity of a model for ancient Incan architecture.

Gollick entered Balv's. Not so long ago he had stumbled upon a crime being committed in the shop. As he had approached the parade, rainlashed and cagouled, on a nasty autumn morning, Gollick had heard the distinct sound of banging. Trepidation augmented by the rigours of training prevented him from running towards the sound, and so he stopped and pressed himself against the shuttered metal door covering the front of the old kebab shop next door. The metal gave a little beneath his bulk and made a sound like a car reversing into a garage door. Gollick kept calm and stepped back out onto the parade.

With great caution, he crept along beneath the stained and unlit shelf of the walkway until he reached the edge of Balv's shopfront window. The banging continued and Gollick could see the door shuddering in its frame. Opposite was a thick concrete pillar, one of eight holding up the walkway. Gollick took a couple of steps back and shuffled over to the pillar. Thus concealed, he could peer around and take a peek at what was going on. His gloved hands gripped the mottled sides of the pillar and he leaned out.

What he saw filled him with amazement. Not content with just locking the door and flipping the CLOSED sign over, a large black man in a hooded jacket was taking the additional precaution of sealing himself into the shop by hammering a fistful of six-inch nails into the doorframe. Gollick could see beyond the man, along the aisle that led up to the till, and noted the presence of a second man who was holding a baseball bat a few inches from poor old Balv's ear as he pressed the proprietor's face into the counter. Balv wasn't struggling.

Gollick had withdrawn at this point. He went through his mental checklist of responsibilities. Under no circumstances was he to intervene in a way that might increase the threat of potential violence at the scene of a crime. That was the job of the police. Finding himself in this situation, Gollick could only praise the wisdom of this injunction. He had powers to detain but not of arrest; he carried no cuffs, no baton, no incapacitating sprays. He wore a padded stab vest, but that was his choice and not a mandatory requirement.

What to do, though? A concern made more pressing as Gollick heard a muted shout of distress from within the shop and the sound of something hollow—the baseball bat had looked aluminium—impacting on something else of a more solid composition.

Gollick decided to investigate the rear of the shop. He crept out from behind the pillar and trotted the length of the rain swept promenade until he arrived at the gated entrance to the Snowcat. He turned and had a look back. The hammering had stopped. All he could hear was the sound of the rain blowing in spattering sheets against the sides of the buildings. He dodged around the side of the pub and went to where there was a wooden fence corralling a small yard full of stainless steel beer kegs and old wooden crates. He stood on tiptoes and peered over the fence. He could see the back entrance to the pub but it was shut, probably locked. No one about. Gollick lowered himself onto the soles of his boots and padded around the back of the building. There was a narrow alley giving onto the rear of the parade and, to the right, the exiguous gardens belonging to a block of bungalows running parallel to it.

Gollick crept along the alley until he came to a gate sentried on either side by piles of bulging black bin bags. The rain was a fine mist and Gollick squinted through it to see that the gate was ajar. The bottom of the gate rucked up a thick lip of mud as he pushed it open and he stepped through into the yard at the back of Balv's shop. Ahead was a door that was inset with a small, filthy window. Gollick stole up to the door, past piles of crates, pallets and saturated cardboard boxes, their sides sunken in like gaunt cheeks and giving off a dim smell of must.

Gollick peered through the window. He could see through the length of the storeroom and could make out the shape of Balv's skinny old buttocks and legs, rickety with distress, as he was being forced to bend over the counter and receive repeated and savage blows to the side of his head from the baseball bat wielded by his assailant. Gollick winced every time the bat chimed off the old man's skull.

Gollick's hand hovered above the handle. And then he remembered his prime directive and pulled it away. He sighed with relief.

And then he remembered something else and backed away from the door as quietly as he could, his heart pounding in his chest. What a fool he was, he thought. All that training, that entire *week*, nearly wasted in the heat of the moment! He turned and went back through the gate into the alley. He pulled the gate shut behind him. Then he trotted the remaining length of the alley and came out into a space bordered on both sides by lock-up garages.

Gollick rested for a moment.

How could he have forgotten that the shop door had been *nailed* shut! That meant the only way out for the robbers would be by the back door and into the alley. Gollick had risked compromising the mission by being discovered. He shook his head and took off at a light jog across a green towards the community centre. He must have appeared odd, a bulky figure, hunched and loping through the misty rain, like grainy footage of Bigfoot shying away from prying eyes.

As he ran, Gollick reached up into his cagoule and unhooked

his radio. He pressed the button and seconds later was reporting hearing a disturbance coming from the Reservoir End Estate general store and he would be proceeding with caution to investigate.

Gollick reckoned he'd give it ten minutes and then saunter back.

Having fulfilled his duty, Gollick nipped up the steps to the community centre and had his first complimentary cup of tea of the morning, care of Maude, the voluntary hostess, who liked to support her local police, and who just happened to be the self same lady to be issued a ticket by Officer Gollick a few weeks later for letting her dog curl a sneaky one down on a verge by the bus stop.

Now, GOLLICK WAS inside the store, and looking at the aisles of goods piled high on the shelves, marked up to the kind of eye-watering prices found only in shops enjoying very little or no competition and patronised by those unable, or unmotivated, to travel further for their shopping.

"We got raspberry ruffles better than half price, boss," someone said, as if reading Gollick's thoughts.

Startled, Gollick looked around. From somewhere below him and to the left, the person said, "And we just got some of them mobile phone facials in, plastic, pretty, innit. For the kids. Up by the till."

Gollick looked down and saw Beanie, Balv's nephew, standing in the aisle beside him. It was gloomy in the shop, and frigid. Light and heating, thought Gollick, detrimental to profit margins. First things to go.

Beanie the dwarf grinned up at Gollick. Since the attack, Balv had been unable to continue running the shop owing to nerves and a steel plate in his head, and had passed the reins to his nephew. Beanie, previously busy with his mobile disco, had taken on the role of shopkeeper with an enormous amount of disinclination and indifference. Takings were down. He bought in a lot from the more diverse suppliers, the kind of unsavoury joke shop tat Balv previously demurred owing to his strict religious observance, and Beanie certainly stocked a great deal more porn. The shop window was covered in posters advertising *BEANIE'S MOBILE DISCO AND KARAOKE, available for weddings, hen/stag nights and children's parties* and displayed a picture of Beanie in sunglasses and a baseball cap manning his decks and giving a stumpy double thumbs-up to the camera.

Today Beanie was dressed in a child's parka, mittens and snow boots. The oblong bulge of his head seemed to squeeze against the hood of the parka like that of some inquisitive savage leering out from a tufted shrub. He was carrying a box of miscellany that he was distributing around the store. He pulled a four-pack of coloured cigarette lighters from the box and poked them sideways into a gap between some tins of vegetable bhuna. They were priced at three pounds but Gollick knew you could pick them up for a quid in the cheap shop in town.

"Just doing my rounds," Gollick told him, squaring his shoulders. "How's old Balv?"

Beanie shrugged with disinterest. "He's just sitting in the back, innit. Jibbling down his chin, like. Don't say nuffin at all though. Hey, you want a free cock mag? Just help yourself, chap." Beanie shuffled past Gollick and disappeared around the next aisle. Gollick heard him muttering and trying to jam things into available gaps.

Gollick approached the counter. In the back of the shop, between the counter and the storeroom was a small room that passed as a kitchen. There was a sink and a table with a kettle on it. Sitting in a grimy, hollowed-out armchair was the old shopkeeper, Balv. There was a pinched, white dent in the side of his head, scarring from where he'd undergone the emergency surgery to shore up his skull.

Gollick coughed.

There was no response from Balv. He continued to sit staring into the distance, his eyes glazed and tragic, with a sheen of saliva coating his chin.

Gollick coughed again, more loudly, and raised a hand. "Morning, Balv," he said.

It was entirely possible that Balv was dead, so negligible was Beanie's attention to him, and Gollick felt suddenly foolish. He'd saved Balv's life after all, and it was terrible to see him reduced to this mindless crust. A small part of Gollick remained sour that the old man had never recovered enough to thank him.

Gollick returned to the shop door. Beanie was watching him from the corner over by the Lottery machine. He was smiling, and looked – as he'd always looked to Gollick – like he was taking the piss. Beanie raised a diminutive mittened hand and waved.

Gollick was about to leave the shop when he was barged aside by a tall figure coming through the door. Gollick wrinkled his nose as the figure pushed past and headed up the drinks aisle.

Beanie ducked behind the counter and climbed onto his stool.

Gollick decided to wait a moment.

The man stumbled to the counter carrying a pair of two-litre plastic bottles of cider which he slammed down like a soldier under fire unloading huge shells of ordnance before returning for two more.

Gollick watched as the man paid with coins and shoved the bottles into two plastic carrier bags. He was mumbling, "Fuckin' charge me for bags you burnt smurf."

Unoffended, Beanie rang up the purchase. "Overheads, innit." He said.

The man grunted and swung around, the bags clenched in his bony fists. He saw Gollick standing by the door and his expression changed, notching quickly up from disgruntlement to aversion. He continued down the aisle and edged past Gollick without looking him in the eye.

Gollick smiled and opened the door for him. "Good morning, Rob," he said. "Stocking up for a productive day?"

The man ignored him and left the shop. Gollick decided to follow him.

He watched the man traipse across the car park and make for a bench over the main road in front of the school. He threw himself down and pulled a bottle from one of the bags. Gollick walked over.

The man looked up, his eyes narrowing.

Gollick appraised him, taking in the long, greasy black hair streaked with grey, and the beard, likewise grizzled with a hint of some uncommon solid diet still clinging to the strands around his mouth. A pallor indicative of a liver the size and function of an old individual meat pie. And army camouflage gear, jacket and trousers; an outfit contrived, Gollick imagined, to imply danger and caution people away. And big black biker boots. Very intimidating but hardly functional as weapons in a fight as the poor sod hardly had the strength to put one foot in front of the other.

"Oh, fuck off, Neil," the man said. "Leave me alone."

"Goodness me, Rob," said Gollick, feigning surprise, "I didn't see you there with all that camouflage gear on. You're nearly invisible. Remarkable feat of concealment. Very effective—"

"I said fuck. Off."

Gollick watched as the man took a bottle from a bag and stuck it between his knees. He unscrewed the top and lifted the bottle to his mouth. He gazed at Gollick with a rheumy expression of defiant content as half a litre of laboratory cider swilled down his throat.

"You can't sit there outside the school and drink," Gollick said.

Rob lowered the bottle and sighed. "It's half term, Neil."

Gollick looked over Rob's head at the empty playground and low, lifeless prefabricated buildings. "Well, you need to move on."

ROB SAT BACK and crossed his legs. He had another swig from the bottle. He stared past Gollick towards the community centre.

"Why don't you just piss off back to the tea shop and harass some grannies, Neil?"

"Don't talk to me like that," Gollick commanded.

Rob sighed again, licked his lips. Once, he and Gollick had been friends; they'd gone to school together, grown up on the estate together. Neil Gollick and Robert Litchin had been *mates*. He recalled the slow deterioration of things, things specific leading to things overall. Things. Rob thought a lot about *things*.

While he sat in his flat, or if the weather was amenable, one of his spots around the estate, Rob drank and thought often about killing himself. That had begun to preoccupy him a lot recently. He didn't question it; it seemed to him to be a logical ordering of thoughts. Once certain paths had been trodden, certain choices made, then it seemed only a matter of time before the mind turned in on itself and began to cascade despair along its pathways. It felt like the passage of some thick, hellish tar, coating an infinite network of flumes until nothing good, clean or useful could pass along without becoming degraded in filth.

Before the booze kicked in and hazed somewhat the bleak itinerary of his downfall, Rob would be prone to early-morning recollections. Staring at the bare, scuffed walls of his flat as he laced his boots, Rob would remember, with a brief and insufferable clarity, the fact that he had once had it all. The house, the job, the girl. Stuff. He'd had some great stuff. And now it was all gone.

Like all heavy social drinkers, Rob had experienced a brief period of ascent as the sauce took hold, a sense of being invulnerable; he had found his peace in the ordered and undemanding routine of customary intoxication.

Rob had money at first, because he had a job, and acquaintances, because he socialised. A sense of well-being suffused him and he felt, for a while, so free—the world, because it feeds him the bright enlightenment liquor brings, is his very good friend and takes him on a new adventure. This adventure is enhanced by a liberating loss of judgment that is mistaken for spontaneity and self-actualisation.

There's a woman down the pub who is also self-medicating with alcohol, in her case to escape the reality of a neglectful and abusive husband. Her eyes are dead but her breasts heave with mountainous, floury warmth beneath her low-cut tops and her décolletage is only just beginning to crease into the loose artex of the fiftyish sunbed habitué, her lips are still full and are yet to display too many of the pinched striations common to the chain-smoker, and it is discovered one evening on a sprung sofa back at hers in front of a grate of cold but still fragrant apple wood logs, following another bottle of cheap white wine picked up at Balv's, that she gives a stupendous gobble, and that's that.

Now things are really looking up because he's out every night, coming back late and getting to slip this woman a length of the old pipe supreme. He neglects his girl and she starts to nag but he feels a bit invincible now even though things are starting to slide, like personal hygiene. He struts; his new piece tells him he's big, even though he's clearly not, and there's nothing like the feeling of popping against the spongy ring of tonsils at the back of her throat. His thinking is becoming a bit limited. Work is suffering because he slips away early, or doesn't go in at all. There's a stool at the end of the bar he likes to get to first. He likes to sit at the sun-dappled bar in the late afternoon and watch the place fill up. He relaxes. He can stop and think, or think he's thinking. By dusk the anxiety's gone and he can think about later, about tomorrow, maybe—just about think that far but really no further—then think about the laughter around him, the fire in the grate, the brisk smell of autumn whenever the door opens and someone blows in.

His girlfriend finds out about the other woman and leaves him. She takes quite a lot of stuff so he's left mostly with the shit. But there's still the record collection—quite a lot of rare vinyl there— and his World War II memorabilia, and his air rifles.

He likes hunting rabbits in the fields that surround the village. One day he takes a friend, a young lad he's met in the pub and got talking to, in order to impress him with his rustic approach to life, but he can't hit a cow's arse with a banjo. In the end he takes out a juvenile rabbit from about four feet. It jumps so high and fast he thinks for a second the fucker's teleported. Then he sees it lying by a hay bale. Its eyes are wide with shock but it's alive. The boy from the pub is watching and is clearly upset; the rifle he borrowed is hanging slack in his arms—he's not fired a shot all morning, just stood enjoying the misty morning light and the clarified air. This was about being up early, about the stealth and secrecy of being with the dawn, not about the focused revulsion of taking something's life.

So with the boy watching, he looks down at the rabbit and feels like he has to act like the hardened tracker, and fires three pellets at point blank range into the side of the rabbit's head.

They walk back to the house in silence, the rabbit thrown over his shoulder like bagged game. In fact it looks pathetic, a furry epaulette. He slings it on top of the chest freezer in the utility room when he gets back, and he imagines the boy is expecting that by dinner time there will be rabbit stew on the menu.

He cracks some beers in an attempt to keep things sociable and they watch some porn together in awkward silence, just the slow sound of lips pinging off the tins and long self-conscious swallows over the ripe sounds of fucking, which all seems terribly misjudged, because he doesn't ever socialise with this boy again after today— and in reality he ends up throwing the tiny corpse of the rabbit into the bin two days later, trailed by a confetti of tiny white maggots before putting a frozen Admiral's pie in the microwave.

So, the job's gone now. His talent got him a job working for a small, independent computer graphics firm. He wasn't getting anything done, which, when confronted, really threw him. He protested, because he was sure he was all over it. But, no. He'd achieved fuck all in six months.

His hair is long, his beard substantial. He's always favoured the old army fatigues as they complied with his self-image of the woodsman-survivalist type. His catchphrases were once the celebration of the pub, now they seem to grate on the regulars and he ends up sitting alone. Now he gets absolutely slaughtered and by then he's feeling okay and the anxiety's gone. The woman he was shagging hasn't been out for ages as her husband has put her in hospital again.

There's a shop in town that buys stuff, so he sells his records, his WWII memorabilia and his air rifles. The money goes on drink; there's a pub near the shop with a stool at the bar he likes to sit on and watch the place fill up. There's a bus back to his village that runs until 11.30.

When it's all gone, he loses the house and moves into a shitty flat on the estate. It's okay.

It's just not okay first thing in the morning.

* * *

ROB WAS ONLY vaguely aware of Gollick lecturing him. He was only one bottle of cider into the day and didn't like being reminded of things. Gollick's presence was bringing it all back. Gollick the betrayer.

He shoved his empty bottle into an overflowing bin next to the bench and set another between his knees.

"Have you got access to the Internet at your mum's?" he said, interrupting Gollick.

"What?"

"The World Wide Web, Neil? Can you go online?"

"Of course," Gollick frowned. "Mother has a high speed connection."

Rob looked up at Gollick and grinned. "Well, when you go home for tea, go on YouTube and type in 'Cowardly copper bottles robbery' and see what you get."

"And why would I want to do that, Rob?" Gollick asked, a brisk current of unease threading up the backs of his legs and into his buttocks.

"Because," said Rob, lifting his second bottle to his mouth, "Beanie put the CCTV footage of you creeping around outside the shops and legging it from Balv's robbery on the net. Everyone's been pissing themselves at you for months. It's got *millions* of hits, Neil. You're a fucking joke."

"*Creeping*?" Gollick said, which, out of all the words in Rob's sentence he could have highlighted, seemed the one most offensive to his sense of self-regard.

"Sneaking," said Rob with relish. "Skulking. Basically, being a gutless twat, which is what we all know you are, anyway, but it's nice to have the proof, isn't it?"

"*Proof*?"

And then both men were startled from their discourse by the sound of gunshots.

GOLLICK FROZE. ROB leaped to his feet just as another shot was fired.

He clenched his bottle in reflex and a pale arc of cider spewed from the neck and splashed across Gollick's boots.

"That's coming from the community centre," Rob said.

Another shot, and now there was screaming. Both men looked across the green towards the block of buildings that contained the community drop-in centre and the indoor play area, Fizzy Willy's. The main doors were open and people were running out.

"Come on, Gollick, you fraud. Come and earn your pay!" Rob started to run across the green, his bottle held in both hands to prevent further spillage.

Gollick looked down at his boots. His head felt weightless, like a bulb of skin tethered to his body. His feet, however, seemed to be anchored suddenly to the surface of a large, alien planet made entirely of iron. His eyes swiveled towards the community centre. Rob was already nearly halfway across the green, his narrow shoulders hunched and his hair flying. He looked back once, and Gollick could see the expression of disgust on his face even from a distance, and then Rob tripped over his great clumping boots and fell on his drink. Another fountain of cider launched itself from beneath Rob's chest as he collapsed onto the bottle. Rob got to his feet and examined the bottle. It was flattened and split along its length but still held about half a litre. Rob held it sideways on his palms and continued jogging towards the centre, the remaining liquid sloshing about like fluid in a spirit level.

There was another shot followed immediately by two more. Gollick did some thinking. His thinking was naïve but steeped in the tradition of self-preservation; what he knew about guns was negligible, so he thought: six-shooter?

By the time Gollick had managed to unstick his feet and start running across the green, Rob was almost at the steps leading up to the community centre. A few people were still running out, and a woman had stopped to talk to Rob. She was crying, and pointing back inside the building. Rob appeared to be reassuring her. He was nodding. Then he gestured towards Gollick, and despite her distress, both she and Rob had a laugh. Then there was another shot, and Rob ushered the woman away. He waited at the bottom of the steps until Gollick arrived.

Panting, Gollick drew alongside Rob. "What's going on?" he asked.

"Some dad just pulled a gun in there and started shooting up the soft-play area."

Again, the content of Rob's sentence seemed to contain information too complex for Gollick to fully comprehend, and he said, "Soft-play area?" His active listening module either hadn't covered paraphrasing adequately, or he'd slept through it.

To simplify, Rob said, "He's shooting the children, Neil. Someone's called the police but you need to do something."

"What do you want me to do?" Gollick cried. "Incapacitate him with my alcohol wipes?"

"I don't fucking know. Come on, cunt, in for a penny!"

Rob climbed the steps and peered into the foyer. There was no sound of movement, but he could hear crying. Some children bawling and adults calling out in distress. "There's people trapped in there," he said.

Gollick lifted his alien boots a step at a time and met Rob at the door. Rob gripped the material of Gollick's coat at the elbow and pulled him through the doors.

They crept through the foyer, past all the posters proclaiming *welcome* in a hundred squiggly languages, and peered into the main hall. At the end of the hall was a desk and a low gate giving access to the play park. Still pulling Gollick behind him, Rob covered the distance across the hall, past the tea and cake counter, and drew up against the wall next to the gate. They could hear crying coming from within.

"Have you got any weapons?" Rob whispered.

Gollick shook his head. He was trembling so hard Rob had to yank on his sleeve to get him to stop rattling.

"Telescopic baton?"

"No."

"Body armour?"

"I've got a stab vest."

"That'll have to do. You go in first and distract him. I'll get behind that Bob the Builder ride over there and see if anyone's hurt."

"We should wait for the police," Gollick whined. "I'm not allowed—"

"Oh, for once in your life stop being a coward. Look at me. I'm fucked and I'm up for it."

Rob swung Gollick around and propelled him through the gate. He shoved the support officer across the floor and threw himself behind the ride, according to plan, but instead of doing anything useful, Gollick just stood frozen, staring at the tall, harried-looking man standing amongst the tables in front of the play area. He was pointing his gun at Gollick, and there were tears streaming down his face.

Rob could see a couple of people hiding amongst the scattered toys. Someone had immersed himself in the ball pit; whether he was protecting his children was unclear but Rob could see the top of a balding head sticking up amongst the coloured plastic balls like a cuckoo's egg in a profligate and fabulous nest.

Others were hiding behind the climbing frames and slides. Rob couldn't see any children. He glanced at Gollick, who was still standing petrified in the middle of the floor. The man with the gun raised it and pointed it at Gollick's head.

"I'm so sorry," he said, and fired.

Gollick screamed but a light fitting behind him and three feet to the left exploded as the bullet struck. Rob figured the guy for a lousy shot, and stood up.

"Hey! Fucker! Over here!" Rob shouted and stepped out from behind the ride. The man swung the gun towards him, and Rob drew back his arm and launched the quarter full plastic bottle of cider at him. It flew fast and true, and smacked the man in the side of the face. He grunted and fell to his knees. Rob moved towards him, but not before the man could fire again. The gun was pointed back in Gollick's direction, and Rob leaped across the floor and piled into Gollick as the gun went off. They both went sprawling.

Rob sat up, Gollick cradled in his arms. They were in the open and an easy target, but were saved from further attack because the man, who was sobbing now, was putting the gun to his own head.

"No," Rob said, but it came out as a whisper. Whether the negation ever reached the man's ears would forever remain a mystery because it was obliterated by the sound of the shot that blew his head apart.

"Ah, fuck!" said Rob. He looked down at Gollick who was trembling in his arms. He groaned. Gollick stirred, looked up into Rob's face. "He shot me, Rob."

Rob held him a bit tighter. "You'll be fine, Neil," he said.

Gollick whimpered. "I can't feel anything," he said in a quiet voice. His breathing was rapid and he was sweating.

"You'll live, Neil, I promise."

"But I'm shot."

"No, Neil, you're not. I am."

"Oh," Gollick breathed. "That's okay." Then he passed out.

3

Phil Trevena already knew Leftley was dead before he got called into the boss's office. A colleague had phoned him at home the previous evening and told him in triumph: "That bloke you saw this morning. He's topped himself."

Trevena went in early. He made a cup of tea in the kitchenette off the main office and dropped thirty pence through a slot gouged through the lid of a large coffee jar by the kettle. He nicked a couple of biscuits from the Christmas tin which had been gifted to the Assertive Outreach Team by a service user's grateful carer, and which was labelled with a sellotaped note encouraging the Crisis Team to get their own biscuits, and then he went and waited at his desk.

Trevena booted up his computer and tried to get onto eBay but the Trust's web blocker had already kicked in and denied him access. He sat back in his chair and sipped his tea. He brought up his emails.

CarolTrevena@aol.com to Phil.Trevena1@hotmail.com

Can u have Lizzie this wkend? I've got a chance to go to France with Clive.

Sorry its short notice. I know you're off this wkend.

He groaned and hit reply.

Fuck off. FUCK OFF. FUCK O

"Morning Phil," said Stibbs from behind Trevena's left shoulder. "Got a minute?"
Hit delete.
Do you want to save this to drafts?
Yes, he thought. *Yes I do*. He hit save.
"Yes, boss. I'll just grab a couple of biscuits."

STIBBS WAS NEW to the team. He'd been seconded from the Later Life Services to come in and shake things up. Everybody knew the Crisis Team was failing. Although the failures were systemic, over time they had become personalised, attributed to individual incompetences, always fertile grounds for scapegoating; because it was easier to blame one person's practice whenever there was a major incident, and it generated a nice little bit of vindication and professional smugness outside the team.

Trevena sat in the proffered chair in the corner of Stibbs's tight little office. There were touches of Stibbs all over the walls: photos, certificates and awards he'd got stuck up there as soon as he'd got the job. Trevena was patronised by motivational poster wisdom everywhere he looked. Stibbs seemed to view the world through a filter of stale aphorisms.

"I know how the grapevine works around here, Phil, so I won't waste your time. Nasty business on the estate yesterday. How do you feel about it all?"

Trevena respected him for his bluntness. He had three pink wafers balanced on his knee and he picked one up and nibbled it while he considered his question.

How did he feel about a man he had assessed the day before and found to have no mental illness, just a difficult context of social problems, having then gone straight out and shot up a play area and then committed suicide? Ed Leftley had been referred by his GP. He was a normal bloke with normal problems. A month ago he'd split up with his wife and had moved into a flat on the estate. He worked as a van driver but was having trouble concentrating so he got a sick note. His doc started him on some anti-depressants and gave it a month for them to kick in. Ed seemed to be doing well; his appetite improved a bit and he was getting some sleep again. He was seeing his kids and thinking about getting back to work. Then out of the blue he started getting suicidal thoughts. Vague at first, just fleeting ideas that everyone might just be better off if he wasn't around anymore. Then they started to preoccupy him and he found himself considering ways to do it. Ed was upset by these thoughts and went back to the docs, which is how he got referred. GPs are okay, they'll normally try to treat a bit of depression but they get twitchy when suicide's mentioned; too much risk. So the Crisis Team gets to have a look at them.

Trevena had seen him at home and he was a nice bloke. Pictures of his kids on the windowsill, a wedding photo on the mantelpiece. No overflowing ashtrays or empty bottles of booze. A well presented man in a clean, if barren, flat. Good eye contact, warm manner. Instant rapport. He was easy to assess. He assured Trevena there was no risk to himself or others and he was happy for the team to keep an eye on him over the next few weeks just to make sure things didn't get any worse. He said he was relieved to get some support because things were difficult sometimes and these thoughts about killing himself were something he'd never experienced before and he certainly had no intention of acting on them. In fact, symptomatically, he was very much on the mend. They had shaken hands and Trevena had said he'd pop over and see him again tomorrow. Ed was sorry to be a bother but Trevena assured him he was deserving of the same care as anyone else, and besides, this was his patch and he had a load of other visits to do on the estate so it would fit in nicely. Ed grinned, a bit abashed. A first episode of depression can really catch you unawares. It creeps up on you. Recovery has an unpredictable trajectory. There's up and downs;

good days and bad days. Don't worry too much, Ed, Trevena said. We'll look after you.

So how did he feel?

He felt gutted, and said so.

Stibbs nodded. He looked up at the pin board above his desk as if seeking guidance from his pantheon of chirpy bollocks. *You don't have to be mad to work here, but it helps… Look busy! Here comes the boss!!*

"Is there anything you need to put in your assessment you might now reconsider?"

Trevena had been thinking about this all night. And *no* was the answer. It's a terrible admission, but it happens. People kill themselves. Although to be fair, in seventeen years as a psychiatric nurse, this was the first time he'd been directly involved. He'd found a guy hanging once when he was still on the wards, but he'd been gone for hours and Trevena had just come on shift. And people he'd discharged, as well as they could be, well, a couple of them had gone off a year or so later and done it, but again, if people really want to do it, they don't present to services, they go and do it. But he'd never lost a patient he'd been working with, and he knew he got them through okay. Had he been lucky? Oh, definitely. But Trevena was also very good at his job.

But the system wasn't as forgiving as it used to be. There was no accumulation of good will or appreciation for the stress you were working under. You were only as good as your last fuck up. Maybe that was right. Maybe that was something they should have got their heads around by now. But…Trevena didn't know. It just all seems so unfeeling, and he was a sensitive guy.

Stibbs was looking at Trevena again. Big brown eyes. Solemn expression. Pathological narcissist.

"I'm asking, Phil, because as you know, there'll be an investigation. The media will be involved. It's looking very bad for the Trust."

God, how Stibbs loved his investigations.

Knowing Stibbs, and knowing narcissists, Trevena tried his best to reflect him back to himself in his response so Stibbs liked what he heard.

"I understand the necessity of an investigation, John, but I don't think I have anything else to add. I asked all the questions and ticked all the boxes. He was risky but he wasn't mad. I've been up all night thinking about this."

Stibbs nodded, all sagacity. "You're a good nurse, Phil. But you've been tired, under stress yourself. Do you think you need some time off?"

I'd love some time off, thought Trevena. I'd love to *retire*, to be perfectly honest. But he couldn't let Stibbs see a weakness.

"I'm okay, John. I need to let this sink in, get some supervision and be here while it goes through. And I've got a student half way through a placement. I don't want to drop Zoë in it now."

"She can work with Graham," Stibbs said.

Trevena must have looked hurt, because Stibbs turned conciliatory. "Just for a week or two. Graham won't ruin all your good work in that short a time." He grinned, but there was surprisingly little humour in it. Clever bastard. Undermine, manipulate, and make you fucking paranoid.

Trevena's wafer was sticking in his throat. "I'll be fine, John. I'll keep it in mind, though." He went to get up. Trevena suddenly felt the panic he'd been suppressing up until then beginning to rise and those posters were really starting to generate a lot of anger.

"Phil," Stibbs said. Trevena was at the door. He turned, hearing scorn in the little prick's voice now, and the implied threat.

"You need to be careful, Phil. This could look very bad for you."

Trevena left the office and went over to his desk.

He sat shaking for a full ten minutes until the rest of the team started to roll in at nine.

GRAHAM CAME OVER and put a hand on Trevena's shoulder.

"Heard about Ed Leftley," he said. "Sorry, mate. Could have been any of us."

Trevena had worked with Graham Knott for years. They'd been through the wards together and landed jobs with the Crisis Team at the same time, seven years ago, when they were setting it up. He was a big lad, six three, a proper old-fashioned mental nurse. He had a good nature but didn't take any shit.

"Thanks, mate," Trevena said. Graham leaned his backside against the edge of Trevena's desk. He folded his arms.

"This'll cheer you up," he said. "That girl up on the ward we banged up a week ago. Little self-harmer from the estate? Got that support worker from some rapey charity. Can't remember what it's called."

"Probably not that."

"No, probably not. Anyway, the night staff found her in her room last night putting broken glass up herself." Trevena looked up, his face a mask.

Graham nodded. "Gave herself a nasty gash."

"Fuck off and make me a cup of tea, Gray."

"All right, buddy."

LATER THAT MORNING, Graham came over again. Trevena was making notes in a Word document for the impending investigation.

"Got a little job, if you're interested."

"I'm not a gangster, Graham," Trevena said without looking up.

"None of us are. Especially you."

"That bloke who got shot at the play area yesterday. He's woken up in EAU and they've referred him to us because he's coming out with a load of mad stuff."

"And you've picked him up?"

"Mmm. Thought you might be interested in coming over with me and having a look."

Trevena stopped writing. He sat back in his chair. Stibbs would never allow it, would see it as *inappropriate*. "I can't get involved in the assessment, Gray. Stibbs sees my name on any of the paperwork he's going to lose his shit."

"I know, I know. Just come over. I've got his history, what they could give me of it, anyway. He's a massive pisshead so this might just be the ravings of a *very* thirsty man, but they've got him boated up on Librium so DTs aren't likely. His name's Robert Litchin. He sounds like fun."

Trevena looked up. Graham was grinning. He already had the paperwork in his hand.

Trevena closed his document. "Okay," he said. "I'm in."

THE EMERGENCY ASSESSMENT Unit was busy so Trevena and Graham were ushered into the ward by a harried staff nurse and pointed towards the bed at the far end of one of the bays. There was always pressure on beds so someone bearing an expression of desperate, calculating hope usually greeted them: *please take this patient away from us. Deliver us of this awful mental nuisance.*

They approached the bed. Rob Litchin was asleep, his mouth open, hair strewn across the pillow in scrawls. Behind his beard, his lips looked dry and cracked, like the perished opening to some old, long-ago emptied pot.

They took two chairs and sat next to the bed. Graham coughed. An eye opened in the sallow face and rolled in their direction. It fixed on Graham and glared.

"I'm Graham and this is Phil. We're from the Mental Health Crisis Team. You were referred to us this morning. Did the nurses tell you?"

The head nodded, just a slight dipping of the chin. The other eye struggled open.

"You look a bit dry," Graham said. "Would you like a drink?" He reached for the plastic water jug on the bedside locker.

"Are you taking the piss?" Rob croaked. He pushed himself up the bed a little so that his shoulders were propped against the headboard. He smacked his lips.

"Sorry, it's just water," Graham smiled and handed Rob a plastic tumbler pearly with age and numberless journeys through the industrial washers.

Rob eyed them with suspicion as he took a drink. "Thanks," he said, and put the tumbler back on the cabinet with a hand afflicted with a coarse tremor.

"Can I call you Robert?" Graham asked.

"Nah. It's Rob. Call me Rob. Robert was someone else."

"Okay, Rob. So, what happened to you, then?"

"You don't know?"

"I know bits. I know you got shot. Must have been terrifying."

Rob sighed and closed his eyes.

"Got shot in the arm," he said. He confirmed this statement by looking down at the bandage covering his forearm.

"Nicked the wrist bone, I hear." Graham said.

Rob nodded. "Didn't feel a thing," he said. "Adrenaline."

"Some chemical like that, I reckon," Graham said.

Trevena coughed.

"So," said Graham. "The nurses told us that when you woke up this morning you were a bit upset. You were talking about monsters on the estate? You were saying you didn't want to go back home and that you'd be better off dead?"

"I remember." Rob said.

"Do you still feel like that?"

Rob shrugged. "I don't know. I suppose. What happened to Neil?"

"Who?"

"Neil Gollick. The bloke I saved."

Graham turned to look at Trevena. Trevena shook his head.

"He's *dead*?"

"No. No, he's fine," Graham said. "We're just not sure where he is now. I suppose he's at home. That's where I'd be."

Rob settled back onto his pillow. He looked relieved.

"Was he a friend of yours?"

Rob shook his head. "No. Well, we go back a way, you know. School. We used to be friends but he let me down."

Graham remained silent. He was letting Rob talk, establishing the all-important rapport. Trevena sat back in his chair and crossed his legs.

"He let you down." A statement.

"Yes. He knew I was knocking off this woman on my estate and he told my girlfriend. Finished me."

Despite his years in the job, Trevena was still regularly taken by how easy it was to get people to reveal the most awful secrets. They were *desperate* to spill.

Graham was nodding and leaning forward in his chair. "It's been downhill since then?"

Rob stared at the ceiling. "All the way to the bottom," he said.

"Okay," Graham said. "Tell us about the suicidal thoughts."

Rob blinked, his eyes moist. "What's the point in going on? I've had it. I see things I can't explain. It scares me. I think about topping myself all the time now. It's become a persistent thought."

Trevena knew they were heading into decision time. They had a duty of care, so it was about risk management now. Graham would probably not offer an admission to the psychiatric ward because of Rob's drinking. The nurses would despise them for offloading that kind of problem on them. If Rob could persuade them he could keep himself safe then it was probably going to be a couple of weeks of Home Treatment. Still difficult but manageable. Medication would be pointless because of the amount of sauce he was knocking back, so talking and rapport would be the way forward, and trying to make a few changes to his lifestyle. Trevena knew the odds were *tiny* that they'd see any recovery, but still it was a service they would probably have to offer.

"What about the things you see around the estate?"

Rob shuddered and reached out for another sip of water. He sat up and took a drink from his tumbler then remained staring off into the distance with the cup held loosely in his lap.

"First time I was sitting around the back of the day centre. I was slaughtered. It was about three in the afternoon and I could hear the kids coming out of school. There were big metal bins and I was sitting between two of them. I think I'd been a bit sick." He glanced up at Graham with an apologetic expression. Graham closed his eyes and nodded.

"I just got a glimpse of it. A shadow, passing over my head. I remember hearing something, like a clicking sound, like something taking huge strides on stilts. I don't know. The next time I was walking back to my flat in the morning and I was sure something was crawling after me up the stairwell. Sounded like someone pushing down on rusty springs. I ran the last bit and shut myself in the flat for a couple of days. Had enough drink in. Then two days ago I was crossing the green going to Balv's for my morning bottle and as I was walking, my shadow changed into a square. A square, like something had flapped in front of the sun. I stopped, all cold, and watched as it just, well, sort of lay there on the grass under me. A big square shadow. And then things started wriggling out from the corners and I legged it. That thing slid after me, you know. Right up till I got to the shops. Then it disappeared."

"What do you think they were?"

Rob clutched his tumbler in both hands. His fingers were long and bony and pale, the knuckles prominent. He spoke in a whisper.

"It's the Angel of Death," he said.

"The Angel of Death."

"In a machine."

"What kind of machine?"

Rob looked up. "I don't know. A fucking Angel of Death machine. Look, fellas, I've got to get out of here." He started to slide his legs out of the bed.

Trevena sat forward. "Rob," he said.

Rob looked up. He was scrabbling under his bed for his boots.

"Have your thoughts about wanting to die coincided with you seeing these things?"

Graham looked sideways at him and raised his eyebrows. Whether he was impressed with Trevena's insight or just amused by his unexpected interjection, Trevena didn't know, but he wasn't going to hang around and wait to see whether Graham was going to ask.

Rob pulled his boots out from under the bed and sat up. He was about to put his feet in them and then realised he was wearing pyjamas. His shoulders slumped and he reached to open his cabinet.

"I reckon so," he said as he pulled a pair of combat trousers and a camouflage jacket from the cabinet. He stood on wobbling legs and pulled the trousers on over his pyjamas. He sat back on the edge of the bed and slid his feet into his boots. "Those shadows, and those sounds, man. They made me feel like I was filthy. Pathetic. I didn't say, but that day in the stairwell. When I got back to my flat and locked the door, that thing stayed outside all night. *Creak, creak, creak.* I could hear it all evening."

"What did you do?" Trevena asked.

"I passed out eventually but there's nothing new there. If I'd had tablets, I would have done the lot. Never felt so... hopeless."

"And this was when?"

"About a week ago." He had his boots on and was struggling with the buckles.

"Need a hand?" Graham asked.

"I need a drink is what I need," Rob said. "I'm drier than Derek Jarman's garden. But thanks. I can put my own bloody boots on." Despite this assurance he spent the next five minutes jangling and muttering until they were done up in some fashion. He pulled his jacket on and stood up. He put out his hand. "Pleasure talking to you, gentlemen."

"Are you sure you want to discharge yourself?" Graham asked.

"Discharge myself?" Rob said. "I'll be back in a hour. I'm just going for a pint."

Graham was about to say something but Rob interrupted him.

"I'm *joking*. I'll be fine. I need to get home. I don't like lying about doing nothing." He shuffled past Trevena and Graham and headed towards the nurses' desk.

"Okay, look. If you're going to go home, at least let us visit you there later. Make sure you're all right. We want to take you onto our caseload and see if we can help with some of the things you're going through at the moment," Graham said as they drew alongside Rob.

"That'll be lovely," Rob said. He waved a hand at one of the nurses standing at the end of the desk writing up notes. She raised her eyes heavenwards and came over.

"I'm off," said Rob. "Thanks for everything. I especially enjoyed listening to you give that old boy in the bed next to me a manual evacuation at three o'clock last night. Sensational. Anyway, these lads will be looking after me from now on, so I'll be on my way."

The nurse looked at Trevena and Graham.

"You can discharge Mr. Litchin into the care of the Home Treatment Team. Thank you, Sister."

The nurse made a face that articulated a complicated combination of professional assent with mild distaste and relief. It was quite a triumph of non-verbal communication.

Rob stumbled off towards the exit and Trevena and Graham followed.

At the door Graham asked how Rob was going to get home.

"Gradually," Rob said. "With a number of refreshment stops on the way."

"We'll pop over and see you in the morning, then," Graham said. Before you've tied too many on, Trevena was thinking.

"You've got my address?"

Graham held up the file. "And take this leaflet. It tells you a bit about what we do and it's got a pager number on the back you can use out of hours if you want some support. See you tomorrow?"

"Okay," Rob said. "Why not? I'm not much of a morning person though, I should warn you." And he turned and walked off, big boots clumping on the tiled floor.

Trevena and Graham followed Rob down the corridor. Rob turned right at the end towards the exit while Trevena and Graham lingered at the corner debating whether to go to the canteen for a coffee. Trevena looked at his watch. Half past ten.

"I'll grab a takeout. I've got to meet Zoë at eleven at Les's to collect a few bits for him." Trevena said.

He was referring to Les Branch, one of his patients with schizophrenia who had recently deteriorated to the point where Trevena had had to get him admitted under the Mental Health Act. Les was never entirely well and was chronically symptomatic, but with the injections Trevena gave him and regular support, he remained able to function. He kept pigeons and rabbits. "Pigeons for racing, rabbits for meat," Les had informed Trevena once, standing with his back turned and his trousers round his ankles, the thin, slightly loamy smell of an unwashed bottom drifting into Trevena's face, while awaiting the jab to his backside; it was only when Les phoned the office in tears to tell Trevena he had killed all his animals that it was time to get worried. When Les's illness worsened, usually exacerbated by stress induced paranoia, he would slaughter the lot because he thought they would be better off dead if he couldn't look after them properly. "I've killed all my animals again, Phil," he'd say. And Trevena would have to drop everything and get round there fast before he did any more harm. Les wasn't cruel, he wasn't a sociopath; he just got scared, and Trevena had known Les a long time and felt a lot for the man.

"You know Stibbs told me he wanted you to take over supervising Zoë?" Trevena said as they headed towards the canteen.

"No way," Graham said. He shook his head. "I can't do that, fella."

"I hoped you'd feel that way."

"She's far too pretty. I'd abuse my position and try and give her one. I'm not the mentor she needs, Phil."

"That's what I thought. Thanks, mate."

AT TEN PAST eleven Trevena pulled up behind Zoë's old Volkswagen Golf and flashed his lights. Zoë waved and got out and met Trevena on the path outside Les's house.

Les rented a cramped mid-terrace from the Housing Authority. It had no front garden, just a communal verge, mostly laid to dry dirt, which abutted the pavement. Next door had tried to enliven their approach by mounting a concrete birdbath the size of a kitchen sink flanked by two roaring stone lions beneath their front room window. The entire installation had been painted an inexplicable cobalt blue. It was quite probably one of the most dispiriting sights Trevena had ever seen.

"Sorry I'm a bit late," Trevena said as they stepped up to the front door. The door was testament to Les's increasingly florid mental state, an early warning sign not only of his worsening symptoms but also of what lay beyond. Les had repainted it bright red. The paint was smeared and blotchy, having been applied with a sponge. It looked like the back of a raw, sick throat.

"No worries," Zoë smiled, her cheeks dimpling. So keen, thought Trevena. Pretty and bright and young and so bloody *keen*. She probably wasn't much older than Lizzie. He sighed at the thought of his daughter, who also was pretty and bright and young, but a little bit fucked up, and keen, it seemed, only on *cock* at the moment.

"I thought you might like a look in here," Trevena said. "Les has been in hospital for a while now and he's asked me to fetch him some clothes and a few toiletries." He held up a roll of black bin bags. "It's like a museum to schizophrenia in there."

Zoë nodded, wide-eyed.

Trevena used Les's front door key and they went into the small, pokey hallway. Ahead was a bare galley kitchen and to the left a flight of stairs. Despite his familiarity with the inside of Les's house, Trevena still felt his skin crawl; he acknowledged the feeling as a primal kind of empathy the intuitive sane felt when confronted with true, tragic madness. An awful, lonesome desolation, encrypted throughout the fabric of the house from years of terrifying symptoms. If that didn't connote a haunting, he was unsure what did.

They went into the living room, which was the only other room on the ground floor. It was narrow and bare and evinced more of Les's attempts to brighten the place up. The walls above the dado rail were a nasty, bilious yellow, those beneath a cold, metallic blue. It had the effect of making Trevena feel he was sinking into a pool of stagnant water encompassed beneath a low sky full of light from a sickening sun. The floor was lino tiled, which increased his disorientation and sense of wading across the bottom of a pool. There was no TV, just a smeary glass-topped desk with a radio on it. Two greasy old armchairs were positioned next to each other against the back wall and faced the bricked up fireplace. The room smelt of biscuits gone soft at the bottom of a barrel.

Zoë went over to the hearth. There was a footstool in front of the fireplace with a stack of ripped-up paper piled on it. Zoë began picking through it.

"It's a Bible," she said. She picked up a chunk still attached to a piece of spine. She thumbed through it. Trevena noticed that the paper had not so much been torn or cut, but hacked apart by a pair of shears.

Trevena said, "Textbook paranoia, Zoë. Religious delusions with persecutory ideation." Zoë was looking at him intently, the fragment of Bible still held loosely in her hand. She's lapping this shit up, thought Trevena. I could make her fall in love with me. Here, in this grotty, flyblown hovel.

The curtains were shut front and back and the room was warm. Trevena had grown quickly accustomed to the dusty smell and now thought he could pick up a few conspicuous motes of Zoë's subtle perfume. The curtains at the back were thin, red material and the weak sunlight that shone behind them tinted the room with fragile pink shadows. Zoë's soft brunette hair, tied up in a ponytail, gleamed for a moment like polished mahogany.

Trevena swallowed. And a voice in his head whispered. *You want to eat her pussy.*

Trevena felt his heart beating with hot, heavy thuds high in his chest. He turned fast, hoping to hide his arousal and said, "Let's go upstairs, Zoë," in a voice that sounded hollow and dry. He caught her expression as he said it, too, and saw her lips part, just slightly, shiny with wetness she put there with the tip of her tongue.

He went upstairs.

TREVENA WAS TRYING to find something resembling toiletries on the shelf in the bathroom. There was a foamy sorbet of excreta unflushed in the toilet. He wadded up a few pieces of toilet paper and pushed the handle down to get rid of it. It left a rusty tonsure around the neck of the bend, but at least it was gone.

Zoë was in Les's bedroom filling a bin bag with clothes and shoes.

Trevena looked at his reflection in the cracked mirror above the sink. He squeezed his eyes shut then reopened them. He looked tired. *What the fuck just happened down there?* he thought. His heart rate had returned to normal and he had shed that odd, suspended feeling he had had for the few seconds he and Zoë had held each other's gaze. *I'm tired but I'm horny. She's pretty and she's probably got a bit of a crush on me I could exploit if I was that kind of bloke. It's normal to fantasize and sometimes the fantasies come without warning. Especially when you haven't had it for bloody ages.*

This analysis seemed to satisfy Trevena. He stepped out from the bathroom and crossed the landing to Les's room. "How you doing?"

Zoë held out the bin bag. It bulged with musty clothing. "This stuff's filthy," she said. "It'll need washing when we get it up to the ward. And there isn't much. He's hardly got any pants. You?"

"I've got lots of pants," Trevena said. Zoë giggled.

"How are you getting on in the bathroom?" she said, enunciating each word slowly.

Trevena held up a Bic razor and a tube of toothpaste curled up like an ammonite and just as fossilized.

Trevena looked around. Just a bare mattress with a grey sheet balled up at the foot of it and a couple of deflated pillows against the wall. A crooked bedside cabinet with nothing on it but a disconnected digital alarm clock. No cupboards or wardrobes, just a clothes drier by the storage heater beneath the window. A proper heart-sink, he thought.

"That'll do," he said. "We can get him a few bits from the shop."

Zoë tied a knot in the top of the bag and toted it to the stairs. She smiled at Trevena and indicated for him to go down first. If there was any residue left of that earlier uncanny arousal, Trevena certainly couldn't detect it. He must have imagined it, he thought, with the joyless and ambivalent disappointment of the forty-six-year-old.

He started down and the phone in the hall by the front door began to ring.

He was startled and felt his heartbeat ramp up again. He nearly missed his step and had to throw an arm out to grip the banister. Zoë bumped him.

The phone was old; faun-coloured and shaped like a wedge of cheese. What were they called? Trimphones? It made an insistent, electronic warbling sound.

Trevena steadied himself and continued to the bottom of the stairs. He paused, in two minds whether to answer it or not. Zoë reached the hallway and put the bin bag down by the living room door. Trevena shrugged and picked the handset up.

"Probably just his mum," he said. "She forgets when he goes into hospital."

But it wasn't Les's mum. *"Hello! Hello! Phil? Is that you? Are you there, Phil?"*

Trevena pulled the phone away from his ear, wincing. He put it back slowly, keeping it about an inch away from the side of his head.

"Les?" Trevena said.

"Yeah. Yeah, it's me, Phil. Listen."

"Mate, we're just on our way back with your clothes. We've got to stop at Balv's and get you some stuff but we'll be back—"

"No. No, no. Listen. You have to go straight to Daniel. Get out of there. Get out of there now and go to Daniel. You're not safe, Phil. There's something there with you. I think it's looking for you, Phil. I bricked it in. But it's destroyed all my Bibles. Get out now and go to Daniel."

Trevena was trying to make sense of what Les was saying. "Who's Daniel, Les?"

"Phil?" Zoë said.

"He's my friend. He's visiting the estate. He has things to do here. Very important things. We knew each other a long time ago." Les was still shouting, his voice hoarse with urgency. *"From our time in the bins."*

"Phil!" Zoë said, this time with more than a hint of fear in her voice.

"What?" Trevena snapped, pulling the handset away from his ear again. He could still hear the metallic scratching of Les's voice captive in the moulded plastic earpiece.

Zoë was standing close, her left side pressed almost against Trevena. She was staring into the front room. The door was ajar and obscured most of the room, but they could both see, strewn across the floor, a thousand pieces of shredded paper. No draught had done that. And then they both heard something from upstairs, from above. The spare room, empty of anything functional, but which shared the chimney with the lounge beneath it.

It was the sound of something falling dead to the floor; something going from vertical to horizontal in the instant it takes gravity to drop it to thinly carpeted floorboards. But not dead. Crawling and scraping.

Trevena glanced up the stairs. He indicated with a flick of his hand for Zoë to get out. She gathered up the bag and opened the front door and went outside. Trevena backed around the door, still holding the phone, his eyes riveted on the gloomy landing at the top of the stairs. He put the phone back to his ear. Silence. Les had gone.

"Les?" Trevena hissed. Les hadn't hung up. There was no dial tone, just silence. And then a dog barked somewhere on the estate behind him and Trevena jumped again and let go of the phone, which flew out of his hand and around the door on its tight little springy lead, to clatter against the skirting board. And he was backing out and closing the door, that bloody neck wound of a door, against the shadows, and the rickety substance of them that had stepped onto the landing at the top of the stairs.

THEY MADE THE journey back to the ward in their separate cars and parked up next to each other in bays outside the main entrance. Trevena was glad of the time alone so he could think.

He had pretty much shooed Zoë into her car outside Les's house, shoving the bin bag full of clothes onto her passenger seat. Their eyes met again, and Trevena noticed how pale Zoë's complexion was, how scared she looked. "Don't worry," he said. "I expect we disturbed something up there and it fell over." But they hadn't gone into the spare room, just given it a glance, and it had been empty, just a cold, neglected space in the house, and Zoë's expression told Trevena she knew it, too.

On the way back to the ward, Trevena immediately started the process of engaging denial, a useful tool to dumb down and cope with the full force of existential dread. He hadn't really seen anything coming onto the landing. He had been distracted by Les's phone call, that's all. He was tired and under stress and although it wasn't a nice thought, he might well have suffered a brief hallucination brought on by recent events. Or misinterpreted the whole thing: an illusion (much more palatable than an hallucination, because that was really a bit *psychotic* and Trevena wasn't going to admit that he had lost touch with reality). And there was definitely an atmosphere in that house, an ambient sickness, a morbid history of psychic distortion, whatever you wanted to call it, and he had been susceptible to its effects because he was drained. Yes, he thought, that'll do for now. He glanced into the rear view mirror as he undid his seatbelt and couldn't help feeling slightly aggrieved that his reflected expression did little to support his cunning refutation of the truth. He knew very well what he'd seen, and so did Zoë.

"Bollocks," he said, and climbed out of the car.

AND THERE WAS awful news for them when he got up to the ward.

Les had died.

"WHAT HAPPENED?" TREVENA asked. He was sitting in the nursing office talking to Cherry Something, an agency nurse he didn't know, who was in charge of the shift that morning. She was sitting opposite him behind a desk and she was trying not to burst into tears again.

Trevena had sent Zoë home telling her he'd catch up with her later. The bag of clothes Les would never wear was leaning against Trevena's chair. He could smell the fusty odour of the contents through the plastic. Absurdly, Trevena felt a sudden urge to pat the bag, to comfort it as though it was an obtrusive old pet nobody wanted to fuss. You just wanted to be washed, he thought. Now you're going to be incinerated. A bit like Les. What a fucking day.

"We checked on him at quarter to eleven," Cherry said. "He was fine. He was sitting on his bed looking out of the window and drinking a cup of tea. He was doing so well, too. He was getting better every day."

Trevena nodded encouragement. Outside in the corridor someone was kicking off. Three nurses ran past. A big-boned woman in her fifties approached the office door scowling, and tapped on the glass. She mimed smoking by holding up two fingers in the traditional form of abuse and tapped them against her pouting lips. Cherry ignored her.

"And then at eleven o'clock we checked to see if he wanted to join the Mindfulness group and... and..."

"He'd cut his throat with a shard of broken teacup," Trevena finished for her. He'd read the incident form but felt an obligation to help this poor girl debrief. No managers seemed to be forthcoming.

Cherry concurred with a snort she buried in a handful of Kleenex. Her wide, watery eyes regarded Trevena over the spray of tissues and Trevena saw more guilt in them that he would have liked.

"What time did you say you found him?" Trevena asked.

"Eleven."

Trevena shook his head. "I spoke to Les about twenty-five past eleven. He rang his own home. He sounded agitated."

Cherry pulled an observation list from the wall above her desk. She slid it over to Trevena. Leslie Branch, fifteen minute obs. All signed off right up to quarter to eleven. No one had bothered to sign the eleven o'clock box.

"Might it have been a bit later than that? Maybe someone missed a check?" Trevena said. He tried not to sound critical.

Cherry shook her head. "Mindfulness group starts at eleven. It was eleven o'clock." She was filling up again. Trevena discontinued his line of questioning. He wasn't investigating anything here. There *was* a discrepancy and it may or may not be uncovered but it wasn't up to him to do the uncovering. He'd have to make a statement, though. Shit. Well at least it wasn't on his watch, like Leftley. That sounded mean but it was a hell of a relief. Two of his patients within twenty-four hours of each other. Hell of a thing. Les must have killed himself within moments of speaking to Trevena on the phone. He was still lying dead in his room on the ward. Two nurses were sitting outside while they waited for the men to pitch up from the mortuary. This was as fresh as it comes. Bit of an eye-opener for young Zoë, there. Perhaps he should comfort her later. Come on her. *Come in her lively little twat.*

Cherry was sobbing. Trevena snapped back from his thoughts. Where had he been going there? What was wrong with him today?

"Look," he said, wanting to put a lid on this and get away. He was feeling cramped in the stuffy little office and claustrophobic. The warmth of the room and his fatigue and a need to urinate had all combined to give him a niggling partial erection and its impatient winching against the cloth of his underpants had become tiresome. "These things happen. People get tired of being unwell all the time and sometimes, during recovery, they get a glimpse of two things. What the illness has taken from them, and what the future holds. And neither thing is good, and they decide to bail out. I know this probably doesn't help, Cherry, but he'd clearly made up his mind. He'd have done it sometime. I'm just sorry it happened here. On your shift."

Cherry muttered a snotty thanks and Trevena got up and left.

AND THEN HE went back to his office, which was just along the corridor from the ward, and really wished he hadn't, because the expressions on the faces of his colleagues when he walked in, and the awkwardness of the silence, and the shuffling of paperwork and tension in the postures, told him that, unfortunately, there was still more shit to come.

"Phil," Stibbs said, stepping out from his office as Trevena walked in. "Can we have a conversation?"

"OH THIS IS just un-fucking-*believable*," Trevena said. "When? *How*?"

Stibbs sat back in his chair and laced his fingers over his paunch. *He looks like he's just finished a good meal*, Trevena thought. Incredulity was amassing and he felt defenceless before it, light-headed and at the mercy of something gargantuan; a stumbling, idiot Fate opening its bowels all over his life.

Stibbs had informed Trevena that another of his patients had taken their own life, and yet another had been brought into Accident and Emergency just ten minutes ago having tried to drown himself in the Invidisham River half a mile away from the estate.

"Dean Brazil's an idiot," Trevena said. "The only reason he didn't drown is because he can swim. But Sally Cross? I can't believe she'd kill herself. She's been well for ages. Suicide was never discussed. She wasn't depressed."

"Evidently she was, Phil," Stibbs said. He picked up a slim green file from his desk and opened it. He didn't hang about, this bastard. Stibbs had already been through all her notes in order to start compiling yet another investigation. He handed the file to Trevena. "Look at your last entry."

Trevena took a deep breath. He wasn't going to get reeled in here, manipulated into saying something he'd regret later. *Think, man. What is Stibbs' getting at?*

SALLY HAS RECOVERED well from her hypomanic episode and is now caring for her children fully and without intervention from Social Services. She is managing her medication without issue and is thinking about going back to work part-time. I will review in one month.

Trevena looked up from the page. He raised his eyebrows at Stibbs, not wanting to commit, wanting Stibbs to spell it out. Trevena was trying to get a grip on what was happening, on losing Sally, on the others, so he missed the essence of what Stibbs said next.

"What?" said Trevena.

Stibbs frowned and snatched the file from Trevena's hand. He held it up and pointed at the hand written note, jabbing the tip of his short, narrow index finger at the date. *You have child's hands,* thought Trevena. *Probably hung like a grain of rice. Explains a lot.*

"*What?*" Trevena said again, more sharply. He was starting to lose patience in a very big way. He glanced over his shoulder to see whether Graham was back in the office yet. If he was, Trevena was going to get him in here as a witness to what could rapidly become a nasty situation. There was a stench of harassment about all this, a stitch up.

"Can I have your attention, Phil," Stibbs said. "This is a very serious matter."

Trevena turned to look at Stibbs. He felt his fists clench around the ends of the chair's armrests.

Stibbs soldiered on, "The date was five weeks ago, Phil. You've missed her review."

Trevena shook his head. "That's not a legal requirement. It's not a 117 meeting. It's informal. It's up to me when I see her. For God's sake, man, you know how busy we all are. She was fine."

Stibbs drew breath through his teeth. He seemed to be making up his mind about something. "Okay," he said. He slapped the file down on his desk. "I have no choice but to send you on leave, Phil." He saw Trevena's expression and raised his hands palms outwards. "It's not a suspension, Phil. Just a bit of gardening leave. You need a break. You need to get onto your union, too. You can't be expected to work with all this going on."

Trevena got to his feet. He felt wobbly.

"John," he said, and it sounded like he was speaking through a mouthful of bubble gum. "I don't want to go off. Not now." And he realised as he said it how utterly pathetic he sounded. He felt the horrible, unmanning sensation of tears pricking his eyes. None of this was his fault. He knew with total conviction that he had done nothing clinically wrong. He felt like he was being slowly and remorselessly assassinated. *Later*, he thought, *please let this all hit me later. Just not here, not now, in front of Stibbs.* He blinked and cleared his throat.

Stibbs was watching him. There was a nasty caution in his expression. Trevena knew he had to be seen to be doing the right thing as a manager, ticking all the right boxes so that if and when Trevena finally imploded it would appear he had managed the situation effectively. But Trevena also knew right there in the very centre of his being that Stibbs wanted him gone. It was his remit, after all. It was why he was there: out with the old, in with the new. An avenging managerial mantra Stibbs might as well have put on one of his chipper motivational posters. Get rid of the old team, the change-resistant, experienced ones and bring in a tame and cherry-picked crop of low-grade yes-people. Cheaper, compliant and grateful for their jobs. A narcissist's dream assignment.

Trevena said, "You're right, John, I need a break. And I want to do things your way." That dry, gummy sensation was back in his mouth; these were words he really didn't want to say. "But I've been here a long time and I can assure you I've done nothing clinically to contribute to any of these deaths. Les was on the *ward* for God's sake. It's unprecedented, and it's going to have an effect on me, certainly, but I need to be working, not sitting at home with the pressure off. I've got paperwork to do, reports to write and there'll be a shitload of stuff coming my way because of these incidents. I'll stick to my desk. You can review it each day. If I'm going under you'll know."

Trevena held his breath. He had tried playing Stibbs and he hoped Stibbs hadn't realised. What decision would give Stibbs the illusion of having the *most* control? He hadn't denied Stibbs the option of sending him off, but he had offered him a way of delaying it that still made it look like it was Stibbs' decision. With any luck, Trevena was thinking, Stibbs might look upon a few days more as an opportunity for Trevena to destroy himself against Stibbs' best intentions. Trevena wasn't even sure why he was fighting so hard to stay at work. Because it was better than being at home on his own all day, pacing and fretting and having to worry about his daughter and his career and the state of his life? (He wasn't going to let Stibbs know that, though. If he gave him the impression he'd be laying around with his feet up then it improved his chances of getting Stibbs to allow him more time at his desk.) Because he didn't want Stibbs thinking he was beaten? Because he needed time to think and find out what the fuck was going on? All of the above.

Stibbs was giving it some thought. He was tapping his pen against the stack of folders on his desk and looking up at Trevena with a bland expression. Trevena was suddenly revolted. That he had to play up to a prick like this, and that the man sitting before him could muster no empathy whatsoever in its purest form while he pondered the best outcome not for his colleague, but for himself.

"Okay, Phil," Stibbs said in a tone that implied that—just for now—he was prepared to treat Trevena like a grown-up. "I think it would be good for you to step down from any one-to-one clinical work until we've had a chance to review this. Office duties only and we'll meet up again tomorrow morning."

Relief, and a catastrophic impulse to laugh, rushed into Trevena. He bit down on the laughter—it was a twisted, fucked-up glee that was far better off being suppressed—but he let the relief soothe him as much as it could. He tried not to let it show as anything other than a species of subordinate gratitude. Stibbs seemed content with it. "Thanks, John," Trevena said, and managed not to add, *I'll try not to let you down*. That would have just been too much shit.

Trevena turned and walked out of Stibbs' office. There must have been a strange look on his face because everyone else seemed unable to look him in the eye as he went over to his desk and sat down.

4

PLAGUED BY SOUSED philosophies, Rob Litchin lurched home. What was going through his head? What moronic ideation sluiced through those tarry ventricles? A book he had read once plagued him like an intrusive, perseverating thought, the initial idea that had begun it long ceased, carking it at the face of some burned-out synapse. How did it start? The book—*Yellow Dog*. Genius. An opening paragraph so clever it was impenetrable, you just had to accept it meant something and move on. Like life. Or not, Rob thought. Perhaps it was a con, to make you think the author was more clever than he actually was. But it was nonsense. Like life. Maybe these last chapters of *his* life, part scripted by some tawdry hack minion of fate, part floundering, improvised stand-up, were meaning only in and of themselves. Meaning implied destination. It was heading somewhere for a reason. But there was nothing at the end to tie it all up, no wry dénouement, nothing to swivel in his direction like a smug villain in a red leather chair in a library in some exclusive club, and say, "Ah, you've arrived at last, Mr Litchin. Join me for a drink, if you so like, and I'll explain what that ex*asp*erating cobblers was all about."

Yellow Dog. But Rob Litchin went to hospital. But Rob Litchin got damaged. But Rob Litchin exerted lethal force on those that damaged him. Male violence does it, indeed.

He stumbled; it's dark, too many pints in the pubs on the way home from the hospital. Terrible thoughts now about Gollick. *Gollicunt. Yellow Cunt.*

He'd had a last one in The Macebearer on the corner of the shopping centre. Some of the windows were still boarded up. Something went down recently, some sort of riot on the estate, but Rob didn't remember it. Probably slept through it. Things hadn't been right since though, for him or the estate. The Polish seemed more menacing, more clustered; an ethnic defence against something they sensed, perhaps. They were more open to that sort of thing, Rob windily surmised. More traditional in their sporadic bouts of violence. There was an Eastern Bloc wintriness about their blunt, Romany bloodshed. Over in seconds. Rob had been clumped a few times, in the pubs, over the years, by big men with heads like the concrete balls that decorate the tops of gateposts. They'd let it go for a while, pores cemented shut with blackheads on the planes of their profiled cheeks, and then: a fast clump. On your arse. And that was if you were a clown pisshead twat. Knives, blunt instruments and vehicles for you if you crossed a different kind of line.

Rob crossed an expanse of earth between two blocks of flats. Children played there during the day. Dogs shat there at all hours, despite Officer Gollick's best efforts to prevent them doing so, and the deep treads of Rob's boots tractored through it in careless disregard. He would, as he ended up doing most days, scrape and stamp it off in ridged strips on the edges of the concrete steps leading up to his flat.

Gollick lived nearby. With his old mum, Ethel Gollick. She'd been a lollipop lady when they'd been kids, Rob remembered. If it was pissing with rain, she'd always let the cars go first if Rob was waiting, shivering, to cross. Her big tin lollipop towering over him, clenched in her municipal fist, rain clattering off its dented, rusty disc. *STOP CHILDREN*. Should have said *FUCK CHILDREN* for all that old cow cared.

One day she'd gone under a joyrider's nicked Citroen. Atomised her pelvis. Rob smiled, the old memories seeming fresher now. It was new stuff he had trouble remembering. Alzheimer's, he thought. No, what was it called? Korsakoff's. He was fucking dementing, that's for sure. And what of it? Anyway, that was the end for Ethel. At least it was the end of her contribution to community service. Might explain Gollick's choice of career. Old bitch living through her son. They didn't have Community Support Officers when they were little. Just infrequent traffic wardens, who were ridiculed and lampooned, but were mostly avoidable because you could park anywhere you liked in those days.

Rob grasped the thread of a memory and spooled it into something coherent. A few years ago he had been sitting in a pub looking out of the window. He'd just sold some rare Zappa, so he had a few quid for a sherbet or two. He was mellow on proper cider. And he watched the world go by through the single frame of the window, and as he watched, into shot came a Parking Attendant, as they were now known, in full uniform. He checks around a car, parked in a time-limited bay outside the pub, and then takes out a little camera and starts taking photos. Having captured the crime, he walks off, head down, checking his digital screens of data, and as he moves out of frame, a man runs past in the opposite direction, loping in a luminous yellow running suit, and pushing his baby boy in a trendy three-wheeled sports buggy. The child is chortling away with the joy of it as dad's long-legged, Ichabod Crane sprint propels them both past and out, and off into the future. Rob stared out at the road, at the now mundane-again world framed by the pub's window and feels that something important has just happened. He actually feels, riding those ciders to a good place for a while, that he's just had a cartoon squirted into his eyes. All sudden colour and incident, and it vexes him that there's a point to this epiphany, and he suddenly gets it: neither man notices each other. They are lost in their own worlds and demonstrate the polarity of humanity that makes us both sublime and absurd; wonderful, hopeful, joyous, petty, stifling and cuntish, all at once. Kafka and Carroll. Legalism versus freedom of expression in one sudden, bright, ephemeral moment. It's a good moment for Rob and he celebrates by having a load more to drink and thus forgets it ever happened. Until now.

He scuffed onto the path that ran alongside one of the blocks of flats and felt those viewpoints, those pickled ideations, coalesce into something coherent, purposeful. Tonight, Rob Litchin was the Cheshire Cat (he stretched his mouth into a grin as he walked the length of the alley, liking how it felt beneath the restrictive bindweed of his neglected beard. And the thought progressed to this: his grin was more like a pike's, pushing up through a mat of black, rotting pondweed. Fuck the Cheshire Cat, Rob Litchin was the Norfolk Pike) and he was going to tear down the civic restrictions imposed by ruling bodies and steering groups and ratifying committees everywhere. The Norfolk Pike was going to take it all back for the people.

Rob kept that grin on his face and turned left at the end of the alley.

Towards Gollick's mum's bungalow.

GOLLICK'S MUM'S BUNGALOW was one of eight in a small square behind the flats. They were quite tidy with well-tended front gardens. They housed some of the oldest residents on the estate and seemed, by some virtue unknowable to Rob, to have remained exempt from the vandalism and depredations found everywhere else around them. There were potted plants and ornaments, wind chimes, bird tables, all sorts of Homebase crap. Neat little flowerbeds dotted the lawns, and the fences were stout and painted and did not lean. A single streetlamp in the middle of the cul-de-sac lit the close with a bright white luminescence. How did they get a white light? Rob wondered as he walked up to Gollick's bungalow. Everywhere else on the estate was lit by dim, flickering orange sodium. If they worked at all. He stopped for a moment and looked around. It was oddly tranquil here and, if you ignored the massive looming flank of the flats that rose behind them, a bit timeless.

Rob opened Gollick's gate and walked up the ramp that led to the front door. Ethel's mobility scooter was parked up on an outcrop of concrete to the right of the door, part hidden under its burgundy plastic all-weather protective cover. It seemed to crouch, that scooter. As if it resented its role in life as much as the old bird that rode it around the estate resented her immobility and need for it. They seemed to have an edgy symbiosis, Ethel and her scooter; her scowling bulk atop its quaking, wheezing chassis, its puny motor pushing them along at a glacial pace through the byways of the estate and the aisles of the VAL-YOU! shopping mart in the plaza. Once, Rob recalled, years ago, he had hidden behind a display of breakfast cereal and watched as she'd tried to reverse the scooter up an aisle, having been thwarted by a blockade of mums and pushchairs down by the Reduced To Clear counter. Her fury at being unable to take *her* rightful place blocking the salmonella counter from all the other shoppers while she laboured over her pick was evident on her face and in the aggressive way she handled the accelerator. Unable to resist, Rob had started making loud beeping sounds interspersed with pronouncing, "THIS OLD COW IS REVERSING! THIS OLD COW IS REVERSING!" in straight-faced, stentorian tones. He was still pissing himself when old Derek, the acting manager, caught him and threw him out for being a childish twat.

Rob stood outside Gollick's home and suddenly felt a little ashamed. His Norfolk Pike grin had gone and had been replaced by a thoughtful pursing of his chapped lips. Ethel had been moved to this bungalow after her accident because it was modified and had a warden-controlled alarm system. But there was more to it. Gollick had had a sister, Rob remembered. Barbara Gollick. She was a year below them at school but she was a big girl. Well, fat really. And very *moley*. *Molier* than Duncton Wood, to be perfectly honest. She wasn't unpleasant at all, in fact she was quite a cheery thing and she used to hang about outside their prefabricated classroom at the top of the playground during breaks so she could spend time with her brother. She mortified Gollick by her very existence but he'd try to be nice to her. Unfortunately, with their innate abhorrence of lack of appeal in other children, their tyrannous misgivings towards any blemishes, pongs or impediments, the rest of the children – Rob included – found themselves *bullying* the poor girl. It was like they couldn't help it. And of course, Gollick got it in the neck, too, just for being her brother, and when he tried to defend her, well, he was finished, really. Rob's shoulders slumped at the memory of things he'd said, and heard said. *Old moley*, and *fat old moley*. Inspired combinations like that.

It had got so bad that eventually Ethel herself had come charging down the playground, her huge yellow reflective coat billowing and her lollipop dragging behind her, throwing sparks off the hopscotched tarmac, bellowing, "Who made my Barbara cry? Who made my Barbara cry?" at the top of her lungs. It had been terrifying. But also, and fatally, quite funny. Gollick had burst into tears, too, at the sight of his mother's wrath, which hadn't helped him, and afterwards, when it had all blown over, and they had all stood there wide-eyed and gasping with the shock and awe, and outright *thrill,* of seeing an adult—an adult in *authority*—lose it so badly, they had recommenced bullying the Gollicks with a renewed and vile fervour. Rob included.

A few months later Barbara had stopped coming to school. Ethel's adherence to the Green Cross Code had become more selective, too, and there were rumours amongst the mums that she might be about to lose her job.

And then Barbara had died.

It was the first time Rob had experienced something like that. He remembered the assembly that morning. Why had they all been summoned to the hall the moment they got through the gates? Teachers were sombre and damp-eyed and irritable. Clouts were applied to the sides of facile little heads. And then the announcement by the head mistress: *Barbara Gollick died last night.*

That was pretty much it. No explanations were given, and in those days none were expected. Things carried on as normal and Barbara was forgotten. Callous, really. And the focus remained on Neil Gollick, even though he was clearly in shock and grieving, because he was now the brother of a sister who had not only been fat and moley, but was also *dead*, which, to his classmates, had a poignant and ostracising enthralment too gripping to ignore.

And then, not long after, Ethel had gone under the Citroen. Rob's brain struggled with a link but finally landed it: she'd tried to top herself, too. It was obvious now.

Remorse suddenly flooded Rob's system like a chemical trapped for decades behind a blocked gland. His knees buckled and he leant against the side of Ethel's scooter and felt tears welling up. Drunkenness and the effects of the recent shock of the shooting overwhelmed him. Through the window behind the scooter, Rob could see into Ethel's kitchen. He watched, through eyes multifaceted with tears, seven or so Neil Gollicks walk into the kitchen and switch on the kettles. Rob wiped his eyes on the sleeve of his jacket and Gollick resolved into just one, who was wearing an *I LOVE HUNSTANTON* tee shirt and baggy khaki leisure pants. Rob stood up straight and backed away from the window. He wiped his eyes again but the tears were still coming because now Ethel had come into the kitchen, propelled by her motorised wheelchair, and Rob could just see the top of her white fluffy hair. He pressed his hand to his mouth to suppress the horror of his own mind. Perspective had made the low altitude of her barnet look like some species of fuzzy rat scuttling along the windowsill.

He bent forward, so he could take the scene in fully. Ethel was chiding Gollick about something; Rob could tell by the defeated set of Gollick's shoulders and his clenched fists. Gollick reached for a carton of milk but knocked it over. Milk spewed across the worktop and flooded down the door of the fridge, soaking a gallery of faded postcards stuck to it with magnets. Gollick fumbled for a tea towel while Ethel shrieked. It was awful. Rob stared wide-eyed, his mouth hanging open, his beard dewy with his tears.

"I want my hot chocolate!" Ethel was screaming. "I can't sleep! I want my hot chocolate!"

"None of us can sleep, Mum!" Rob heard Gollick say. "Don't know what's wrong with me. Must be the shock of nearly being bloody *killed*!"

"Don't give me that! I've seen that video on the Internet. You're *yellow*, Neil Gollick! *Yellow*!"

Gollick rounded on his mother. She flinched but Gollick slipped in the pool of milk on the lino and went down. Rob gasped. Gollick clambered to his feet and stood glaring at his mum. His left hand reached out and went for the bread knife by the toaster. No, hang on. It was a spatula. Rob squinted and wiped his eyes again. It wasn't a spatula, nor was it a utensil of any kind. It was a *purse*. It was his mother's purse. Rob groaned with relief. How Gollick kept his hands off that old woman, he'd never understand. Gollick raked around until he found some coins and then stormed out of the kitchen.

Rob was seized with panic. He looked around for somewhere to hide. Gollick was in the hall, putting on his coat and shoes. The front door opened. Rob leaped behind the scooter and cowered down.

Gollick thundered down the path and through the gate. He was wearing his Community Support Officer jacket over his tee shirt. Rob watched him turn right out of the cul-de-sac and head across the green.

Relieved, Rob stood up and followed him.

GOLLICK TRUDGED ACROSS the green with his head down and his hands stuffed in the pockets of his coat. Rob kept a distance of about fifty meters between them. He wasn't sure why he was following Gollick at all. More than once he decided to duck away down an alley but changed his mind. There was something he needed to do, something that might at least give the last couple of days some closure. He needed to talk to Gollick. They'd nearly died and that needed acknowledging, didn't it?

The single lit unit of Balv's emporium was ahead. Rob was unsure of the time but it must be midnight and Balv's often stayed open until gone one, selling booze and tobacco to the gangs of kids that roamed the estate in the small hours now Beanie was running the show.

Gollick walked up to Balv's and went inside. Rob lurked at the corner of the walkway and tried to look offhand, as if he had just popped out to do a bit of shopping himself. He checked his pockets as an afterthought. Actually, why not? He had a few quid left and he wasn't sure what he had available at home. He was hungry and hadn't eaten all day. A couple of bottles would sort that out.

He went up to the door but didn't get a chance to go inside, because Neil Gollick came out carrying a carton of milk, and stopped and looked at Rob, and grinned with a mouthful of teeth like glass.

Rob stumbled away, arms raised. He felt his remaining strength drain off through his boots. He collapsed against the window of Balv's shop and opened and closed his mouth, wordless with horror.

What stood there, half-turned towards him beneath the flyblown lamp embedded in the concrete roof, was wearing Gollick's coat and boots but it wasn't Gollick anymore. Its jaw was jutting and crammed with those sharp, glassy teeth, angling over each other in a gaping, benthic maw. Its eyes gleamed a bioluminescent white. Its hands were blunt and fingerless but with huge thick claws like toggles on a duffel coat protruded from the knuckles. There was a sudden *pop* and Rob nearly passed out, but it was just the sound of those claws bursting through the milk carton as Gollick-not-Gollick clutched it against his chest. The milk that poured from it was yellow and lumpy and stank like cheese soaked in blister fluid.

Rob gagged and pushed himself away from the window. He backed away until he had a concrete post between them. Gollick-not-Gollick remained standing outside Balv's, the curdled milk soaking into his coat and the legs of his leisure pants. His white eyes shone with a horrible alien patience.

Rob turned and ran.

GASPING, ROB REACHED the stairwell that led up to his flat. He took a look over his shoulder but could see nothing coming for him from out of the darkness, no Gollick real or imagined. He ran a trembling hand over his face. He was sweating and the hospital pyjamas beneath his jacket were clinging to his back and chest. The stairwell was at the end of an alley between two ranks of lock-up garages and he had run the dark length of it without looking back, sure Gollick would be following. His guts churned; a bit of reflux rose up, a sizzling throatful that he swallowed back down with a wince. He closed his eyes but then opened them again, wide and staring, trying to absorb as many of the scanty photons available to him at the end of that dank, secluded passage. He reached out and gripped the pitted iron banister.

Something was coming up the alley.

Its footsteps gritted on the broken flagstones as it came. Its white eyes shone, two smoking pinpricks in its distended face. It seemed in no hurry. And why should it be in one? It knew where Rob lived.

Rob uttered a small shriek. It seemed to get tangled in his beard and would have been unheard by anyone not standing an inch away from his mouth. It went: *brrrffh*. It was more of an exhalation than a shriek but Rob had the distinct and commensurate feeling that he was yelling his head off in a nightmare. He found that he couldn't move.

Gollick drew closer, stepping through the evil slush seeping from bin bags plundered by rodents and foxes that lay stacked along the backs of the lockups. Gollick's arms hung by his sides and the associated movement as they swung slightly with each step dragged those inward curving claws against the fabric of his coat making short, harsh plastic scratching sounds.

Rob pulled his eyes away from the sight and turned to run up the stairwell. He fully expected his flight to be hampered by the dream-sensation of ploughing through treacle, but he accelerated up the stairs so fast that he smacked his head on the facing wall of the landing. He staggered up the next three flights and swung himself onto the narrow walkway that overlooked the roofs of the garages. He took a moment to peer over the low concrete balustrade but could see nothing moving below. Then he heard movement in the stairwell. He moaned again and took off along the walkway towards the door of his flat. Rob's was the sixth flat along and as he passed those of his neighbours he thought about knocking on their doors to try to get some help, but it was a fleeting thought; most of them were in a worse state than he was.

He reached his front door and pulled his key from his jacket pocket. It was a lone chub key on a chipped and dented Mr. Napoli ice cream key ring he'd had since he was a child. At least the isolated nature of his door key prevented any clichéd horror-film fumbling, and it slid home and turned without issue, but it was a sad reflection of his downward trajectory however convenient at that moment. Once Rob had been the owner of a fistful of keys, the like of which any man should possess; house keys front and back, garage key, car keys, suitcase key, gun cabinet key, shed key, a whole bunch of small metal emblems giving access to things and spaces owned, collected and valued. The depletion of his key ring was still a tart reminder to Rob as to how far he had fallen every time he reached into his pocket and let himself into his grotty flat.

Inside, Rob stood panting in the hallway. He stepped into the kitchenette and yanked the curtains across the window above the bilged sink. Then he went into the living room and stood there for a moment and looked around with little hope of finding anything there to protect or defend himself. He pulled the blind down over the window in there, too, then went into his bedroom and did the same again. Then he went back into the kitchen and grabbed a two-litre bottle of White Lightning and took a long swallow.

As he was gulping his drink, he heard a noise on the walkway outside. He froze. It was footsteps; slow, gritting footsteps. They stopped outside the window.

Rob backed away into the hall and, trembling, stood on tiptoes and took a quick peek out through the dirty glass panel set in the top of the front door. He dropped back onto his heels and continued down into a crouch, the plastic bottle held in his arms. He had another quick sip, his eyes shut tight.

Gollick was out there. He was just standing on the walkway, facing the window, arms slack at his sides. He was grinning, or appeared to be, but it was impossible to ascertain his general humour with his jaw jammed open by all those shards of teeth.

Rob shuffled in a crouch into the living room and kneed the door shut. He went over to the sofa and slid onto it and sat there cradling his bottle. As he sat there he became aware that he was filthy. He gazed with bewildered, damp eyes around the flat. No photos, no pictures, no belongings of any value. No carpet. Just a sunken sofa, a second-hand coffee table sticky with sour drink and a twenty-year old TV in the corner with no remote control. He was wearing hospital pyjamas and his supper was booze. Dirty bastard.

He began to cry.

TREVENA HAD GOT home around half five. He had about twenty minutes before he had to go to his therapy appointment. Stibbs had referred him to Occupational Health two months ago because he though Trevena might be 'struggling' after his divorce was finalised. Trevena didn't lack self-awareness but still bridled at the suggestion that he wasn't coping. He'd had a bit of sick time off though and Human Resources were staring to get on Stibbs' back about it. It was kind of a done deal. Trevena took the referral and spent an hour a week in counselling, talking to a psychiatrist. His name was Doctor Mocking, and despite his initial misgivings, Trevena had to admit the doc was good.

He was pouring himself a large glass of merlot when the back door crashed open and a shirtless boy staggered into his kitchen carrying a crate of lagers. He was runty but sported the requisite well-developed pecs and abs youth culture demands, and his forearms were cinched with a black ironwork of tribal tattoos. His jeans looked three sizes too big and hung around the tops of his thighs. His Calvin Klein underpants were blindingly white against the cramped little muscles of his belly. Trevena watched him cross the kitchen and dump the crate of tinnies over by the fridge. Just stood there with his glass raised to his lips, one hand in his trouser pocket, eyes narrowed above the rim of the glass.

The boy reached out to open the fridge and then started when Trevena coughed. He turned around glaring. He had a stupid face,

Trevena thought. *You dim little cunt.* Anger was rising in him and he took a slow sip of his wine. Yet another jobless twat coming and going as he pleased like he owned the place. Stock up on the cheap drink, party on his daughter and then go down the pub and bring back a load of mates.

"Oh," the boy said in a strange high voice. Trevena bridled at its artifice. "A'ight, *chap*?"

Trevena took another sip of wine and set his glass down on the kitchen table.

"My name's Mr. Trevena," he said. "Not chap, or buddy, or *guy.*"

The boy's face went blank. All grasp of the situation just dropped away, like the remains of an unappetising meal being scraped off a plate into a bin.

Trevena stepped around the table. The boy flinched and reached for his beers.

"Leave the beers," Trevena said. "And get the fuck out of my house."

Keeping his back to the worktop, the boy edged away towards the door. Trevena followed him, kept his pace slow and his face expressionless. He stared hard at the boy, daring—wanting—him to say something, do something. Trevena felt all of the day's rage piling up inside him. He hoped he wouldn't have to speak again, because he was sure his voice would be shaky with adrenaline.

But the boy didn't do anything, and he backed away to the door and disappeared up the garden, his narrow back with its caramel, layabout tan rising out of his pants like a wafer in a pert little dollop of ice-cream.

"Pull your trousers up, you prick," Trevena said loudly enough for the boy to hear him and, in reflex, reach around to yank up the waistband of his jeans.

Trevena was relieved to hear that his voice wasn't shaking after all.

At half past one in the morning, Graham Knott awoke to the sound of his pager going off.

He groaned and rolled onto his side. He plucked the pager from his bedside cabinet and squinted at the luminous green display. His heart was racing, as it always did when he was pulled from sleep like this; Graham hated being on call. He always had trouble going off to sleep, knowing there was the potential for the pager to go off at any time in the small hours; he slept fitfully if he slept at all, and he couldn't even have a drink. He frowned as he read the message scrolling across the screen, his heart sinking.

PLEASE HELP URGENT I CANT GO ON NEIL HAS TURNED INTO AN ANGLER FISH THIS IS ROB LITCHIN URGENT

He'd heard it all now. Graham sat up and yawned and began to get dressed.

AN HOUR LATER, Graham pulled up outside Rob's block of flats. His eyes still felt grainy but he'd had a couple of cups of coffee before he left and felt a little more alert. He had tried phoning Rob back on the number he had provided at the end of his garbled text but there had been no reply, just voicemail. Graham had left a brief message to say he had received the page and he would be responding within the hour. If possible, Graham liked to try and de-escalate over the phone; it often prevented him having to go out until the next day, but in this case he was frustrated. He lit a cigarette and got out of the car.

It was cold and there was a low, orange-tinged mist seeping around the grounds of the estate. He zipped up his leather jacket and squinted up at the block facing him through a cloud of cigarette smoke. He tried his phone again but still got no reply from Rob.

Graham trudged across the green and approached the stairwell. The block was large and had at least three legal means of access. There was a back stairs at the end of a row of lockups and a tiny, cramped lift in an entrance hall at the front of the flats but he didn't fancy either of those at this time of night. He started up the stairs dodging flakes of dog muck scraped off on the edges of the steps and other assorted bio-litter; rivulets of urine, sick, and an extra-large condom curled in the corner of a landing like a dozing slow worm.

Usually, Graham would have called for a second worker to support him on a night call like this, but he couldn't be bothered dragging someone else out of bed to end up waiting even longer while they pitched up. It would probably have meant waking up Stibbs, who was manager on-call tonight, and he could well do without that tosser giving it large about wasting resources. And Phil should have been on with him tonight but he was on light duties now so he wasn't an option. Graham was confident he could handle this Rob character. Probably just off his tits on economy pop.

Phil was fucked, though. Graham couldn't help feeling sorry for him. Graham liked Phil; they'd known each other for years, but the bloke was on the edge. He might have felt a bit of guilt, having been the one to mention to Stibbs in supervision how concerned he was for Phil's well being, and offering to take Zoë off his hands for a while to give him a break, but in the end, you had to look after yourself, and the job wasn't about to get any easier over the next few months. People were going to lose their jobs and with his habits and lifestyle choices, Graham really couldn't afford to lose his. Dog eat dog. Or dog at least takes a little nibble when the other dog's not looking. No harm done.

Talking of little nibbles, he was looking forward to working with that student bird Zoë. *That* was tasty. The mouth on it. Graham thought about a student they'd had in the team a few years ago called Zara. No tits, but *legs*. It wasn't long before he was up to his guts in it. It used to be easy, he was a good-looking bloke and the female students loved the experience he had, the knowledge. Psychiatry could be a sexy language. You could sound like a fucking scientist just by knowing the right words. *Phenothiazine naïve, tardive dyskinesia, extrapyramidal side-effects*. You could even get away with bandying that shit around in front of psychiatrists. You could see the affect it was having on the girls. They'd go all still and studious, their brows furrowing and their eyes taking on a serious, burning cast. Trying to look like they were learning but feeling it all downstairs. They always fell in love with their gurus eventually. Just a bit, maybe, but a bit was nearly always enough. Graham smiled as he rounded the last landing and started down the walkway towards Rob's flat.

He passed a narrow corridor that led off into an atrium that housed the lift. He glanced down there but all was in darkness. He continued along the walkway until he reached the door to Rob's flat. He knocked on the glass set into the top of the door. He waited. No reply, no sound from within. He checked his watch. Three o'clock in the morning. He sighed. Good job he was on a late shift tomorrow.

He stood on tiptoes and peered through the glass. He could see into a small, darkened hallway. To the left was the kitchen and straight ahead the living room.

And then he saw movement. Something low and pale had just peered around the door into the lounge. Graham squinted. It was about two feet off the ground, just a smudge against the gloom. He rubbed a couple of fingers against the glass to remove some grime and peered in again. Something was crawling towards him up the short hallway. Graham stepped back from the door until the backs of his legs bumped the low parapet that ran along the edge of the walkway.

Then Graham heard something: *reeeeeeeeeee*.

He turned to look out across the estate.

Reeeeeeeeeeeeee.

Something was coming across the green towards the flats, bumping and waddling over the uneven ground. He could hear the arduous sound of its tiny engine as it struggled to propel the bulk of its rider. A headlight was mounted to the front of it giving off a dim, brownish glow. It looked like it was smothered in a thick film of grease. Graham frowned as he watched it approach the ground floor beneath where he stood. Whoever was on board was hunched over, their face obscured.

Graham watched it disappear beneath the parapet. The sound of the engine continued, blatting away at a slightly higher pitch, growing quieter as it trundled along the corridor towards the lift.

Growing irritable, Graham went back to Rob's door and looked through the glass again. The hallway was empty.

He was about to call it a night and go home but then he heard someone say, "Are you a nurse?"

"Is that you, Rob?" Graham said. He tilted his head so that he was listening an inch away from the door. "It's Graham. You met me with Phil on the ward."

There was silence. From somewhere below, the squat and dented lift clanked and began to ascend its narrow shaft up the middle of the block. Graham heard the low groan of its unmaintained motor and the squeal of its pulleys.

Now Graham could hear sobbing. "You going to let me in, Rob? It's a bit chilly out here, mate."

"Is there anyone out there with you? Have you seen anyone?"

"Just me, mate."

"Have you seen Neil?"

Graham remembered that the name of the man who had been with Rob when he'd been shot had been Neil. This bloke was creating a proper delusional system about all this.

"No, Neil's not here. I'm alone."

There was another sob and a sniff. "Thank God!"

Graham waited for another moment, hands stuffed in his jacket pockets. His toes were cold. He heard the lift reach its destination and grind to a halt. Its door shuddered open and Graham heard: *reeeeeeeeeee.*

"I'll just get my key," Rob said, and Graham heard him shuffling off back down the hall. He looked through the glass and watched Rob crawling back into the lounge.

Graham's patience was diminishing; he knew taking this bloke onto their caseload was going to be a waste of time. Nothing worse than a pisshead to suck the life out of you. He'll probably just crawl into the lounge and go to sleep on the floor.

"Bollocks to this," Graham said. Rob was alive, that was established. He'd give him a ring in the morning. Graham turned intending to walk back towards the stairwell but found his way blocked by the figure riding the mobility scooter. It had emerged from the corridor and turned onto the walkway. Graham frowned. The scooter looked odd. The rider was still hunched over the handlebars, its face obscured. Graham took a step towards the scooter. The rider gripped the accelerator and revved the tiny motor. *Reeeeeeeeeeee.*

Graham stopped. He smiled, despite the peculiarity of the situation and the lateness of the hour. You never knew what you were going to find on this estate. Now it was some old fucker wanting to play chicken on a mobility scooter. Like the gentleman he was, Graham stood aside and beckoned the driver to come past.

The scooter lurched forward. Again, Graham got the impression that something was wrong with it. At first he thought it was just an old wreck but as it trundled up the walkway towards him he noticed that it seemed to have things bolted to it. Whoever was driving it had souped it up. Graham chuckled. *Good for you, granddad,* he thought. *Bet the grandkids love it.*

The scooter rolled on. It passed beneath a lit kitchen window and Graham got a better look at it. There were definitely bits of metal and rods of some sort fixed to it. They looked serrated, rusty and sharp. Not quite so cool. Graham pressed himself into Rob's doorway to allow the scooter to pass and as it came within six feet, he noticed what was smeared over the headlight, dimming it to a reddish glow.

There was blood on the light. And bits of skin and hair. Graham sucked in a harsh breath. Was it hair? It was white and fluffy and stuck to the metal grille that covered the headlight. It reminded him of the chunks of wool sheep leave on barbed wire fences at the sides of fields.

And then the driver looked up, revealing its fuming eyes beneath the hood of the blood-flecked reflective jacket, and it showed Graham its teeth.

Graham froze. He wasn't the type to make a fuss. He thought he'd seen it all. But then he did scream, in shock and horror, because as the scooter drew level with him, something sharp slid out from beneath the chassis and took his right foot off at the ankle.

A MIDDLE-AGED man of slight build wearing a trench coat and suede desert boots heard the man on the walkway scream. It was a choked, throaty sound, surprisingly low in pitch, but nevertheless loud. It was more a primal bellow than a shriek. It contained both surprise and terror. His ear, attuned to the taxonomy of distress, found this unusual but explicable. It was a virgin scream, penetrating the air from a throat unused to exultations. This was a man who spoke quietly, who kept his thoughts and emotions deeply contained. A good man? Not necessarily. If this man laughed, he laughed at others, and that was often a suppressed, internal glee. No great cheers from this man, no ovations.

The man in the trench coat listened for the echo of the scream as its blunt wave ricocheted around the estate. He started walking towards the flats. He looked back once. The woman was still standing in her doorway, lit by the glow of a lamp on a small table in the hall. She made a shooing motion with her right hand. *Hurry up!*

The man smiled. He had a handsome face, but much lined, especially around the eyes and across a forehead etched from decades of worry and uneasy sleep. He wore a beard that was mostly grey. It was neat but not with any vanity, just a rough scissor trim to keep it in check. The woman had wielded the scissors, tipping his chin back and fussing at him, earlier that day. He had laughed when he had looked down, as he had sat on a stool in her kitchen, at the thick pile of grizzled down that had settled in his lap. He scooped some up and examined it. It looked like a bowl of tiny birds' wings. He resisted the impulse to throw them into the air and watch them drift around his head. Considering what the woman had told him earlier, that would have been *provocative*, to say the least.

He picked up his speed and reached the entrance to the stairwell. He loped up the steps, three at a time, the soles of his desert boots making flat, gritty slaps on the concrete. He sprinted across the landing and onto the walkway, his long coat swinging around the backs of his legs like a cape.

ROB WHIMPERED AND slid his key into the lock. His eyes were closed and his lips were moving, uttering a mumbled version of the 23rd Psalm. He was still drunk and some of the verses were slurred, or obscure interpretations of the original.

He pulled on the door, intending to open it a crack and peer out, but the weight of something heavy leaning against it pushed it fully open and he stumbled backwards and landed on his backside.

The body of a man fell into the hall, his head and shoulders landing between Rob's splayed boots. Rob shrieked.

He scrambled backwards until his spine connected with the living room doorframe. He stared down at the body. It was that nurse who had visited him on the ward. Gregory or something. Rob's eyes were wide in the gloom.

"*Greg!*" he hissed. "*Greg, mate.*"

Rob shifted around and crawled over to Graham Knott's body. His hair hung over his face as he looked down at it. He gripped a shoulder and gave the body a quick shake. It groaned.

Rob gripped the padded shoulders of Graham's jacket and started to pull him into the flat. He had succeeded in getting most of him through the door when he looked up. His heart was trying to burrow out of his chest and he was sweating, both with exertion and fear. Whatever had done this might still be outside. It had been Gollick, he realised with horrible certainty. He squeezed his eyes shut and recommenced misquoting scripture.

Rob dragged Graham backwards into the hall and stood up. He groaned and pressed the palms of his hands into the small of his back, and then he looked down and saw the thick trail of blood that had followed the unconscious nurse into the flat. For a moment,

Rob just stood there, perplexed and confused. He was weaving in and out of a kind of sobriety brought on by seemingly endless mindfucks. He didn't seem to be able to stay drunk for very long and this was a new cause for concern. He took a step forward and wondered why his enhanced perspective was failing to bring the nurse's right foot into view.

And then he saw why and fell to his knees.

"No, no, no, no, no," Rob said in a hoarse whisper. He plucked at Graham's trousers, revealing the shredded flesh and splintered bone where his foot had been. A blood-darkened, sodden ring of sock still clung above the stump, neatly sheared off from the foot two inches above the anklebone. Blood was still pumping from the wound, but slowly, as if the instrument that had inflicted this had been hot as well as sharp and had partially cauterised it.

Rob looked up, swiping his hair away from his face, his eyes wild. He pressed his hands together over his mouth and moaned.

The amputated foot, still clad in its casual loafer, was on the doorstep, toe facing away from the door. Nearly out of his mind, Rob reached a trembling hand towards it, meaning perhaps to retrieve it, or poke it out of sight. He wasn't sure what he was doing. And then he heard a noise, a mean-sounding *reeeeeeeeee*. It was loud; it was outside his flat.

Rob froze.

Grinning his splintered-glass grin, eyes smouldering with that soulless oceanic radiance, the thing that had once been Neil Gollick slowly rolled back across Rob's doorstep riding a mobility scooter. Its back wheel reversed over Graham's foot, crushing it with a sharp chicken-bone crack.

"Oh," Rob was saying. "Oh."

With a sudden wrench of the handlebars, Gollick accelerated forwards and swung the scooter in a tight arc. It drove into the doorframe and smashed a four-foot portion of it into a flimsy sheaf of splinters. A chunk of plasterboard the size of a paving stone blew out and hit the floor with a dusty smack. Gollick reversed, twisted the handlebars again and shot forwards. The front wheels bumped up the step and propelled half the scooter into the hall. Its low chassis caught on the lip at the bottom of the doorframe and it rocked there, back wheels whirling an inch above the ground. The engine squealed as Gollick twisted the accelerator. *REEEEEEEEEEEEE.*

Rob was still rigid with fear but somewhere in his brain thoughts were forming, like a poor person's meagre firework display in a cold back garden for a child who never had much. A couple of Roman candles and a sparkler were Rob's last thoughts, but they were valid.

I don't know how many times I've tripped over that fucking step.

And: *What are all those metal things sticking out of that scooter? They look horribly sharp.*

And finally: *What's that fluffy thing rolling about in the shopping basket on the back of that scooter?*

It looked like Ethel Gollick's head. Surely *not.* Rob's face took on a serene expression and then his eyes rolled up in their sockets and he fainted.

THE MAN IN the long coat could see the scooter rocking on the step trying to get purchase. He was still running and as he approached, he leaped and hit the rider in the side with both feet. The rider shrieked and spilled from the scooter where it lay stunned on its back on the walkway. The man in the long coat landed neatly, legs astride the body.

He held out a hand, as if to help the creature up. It stared at the man, eyes glowing, teeth grinding and scraping together with the bitter sound of nails on a blackboard. It lifted a black, taloned claw.

The man smiled, and then slapped the hand aside. He reached down, took the hefty reflective jacket it wore by the collar and lifted the creature one-armed so that they were face to face. The creature's boots dangled a few inches from the ground.

The man spoke again. The creature cocked its head and hissed. Its eyes burned with an even greater intensity and it started to raise its arms, its claws reaching for the man's throat.

The man leaned forward so that his face was an inch away from the creature's and he said, "*I am the Hypnopomp.*"

The creature's arms fell to its sides. The light in its eyes dimmed and its jaw hung open.

The man smiled again and held the creature at an arm's length, and then dropped it over the side of the walkway.

THE MAN TURNED back to the doorway of the flat. He raised his eyebrows at the spectacle of the two men sprawled in the hallway. They were both unconscious.

He stepped over the threshold, past the scooter that had toppled against the doorframe. It was still running and the man reached over and turned the key, cutting it off. He knelt and examined the wound to the leg of the man nearest the door. This was the one who had screamed. No wonder. The man pulled a rag from his coat pocket and pressed it against the stump. There was now hardly any blood loss and when he took the rag away and looked at it, it was only blotted in a few places with a sticky, pinkish serum. He stood up and stepped over to the second man. He was snoring and otherwise unharmed.

The man returned his attention to the amputee. The man searched through the amputee's jacket pockets until he found a mobile phone. He scrolled through the address book until he saw the name he had hoped would be there. As he thumbed the dial button he thought, as he often did, about fate, and hope, and synchronicity. These, and faith, were the tools of his trade. And, as it says elsewhere, without faith it's impossible to please God.

"Hello, Phil," the man said when the phone was answered. "My name is Daniel. We need to meet."

The Night Clock hangs from rusting chains, from the roof of some immense and desolate terminal, its painted face upon a disc of slats of wood cut from reclaimed gallows planks. Its painted hands say ten past three.

5

MY FRIEND ELIZABETH has one eye. She lost her left eye when she was a child. She was playing in the unruly cottage garden at the back of her grandmother's house and tripped on a verge and fell headlong into a blackberry bush. Her face had been terribly scratched, as had her shoulders and upper arms, but the worst injury had been to her eyeball. It had been lacerated by the prickles. That's how she describes it: lacerated by the prickles. Maybe that's how the doctors described it to *her* as they tried to explain to a five-year-old girl that the eye was so badly damaged by infection it would have to be removed. If she hadn't turned her head as she'd fallen, they said, she might have lost both eyes.

At first, Elizabeth had experienced hallucinations. Her eye was dead in her head and sightless but still it saw things: vivid, complex and recurrent visual phantasms. She saw shapes and colours, scaffolding patterns and swirls like piles of wings taking flight, lifting off from the ground. She was diagnosed with Charles Bonnet syndrome and six weeks later the eye was removed and the visions stopped. This had made Elizabeth sad because she'd thought that the visions were perhaps the beginning of some special extrasensory gift, but it had just been a mundane neurological phenomenon, and that was it.

Elizabeth has a glass eye. She calls it an *ocular prosthesis*. It's made from cryolite and it fits over an orbital implant and under the eyelids. It doesn't have much motility but it's quite lifelike if she stares straight ahead, and she's a pretty woman, so people tend not to notice or remark on it very often.

I met Elizabeth on a boating lake in Eastbourne when I was there on holiday with my parents as a child. It rained for the first few days of the week and we were staying in a guesthouse near the front. We had breakfast and an evening meal provided but between times we had to be out of the house. Across the road from the guesthouse was a little park. There was a playground with some swings, a seesaw and a tall iron slide, and the lake itself. It was more of a large pond but it had a wooden jetty with a modest fleet of shabby fibreglass pedal boats moored to it.

It had been a dry afternoon and so we wandered over to the park and had a look at the boats. There was a man and a woman sitting on a bench at the edge of the path eating sandwiches from out of a blue fabric shopping bag. A thermos flask sat erect between them like a dutiful tartan-clad pet. They both smiled as we passed. They were getting on a bit but seemed happy enough. We all smiled back.

We walked over to the jetty. The pedal boats were shaped like little snub-nosed speedboats and there seemed to be quite a bit of dirty rain water slopping about in the bottom of them and wet shoeprints on the seats. I turned my mouth down and looked up at my folks. They seemed intent that I should have a go on the lake though, and Dad pointed across the water at something labouring out from behind a screen of rushes in the middle of the lake.

"Look, Dan," he said. "That little girl's having a go. Jump in and have some fun before it rains again."

I was doubtful about the whole thing. I looked across the lake again, at the girl in the pedal boat. I could see her struggling, her narrow, bony knees pumping up and down as she worked the pedals that moved the paddles at the stern of the little tub. She was gripping the steering wheel and I could see how her teeth were clenched with the effort of controlling the rudder.

"This is shit," she muttered under her breath as the boat drifted up against the jetty. She climbed out and stood beside me. She was wearing flared jeans with turn-ups above a pair of red wellies and a pink fluffy jumper. The turn-ups were soaked. She stomped up the jetty and sat down on the bench next to the old couple.

I returned my attention to the boats. They were two-seaters with a set of pedals either side of a raised plastic hump in the prow, perhaps where a gearbox would be housed if this thing had any workings. The steering wheel was above the right-hand set of pedals. One person to steer, then, and two to drive the thing. No wonder the girl had been struggling.

I turned to point this out but Mum and Dad were over by the bench talking to the old couple. The woman was pouring steaming brown liquid from the little tartan flask into a small plastic cup and nodding and smiling. The old chap looked quite animated. He was nudging the girl who sat next to him so hard she nearly slid off the edge of the bench. I watched all this with curiosity and a strange sense of dread in my heart.

The girl stood up. Mum and Dad smiled over at me. Dad was making exaggerated pointing gestures towards the boats. I sighed as the girl walked back down the path, the soles of her boots dragging with slow rubbery scrapes against the concrete. They sounded like hate-filled, bitter kisses.

She walked up to me and stood staring at the boats.

"They want us to take one out together," she said. "They think it would be fun for us to make friends." She glanced up at me and for the first time I noticed something wrong with her eye. It remained fixed, as if glazed with defeat.

I didn't say anything. Girls filled me with palpitating despair. Especially pretty ones.

"Come on, let's get this over with." And she stepped lightly back into one of the boats. Rainwater sloshed around her boots and the boat pitched and she gritted her teeth and hissed, "Come on!"

Resigned, I took one last look back at the adults. They were all grinning away. The old boy was offering around some biscuits from the picnic bag. Dad was munching on a Bourbon. He waved. I lifted a hand, and then I turned and got in beside the girl.

I was in the driving seat, so I gripped the wheel and put my feet on the pedals. The girl jammed her boots onto her pedals, looked across at me and nodded, her expression grim. We pushed off.

It was fun. We got up a good head of steam between us. The nose lifted a bit and we scudded across the lake towards the screen of reeds. I kept my focus straight ahead, guiding the boat with the wheel and liking the feeling of resistance against the rudder and of the suspension above the water as it fashioned and slid beneath the fibreglass hull sending a widening, rippling 'V' in our wake.

I twisted the wheel and we glided right, around the reeds. A duck, caught napping, uttered one cartoon 'Quack!' You could almost see the word written in a speech bubble above its head. It lifted its chest and belted off across the lake like a rocket. We both laughed.

"I'm Elizabeth," the girl said.

"I'm Daniel," I said.

Laughing we came back around the screen of reeds and began to push for the jetty.

When we got back Mum and Dad had already made great friends with the old couple. They were laughing and joking like they'd known each other for years.

I looked at Elizabeth. She smiled at me. I blushed.

"Don't do a cherry," she said, which made it so much worse. Now Mum and Dad were looking at me.

"Have fun? Dad asked. I nodded. I looked down at my shoes. "That's great," he said. "We're all going for tea on the pier. Come on."

The four adults started walking off down the path. The old boy held the bag with the flask stowed away in it. The old girl took his arm. Dad looked at Mum and reached out to hold her hand, but she didn't take it. Dad looked sad for a moment, but he put his hands in his pockets and carried on down the path to the gate. He started whistling, which was always a sign he was feeling a bit self-conscious. I wanted to tell him not to do it. I guess it embarrassed me a bit. It drew attention to him and I don't think that was what he wanted. *Look at me, I'm being unobtrusive.* A bit of a contradiction there, I think.

He was so gentle, my dad. And I loved him so much. And if it hadn't been for him I'd have never met Elizabeth and we wouldn't have had that last, funny, happy holiday, just being together in easy company, hanging out every day doing silly, fun things.

It's my best memory, and it saved my life. I just wish it had saved his.

THE OLD COUPLE were Elizabeth's grandparents. Their names were Dolly and Gordon. To me, Dolly was just a big, soft, unremarkable grandmother, sweet and fretful and vague. Gordon, however, was a fascination. With his long, weathered face and large features, bright, restless hazel eyes, his compact wiry frame and short bandy legs, Gordon was constantly on the look-out for things to do to entertain us that were borderline dangerous, or at the very least distasteful. One afternoon he came springing down the slope that led from the promenade to the beach with a handful of tiny coloured flags, the type used to decorate the tops of sandcastles. He thrust a couple in our hands and bounded back up the slope. He stood framed by a row of beach huts, beckoning us. We got up off our towels and crunched up the pebbles. The slope was gritty and hot beneath our feet.

"I've put flags in all the piles of dog's muck along the promenade all the way up to the pier," he said. He spoke with the air of a commanding officer briefing his men on the deployment of tanks.

We looked at each other, and then looked along the prom. Indeed, at intervals, against the walls, in the shadows between kiosks selling gifts and renting deckchairs, crouched on verges and curled like sleeping rodents beneath the beach huts, turds lay, each impaled with a cheerful little pennant.

Another time he found a dead seagull on the shoreline and insisted that it would be fun to tie it to a length of twine and run up the beach dragging it behind us. I'm not sure why. At this point, at the height of Gordon's schoolboy ravings, Dolly would say, "That's enough, Gordon!" and it would quiet him and we could go back to doing normal things like skimming or digging holes and filling them with buckets of seawater. But he was always atwitch, those bright little eyes darting about for iffy things to do.

Many years later I recall reading an article about culled animals left to rot by rubbish bins in a safari park in Merseyside. The article came with photos and they were pretty bad. Piles of deer and antelope in crates and sprawled by bins, carcasses rotting and maggoty. But the most dreadful thing was the last picture. It was labelled *Baboon's head explodes out of bin bag*, like some callous display at a modern art exhibition. It was a picture of a baboon's head and shoulders which had slid stiff from a black bin bag, as per the title, but what made it so horrible—or more than *just* horrible— was the expression on its face. It had its mouth slightly open and its eyes shut and it looked like it had realised with a dawning yet amused certainty (*doh*!) that it had just been made the butt of some inoffensive joke. So expressive, that face. Except there were gouts of blood on its face and the side of its head, and it was dead and those heavy blue-lidded eyes were never going to open again.

I imagined Gordon finding a dead baboon in a bin bag.

The fun he'd have had with that.

ON OUR LAST day we met in the café on the pier. It was raining again and the planks underfoot were shiny and slippery and the rainwater dripped and hung in wobbling, wind-blown beads from the underside of the blue iron railings. A herring gull perched on one of the posts glared at us with its incensed spiv's eyes. Dolly and Gordon were sitting at a window seat looking out along the pier and they waved as we battled towards the entrance to the café.

"Nice end to the week," Dad said as we sat down at the table with them.

"Where's Elizabeth?" I asked.

Gordon looked up and nodded towards the counter. There was a one-armed bandit standing on a table next to the hatch. Elizabeth was plugging pennies into it and watching the cylinders rumble round each time she pulled the handle.

I went over. There was a tall glass containing the remains of a banana milkshake on the Formica-topped table. Elizabeth scooped it up and sucked a last mouthful of yellow suds from the bottom of the glass through a straw with a wet clattering sound.

"Hello, Bert," she said. She'd taken to calling everybody Bert. It was something she had picked up from her grandfather. "Granddad had some winkles earlier," she added before I could say anything. "And there was a hermit crab in one of them. He's kept it to show you."

"Right," I said, and before I could add to that, Elizabeth squealed with delight as the cylinders plunked down three lemons in a row and the bandit evacuated itself of a slew of dark brown pennies into a small brass cup at the bottom of the machine. Elizabeth scooped them out then turned and ran back to the table where our folks were sitting.

"I won, Granddad," she said, holding out two cupped palmfuls of coins.

"Drinks are on you, then, Bert," Gordon said.

"That's where you're wrong, Bert," Elizabeth said to Gordon.

Gordon laughed. Dolly said, "Don't talk to your grandpa like that, Elizabeth," in a resigned tone.

"Sorry grandma-*Bert*!" Elizabeth blurted, spluttering laughter, and turned and legged it out onto the pier clutching her winnings. "I'm going to the arcade!" she shouted back at us. Her red wellies clumped on the long boards and the wind dashed a spatter of rain against the window.

"We're having tea," Dad said, "but you go if you want."

I made to run after Elizabeth, but Gordon said, "Hang on, little Bert." He reached into his coat pocket and pulled out a handkerchief folded into a tight white lozenge.

Dolly narrowed her small bright blue eyes.

"Here you go," he said. He unwrapped the handkerchief and held its contents out to me. I had a look.

Nestling in the middle of the fabric was a small conical shell, darkly banded with a pointed tip. Retracted into the aperture was a tiny orange crab. It was only about the size of my little fingernail. It was dead. I looked up at Gordon. His expression was sage. "In with my winkles," he said. "Thought you'd be interested."

I peered closer. It had tiny eyes like full stops and a ragged little mouth surrounded by pale pin-thin stalks. Two delicate, bright orange claws no bigger than beetle's feet but clearly sharp, and articulated like pieces of fine clockwork. Peering back at me as it seemed to lean in a neighbourly fashion upon the shell's curved lip.

I looked up at Gordon. He nodded. "Go on, Dan. Take him. He's yours if you want him."

"Don't give him that, Gordon," Dolly protested, looking with some anxiety at my folks. Mum seemed to be with Dolly on this. "It'll stink," she said.

"Nah," Gordon said. "Might be a bit fishy for a day or two but it'll dry out. Leave it on the windowsill in the sun and he'll last forever."

I looked up at Dad for the approval I wanted. There it was, shining in his eyes. He nodded and winked at me. "What'll you call him?" asked Gordon.

I held the shell on my palm and said, "Bert."

What else?

BEFORE MY DAD died, he made sure I kept up my correspondences with Elizabeth. He was tireless. Elizabeth would write me long, rambling letters framed with dense borders of doodles and sketches; they'd arrive folded into tight squares in bulging pink envelopes. Sometimes she'd send me pages cut out of magazines, or photos, or postcards. Dad didn't ask to read the letters, but he'd know when they arrived and would keep on at me until I replied—with my own notelets of limited interests. In comparison they seemed measly, childish, *boy*ish, especially considering the detail and baroque generosity of Elizabeth's letters. But it didn't seem to put her off. She had clearly taken our solemn end-of-holiday pact to keep in touch to heart. She'd just write back again almost by return of post and another wad of burbling fairyland would thud onto the doormat.

"Very important to keep up your friendships," Dad would say. And then he'd put pens and paper in front of me and keep bugging me until I'd knocked out another grudging minimalist reply.

The week before Dad died I got a letter from Elizabeth containing a homemade birthday card. It was a bit early. I wasn't seven for another month. The picture she'd drawn on the front of the card was strange. It looked like a pylon standing on a hill against a starless black sky, and at the top of the structure was a clock face with hands at twenty past three—and there was something so bleak about the isolated skeletal structure that it made me turn my mouth down in a shudder. I opened the card and it read:

Happy Birthday Dan. Seven's a magic number!! This is the Night Clock. Time's ticking. Love Elizabeth. Xxxxxxxxxxx
Xxxx

To be honest I was probably more disconcerted by all those kisses, but nevertheless showed Dad (hoping he wouldn't mention them) and he said:

"Dear God!" And then he started crying.

It was just a few tears, but they shocked me. I must have looked shaken, because Dad threw his arms round me and hugged me and told me he loved me; he told me he was very proud of me and that whatever life threw at me I mustn't be frightened. Then he straightened up, coughed and handed me back my card. He smiled. It was a sweet smile, and his eyes were clear again. "Look after that one," he said, and winked. I assumed he meant Elizabeth.

I know he was right to say that. They were the wisest words he ever said to me. They were also among the last.

Four days later, Dad killed himself.

*   *   *

IN 1961, IRVING Goffman wrote a book called *Asylums*, which was a seminal educational book describing the effects of what he called 'the total institution' on patients in mental hospitals, how institutionalisation leads to the mortification of self. But my experience was different; to me these places were citadels; their walled perimeters contained a discrete sanctuary from the predatory undead roaming the world outside. They were self-sufficient places of safety. There were farms and allotments, fields, meadows and sports grounds, stores, great engine rooms, laundries, ball rooms, shoe menders, carpenters, hospital wings, and huge voluminous wards like hangers where we could froth and convulse and scream and slope and creep and lurch and pester; where nurses really did wear white coats and consultants had mystifying, unpronounceable Mauritian names which were by necessity abbreviated to their first syllable: *Dr Widge, Dr Sat, Dr Kun.* It was uncertain what they were treating as the inmates had such a range of bizarre and monstrous syndromes that all they could modify with any kind of success was their complex and often gruesome behaviour. Shrieking, befouling, masturbating, buggering. Cretins drooling, steeple-skull monstrosities whooping and whistling with their bulging eyes, twisted spines and fused yet unfathomably dextrous fingers. Idiots wandering the grounds with their wirelesses and *Bunty* annuals, vacant and sated from a transgression in the bushes or behind the pavilion. Imbeciles supple as yogis cross-legged and rocking in their shit-wadded pads in the dirt outside their wards. We were all given drugs. Huge, thick draughts of them, which made us shamble and sleep.

I offer no apologies for the language; these were the names—the *diagnoses*—by which we were known. Less than thirty years ago, I was a certified lunatic. Admissions to the bins were often for life. You were forgotten. My stay was only curtailed by their sudden and brutal closures. I was propelled from a timeless, shuffling routine into a world of community care. I had a flat and a fortnightly visit from a nurse to keep me going. That was my treatment.

Once, when I was suffering a particularly florid episode of psychosis, I imagined that the dead that walked the ruined world outside the walls of the asylum had turned their attention to the hospital and were gathering in sopping ranks beyond the high, red-bricked walls. I spent an evening working my way around the perimeter tying all the gates together with rolls of rusty wire I had found amongst the ashes of a bonfire. They were probably bedsprings from a burnt mattress but the heat of the fire had rendered them brittle and soft. They kept snapping in my hands as I twisted them around the latches on the gates, stabbing my palms and the backs of my hands. I stood back and watched the faces of the dead push against the bars, smelling the blood that dripped from my fingers. I remember the sun setting behind me; it was autumn and the grounds were exposed and damp. But the sky was a clear blue above, darkening in an arc beyond the bulk of the wards at my back and the setting sun threw the buildings into hellish relief against that sky as it sank away from my ruined world.

I saw the face of my father, there in that throng. He struggled to the front and reached arms through the bars.

Sometimes I thought of death as a slot through which all things were removed, all time and space, as it sucked you away. If time and matter and energy could come from nothing then was each individual slot a reclamation of that previous state? Was death a fuel for other universes? Were we just a by-product of an alien fatality in some cosmos beyond our own? Was creation elsewhere nothing more than an unremitting sucking away of our memories and personalities, a steady state of bereavements and loss?

You see, my father's suicide had left a profound impression on me. I loved him with all of a child's broken heart, and I hated him with an adult's entire broken mind.

I rushed towards the gate, to take my father in an embrace, to hold him, to choke him; to kiss him and bite him.

Much later, nurses found me curled into a ball at the foot of the gates and took me, without a great deal of tenderness, back home to my ward. It was time for a more *invasive* treatment.

* * *

THROUGHOUT MY TIME in the asylum the only constant link to the outside world was Elizabeth.

She wrote to me every month. Her letters were more cautious, gentler than the girlish stuff of her youth, but no less full of love and concern. I rarely wrote back. When I was experiencing moments of lucidity I hid myself beneath the covers of my bed and wished the world would blacken and die; I longed for my slot to appear and drag me away to form a universe of my own. Would I be its God, or just one of many? Would I create paradise or would I be barren and expand forever through unformed darkness?

If I wrote to Elizabeth it was usually when I was starting to lose my grip again, when the drugs stopped working or some unusually bad combination of events triggered a relapse. That grey area when hallucinations and delusions began to colour reality like drops of blood spreading in a lake of disturbed water; angry, crimson-tipped waves rippling at the edges of the mind heralding the incoming storm.

And as my delusional system became more complex I incorporated more and more of my memories, experiences and ideas into them. It was my mind's way of keeping me out of reality for as much time as possible. I was harmless, although often disturbed enough to be restrained for my own physical safety. I wished no harm to others and my delusions were not particularly persecutory; in fact as they grew in scope I became more amenable, more at peace in a world I was creating. I had decided, somewhere in the fissures of my unconscious, to become something new, someone of stature. If the slot would not manifest, then I would dig it out of the air in handfuls. But it wasn't a slot to Heaven I opened. It was to somewhere else entirely. And I found a use for myself there.

As the asylum wound down towards its closure, wards and wings and blocks of offices became untenanted and derelict. The corridors between the wards, which were little more than draughty, elongated conservatories roofed with corrugated tin, lined with old, locked doors leading off into rooms and compartments and areas of the hospital unexplored for years, were passage to fewer and fewer people as patients died off or were displaced to other, smaller units outside the hospital and staff left or were laid off.

It was easy to find and break into a small, cold room at the end of one of these corridors and use it for my purposes. It contained an old wooden desk and a couple of chairs. A metal filing cabinet stood in a corner beside a window that looked out across the overgrown cricket field. It was perfect for my needs. It became my office.

And it was there that I met my best friend and started taking him back in time.

6

TREVENA SAT ON a stool next to the breakfast bar in Elizabeth's tiny kitchen and listened to the man named Daniel as he told his story. He sipped at a hot mug of tea that Elizabeth had replenished twice already.

He had taken the call from Daniel an hour and a half ago and despite his initial bewilderment—he had awakened from a deep dream-lashed sleep fuelled by alcohol and wrath—he had listened with care and a mind open to all possibilities following the events of the last few days. He recalled the last conversation he had had with Les, how he should find this Daniel because he had very important things to do. When Daniel told him that he knew why his patients were dying, Trevena had agreed to meet, and had driven to the address on the estate he had been given in less than fifteen minutes.

A small, attractive woman in her forties had opened the door to him. Trevena immediately noticed that she had a glass eye. It was a good one and detracted nothing from her prettiness. She smiled and shook his hand and ushered him into her kitchen where Trevena was introduced to a handsome man of medium build wearing a long coat who appraised him with the most care-worn eyes Trevena had ever seen.

Daniel explained the circumstances prior to his call. Trevena was glad he was sitting down. There was something utterly compelling about the man and Trevena was experienced enough to recognise actual truth from the delusional truths believed and expounded upon by a proper madman. Daniel had called an ambulance for Rob and Graham and then left the scene to return to Elizabeth's house. What the authorities would find beneath the walkway would be a recently deceased Neil Gollick. Daniel was unconcerned what they would make of the entire scene as once sufficiently recovered, Rob's rendering of events would make nonsense of any careful cover-up, so he hadn't bothered. Just let them get on with it. Graham might make more sense, but having been through what he'd experienced, Daniel admitted he probably wouldn't be the same man when he recovered. Trevena was initially saddened, but Daniel counselled him not to waste much energy grieving for a man who cared little for him. It was comments like these that made Trevena listen and not look too hard for madness. Daniel's insight was robust.

Despite what followed, Trevena could detect no insanity in Daniel's demeanour. He sipped his tea and watched the man with a keen assessor's eye but couldn't find anything he could nail down as symptomatic of an illness. And there was this woman, fussing around, concurring with everything he said. Again, Trevena looked for conspiracy, co-dependence or collusion, but found none at all. So he listened.

WHEN HE HAD finished telling Trevena about his history, Daniel reflected that his first thoughts had been that his delusions had been an attempt to make sense of his past, to somehow modify the effects of his trauma and loss. That time was an element he could control and therefore strip of power, a textbook coping strategy, however unbalanced and, according to the psychiatrists, maladaptive.

Elizabeth went over to Daniel and put a hand on his arm. He looked down at her and smiled. It was such a sweet smile, communicating such old friendship, that Trevena felt his eyes mist up. He took another sip of tea and let the steam blur his vision for a moment. He felt very tired.

"You were never mad, though, Daniel," she said. "You really could stop time."

Trevena looked up. Elizabeth turned to him and spoke again. Her expression was very serious.

"Those places he went, they were real. He just needed time to understand why he could go there. But something stopped him before he could fully realise it."

Daniel nodded.

"What happened?" Trevena asked.

"They gave me ECT," Daniel said.

ONCE THE HOSPITAL had closed and Daniel found himself in a flat above a shop on the outskirts of town, the medic looking after him decided that he needed a more *vigorous* treatment regime to keep his symptoms in check. Against his wishes, but within the framework of Mental Health law, Daniel was forced to undergo lengthy courses of electro-convulsive treatment. It worked. Within weeks he had lost all ability to travel back in time. His mind became fogged, his thoughts slow and impoverished. He began to gain insight into his condition and the memories of his pain returned and he had nowhere to go to escape them. He began occasionally to see the dead again, brief incursions, flashbacks that clouded his vision with a green vapour and introduced shambling figures of rot. One small mercy was that his father was no longer amongst them.

It was too much to bear. Daniel had made a decision. He took a train to the coast, to a place where his last sweet memories had been laid down, and, with hope and the final thought—*can love make a moment last forever?*—he ended his pain.

Daniel went through the slot.

* * *

"YOU WENT THROUGH the slot?" Trevena said.

Daniel nodded. His tired, ancient eyes brightened a little and he smiled.

"I did," he said. Elizabeth, still standing at his side, put an arm around his waist.

DANIEL STOOD BETWEEN the tracks and watched the train approach. He closed his eyes and waited for his pain to end.

Following his father's suicide, Daniel had suffered terrible nightmares. Paralysing visitations of a great face hanging beyond his bedroom window, the face of a woman with furious eyes and a mouth bleeding a torrent of black fluid. It screamed at him, blaming him for his part in his father's death. How his very existence had caused his father to take his own life. This was untrue—as vile a lie as his unconscious mind could make up—but Daniel's child psyche believed it, believed, as children do, that the blame for such catastrophic events must somehow lie with them. And there had been a sound, too. A noise that heralded her presence so jarring and hostile and filled with menace that he was unable to describe it. It was a machine sound; a shrieking vibration generated somewhere deep and terrifying, its source unknowable.

Daniel heard that sound now as the train came. He opened his eyes and the train was ten feet away. It was the sound of the brakes grinding against the wheels, thunderous and full of pressure and sparks. It was the sound he had heard all his life and it triggered two things: an opening in his mind that revealed in extraordinary detail all the events of his past, both real and imagined, and in a moment—in a singularity—expanded them to form a periodic table of experience, an accumulation of shells that allowed him for a brief second to glimpse the possibility that order and goodness existed and that he was a part of it all.

And it opened a line of light in the air in front of him.

Daniel blinked, his eyes filling with tears, held his breath, and discovered that he could stop time again.

The front of the train was frozen, shimmering in its own heat. Daniel could smell its hot metal. It *bulged* like an image straining to propel itself from a cinema screen.

The slot opened in the air and Daniel peered in. Love, the emotion out of all so easily crushed in its endless search for rapture, burst through him. He could see what lay beyond the slot and it wasn't darkness, and it wasn't for him to fill it because it was already full, and it wasn't for him to people because people stood there now.

Daniel breathed, and went through.

TREVENA PUT HIS mug down on the worktop and rubbed his eyes. He was glad he wasn't going to have to write this all up. This was definitely off the record. Daniel was smiling and Trevena got the impression that he knew what he was thinking. It was an unsettling feeling but not a particularly invasive one.

"Les was the first to find me," Daniel said. "He came to my office one afternoon. I was sitting in my old broken wooden chair behind my empty desk and I remember staring out of the window across the cricket field and watching starlings flock above the pavilion. He knocked once, and came in."

THE MAN WAS about forty and Daniel recognised him from seeing him around the asylum for as long as he had been there. His gait was unusually erect and rhythmic. Daniel assumed that he perhaps needed less medication than others. He always seemed quite serene; maybe his breakdown had done a perfect job of erasing his worries in one great sandblast of an event.

The man walked over to the desk, his old, soft and faded shoes treading through drifts of leaves and bits of paper strewn across the concrete floor. He looked down at Daniel with his peaceful, pale brown eyes. He smiled.

"What can you do?" he said.

Daniel shrugged. "I'm not sure," he said.

The man smiled more widely. His teeth were quite clean and bright in the dimness of the room.

"Have you got your Instrument?" he asked.

Daniel reached into his coat pocket and pulled out a worn and battered matchbox. He placed it on the desk. "I've got this," he said.

"Open it."

Daniel held the sides of the box gently between thumb and index finger of his left hand and slid the drawer open with the index finger of his right.

The man leaned forward and looked at what had been revealed, in its tiny manger of cotton wool.

"Lovely," he said. "That's it."

"What do I do?" Daniel asked.

"Don't you know?"

Daniel looked down at the matchbox. "What do you want me to do?"

The man straightened up. He raised his hands, the palms grimy and lined. It was a gesture that communicated total confidence. "I want you to take me back to the happiest day of my life," the man said.

Daniel understood. "Okay," he said.

The man closed his eyes, his expression sweet delight.

Daniel reached the tips of his fingers into the matchbox, took out what nestled within and held it up in front of his face, inspecting it, as he did every day.

Still perfect, despite the years; still so reminiscent of happy times, delicate as clockwork and many times more complex and important, Daniel smiled at the tiny hermit crab crouching in its conical shell. It was as dry and hollow as a fossil and its brilliant orange colour had faded to a distant pink, but it was still whole. Even its minuscule eyes, on their hairsbreadth stalks, remained.

"This is Bert," Daniel said.

The man nodded. "Bert," he said, "I'm Les. Shall we?"

"Close your eyes," said Bert. They both heard him. It was the unmistakeable voice of a long-dead crab. It was bossy, it was comical, it had the sound of the sea, and of brine flaking from rocks dried in the sun. There was orange in it, a perfect synaesthesia both men could apprehend.

They closed their eyes and went back.

Outside, entirely covering the dome of the pavilion, the starlings had settled, all their slicked little heads tilted towards the window set into the wall of the now empty office at the end of the deserted corridor.

7

I OPENED MY eyes and saw that I was standing on a path at the side of a narrow, dusty road running through a village surrounded by hills. Les stood beside me, his face turned up to the sun. His eyes were closed and he basked there for a moment, the most composed expression on his face. Then he opened his eyes and looked at me.

"This is it," he said. "Thank you."

I shrugged. I hadn't done anything.

"Who's that?" Les asked, nodding his head towards what I held in my hands.

I held up the large glass jar and peered into the murky fluid it contained. It was heavy, that jar. Something peered back at me, a momentary glimpse of an eyeball hooded with a translucent lid. Something forever dead, having never really lived, yet lived now and always had.

I knew its name, too, knew it intimately; and always had.

"Dr Natus," I said.

Les nodded, but his focus was gone from me now. It was all on the corner of the road and the sign that hung there: Tнe Dog With its Eyes Shut

I looked across the road. There was a scrubby lot and another pub to the rear of it. It looked derelict. There was an old wooden bench beneath one of the windows. Someone was sitting there smoking a cigar. I couldn't see his features because he was wearing a parka coat with the hood up. As we walked towards the corner of the road the figure in the coat did something startling.

Holding the stub of the cigar between the fingers of his left hand, the man—I assumed it was a man, because of the cigar and the evident size of his hands—reached up and gripped the sides of the hood of the parka and pulled them across his face. And then he shouted, an unintelligible sound muffled from within the hood, and stood up and darted around the back of the building.

I stopped and looked at Les, but Les was now standing at the door of the pub on the corner and had lifted a trembling hand to the latch. His face was still serene but there were tears in his eyes.

"Don't try and follow him, Daniel," Les said. "He's not really here yet."

I wasn't intending on following him. The man and that empty pub had given off a vibration that had deeply unsettled me. The sun gleamed off the windows like pools of white, milky scum. If there was life inside it moved with the slow dreamlike glide of fish dying in dense, polluted water. Yes, it was polluted, that place, I could tell. It had a hole at its heart and dark dreams were welling up inside there, dreams from others like me, but not like me. They had been like me once, I realised, but what they brought here was foul and full of despair. There was a sign hanging from a chain on an iron rod attached to the wall above the door. It was faded but I could read what it said: The Night Clock. There was an illustration beneath the words of a clock face with no hands. The numbers were all there but ordered randomly around the edge of the face: 11,2,6,8,4,3,12,7,10,1,9,5. Somehow those muddled numbers disturbed me more than anything else, their sequence an equation mocking good order and progression.

Les had opened the door and was standing on the threshold. The sunlight illuminated an oblong of worn green tiles on the floor and Les stepped into the pub and the sounds of raised voices and laughter. I approached and came behind him. I could see the place was full; I could smell the stale yet contented aroma of beer and cigarettes. There was a low plaster ceiling stained brown and ribbed with thick dark beams. The bar was packed.

Les continued standing for a moment. He was looking around. And then his knees buckled slightly and he reached out and held onto the doorframe. He gasped, almost a sob and said, "There they are." He spoke in a hushed, reverential voice, as though he had just spotted something incredibly rare and wonderful, something he felt he might never have had the chance to see, and might never see again. It was like he had glimpsed a portion of God and apprehended what holiness really was.

As he turned to me, I expected somehow that his face would be glowing like brass, like an angel, reflecting glory, but it was just Les, in partial shadow, the only gleam the sunlit tears on his cheeks.

"Thank you, Daniel," he said. "Thank you again, so very much."

Across the road that rundown building hunched beneath its roof of moss and broken tiles.

"What do you want me to do?" I asked Les.

Les smiled. "Do what you want. If you want to go back, shake the jar. If you want to stay, then stay and look around. This is your Quay, Daniel. Dream it as you want it. But watch out for that thing over there. It's an incursion. There have always been incursions. Get strong. One day you'll have to fight what comes out of there."

I held the jar closely to my chest. The sediment had thinned, settled. I could make out better the grey, suspended shape of the preserved foetus, forever floating, its mind somehow alive and glorious within the billion dead cells of its unfired brain.

"Will I have to come back for you?"

"Yes, this time you must."

"How will I know when to get you?"

Les pointed to something on the wall next to the bar. It was an old Bakelite payphone.

"I'll call you," he said.

I didn't question this because everything here made sense.

A man's voice sounded above the general noise: "Les! What do you know?"

Les turned and grinned. "All I need to, Andy. All I need to."

The man laughed. "They're over there, Les. they've been waiting for you."

"I know," Les said. "I'm coming."

He turned and lifted a hand and then walked off through the crowd, his arms already raised for an embrace he had longed for, had dreamed of, for so many years.

THE DOOR SWUNG shut and the voices and the laughter were muffled. Despite what Les had advised, I crossed the road and stood looking at the derelict building. I put the jar down on the pavement in the cool shadow of a low, crumbling wall and walked onto the lot. It had been a beer garden once, I assumed. There was that bench beneath the window and this scrubby terrace on which I stood was scattered with pieces of broken crockery that spewed hunks of dry, root bound soil. There was a concrete trough filled with a knotted rug of vine that had struggled to lift itself from the earth and had died trying to climb the cracked plaster on the wall at the corner of the pub.

And then I heard footsteps. A tip-tap sound, trotting, non-human.

I turned and saw, coming along the path, a large, handsome-looking dog. It stopped when it saw me and barked once, and wagged its tail.

"Hello, boy," I said.

The dog lowered its head and woofed, its long elegant tail doubling its efforts. It came onto the lot and approached me. I squatted down and opened my arms. The dog came over and let me stroke the dense fur of his neck. I could feel his warm breath panting against my cheek.

"What's your name?" I asked.

"My name is Bix," the dog said.

I remember feeling a frisson of shock when he spoke, but it was a thrill rather than a feeling of alarm, and I remembered the voice of the crab and how right that had been. In the depths of my psychoses I had heard voices, commands and commentaries, ideas of reference from inanimate objects, but this was very different. Despite the circumstances, I knew this was real.

I stood up and looked down at the dog. It was a beautiful animal. Tall and slender with a barrel chest and a long, graceful snout. He looked like a greyhound but a more stylish version. I think he was a Saluki but I wasn't sure.

Bix was looking up at me, his head tilted slightly to one side. What are you thinking? His expression asked.

"Are you a Saluki?"

"You know your dogs," Bix said.

"I've surprised myself."

Bix laughed. A proper doggy *ho ho*.

"Come with me," he said, and started off towards the side of the pub, where previously the man in the parka had fled.

"Les said I shouldn't."

Bix stopped and turned his head. "Les is being cautious for your sake. But Les has other things on his mind. If you want to go, just shake the jar. If you want to see more, come with me."

"Who is Les?"

"He is your Paladin, Daniel," Bix said. "A guide, and a protector."

"Why did he want to come here?"

Bix lowered his head. "I'll let him tell you, when he's ready."

He trotted off. I decided to follow him.

IT WAS SHADY around the side of the building. We walked past the cellar doors, set into a sloping concrete bunker. They were chained and locked with a rusty padlock. There was a pile of dirty aluminium kegs spilled across the path like mines. We went through them and reached an area behind the pub.

Bix stopped, and his tail went between his legs, and his muzzle curled up into a snarl.

Sitting on a bench, his back to us, hunched over and shaking like a frame in a jammed projector, was the man in the parka coat.

Bix let out a sudden, sharp volley of barks and bounded towards the man.

As he did so, something broke away from the roof of the building above us and soared into the air, sunlit and glittering.

The man raised his head, still encased within the hood of the parka, and let out a sound. It wasn't a word, merely a harsh croak, but it had an effect on the creature hovering above the lot.

It reared up, exposing a gleaming abdomen that shone like a searchlight bulb. At its heart a ball of fire glowed. It was small, the size of a fist, but to look at it hurt my eyes. It wasn't the brightness that hurt, it was the quality of the light that felt wrong. It felt as if the photons themselves were *strange*, that they hit the backs of my eyes and crawled into my brain, making the nerves itch and inflame.

It hung in the air, suspended there on wings that were panes of rippled glass. Its head was unformed, a cone-shaped tuber of softened glass pitted with a ring of dark, pest's eyes.

The man croaked again, more loudly, and stood up. He leaned forward, head down, his palms flat on the bench, his arms locked, shaking.

I shielded my eyes as the creature dipped in the air and flew slowly over our heads. It made a nasty clanking sound, metallic and hollow; it sounded like a sack of cracked iron bells being shaken. And then it took off, tilting and swerving through the air, and disappeared down the alley we had just emerged from. I could hear its wings clattering through the high, overgrown bushes and brambles that choked the side of the alley opposite the sidewall of the pub.

We followed, leaving the man in the parka standing beneath the sun in that weed-choked yard, and chased the creature back along the alley. As we emerged onto the ground in front of the building, the creature swung in an arc, out across the road and stopped, its glass wings moving in slow beats. Its head switched about and then it seemed to focus on something. I remembered that I had left the jar containing Dr Natus in the shade beneath the wall at the edge of the path and my breath caught in my throat. I moved forward but Bix said, "Wait."

We could hear voices in the pub garden opposite. We could smell the aroma of a barbecue and hear children laughing.

The creature above the road dipped towards the jar behind the wall. Its wings gleamed and darted spears of sunlight.

There was a sudden stillness. I could feel Bix breathing, my leg against his warm flank.

And then the door to the pub across the road opened and a group of men emerged carrying pool cues. Les was there, and he carried a fire iron taken from the hearth.

They walked as a group across the road and surrounded the creature as it tried to get to the jar, to either smash it or carry it away. It jabbed at it with the claws that had formed like spines at the ends of its fragile legs.

And then it sensed that it had company and turned slowly, the blades of its wings humming as their speed increased. The light at its heart beat and fluttered. One of the men shielded his eyes and as he moved, the creature darted at him. He stumbled, his raised forearm taking the hit. He yelled and dropped to his knees, a splatter of blood raining down his shirt.

The men swung their weapons.

One of the creature's wings shattered. Glass crashed to the pavement around the feet of the men as they closed in. They hammered the creature with blows. Les ducked beneath the smooth beam of the thing's abdomen as it swung towards him, and came up dealing it a heavy blow to the heart. The creature collapsed in the midst of them, the sound of its defeat a sonic peal of ruined blades and edges.

The men continued to pound it until nothing remained but a wide scattering of ground glass. When they were satisfied the creature was reduced to dust they scuffed the remains into the curb and toed as much of it as they could muster through the grille of a drain.

The men stood in a huddle and then turned to us.

Les lifted the hand holding the fire iron.

"Hi, Bix," he said.

"Good work, lads," Bix said.

The men grinned. The injured man held his arm against his chest pressing a hand to the gash to stem the blood. He looked pale but smiled back at us.

"How's the arm, Andy?" Bix asked.

"Flesh wound," Andy said. "It'll heal."

"Before you know it," Bix said.

"We'll be getting back," Les said. "I'll see you later, then, Daniel. I'll call you."

I nodded, my left hand resting idly on the fur at the back of Bix's head.

The men turned and went back across to the door of the pub. When they opened the door and went inside a huge cheer went up. The stillness broke and I could hear the bright sounds of laughter and children playing again.

Bix trotted off towards the road. He stopped at the path.

"See you again soon, Daniel," he said.

"Okay, Bix," I said.

The dog made to go but then stopped. "Remember Elizabeth," he said. "Got to keep your friendships up."

I'm sure he was smiling as he ran off down the road.

I SAT AT my desk staring down at the matchbox.

"Close your eyes, Daniel," the hermit crab said. I did as I was asked.

A telephone rang. It was distant, as though coming from a deserted room somewhere else in the hospital, perhaps in one of the boarded up rooms along the corridor. An old bell system: *ting-ting, ting-ting*; it sounded ghostly, abandoned.

"Hello," I said.

I heard nothing, but the ringing stopped. And then the sound of a door opening, and footsteps coming up the corridor. They stopped outside my office. I opened my eyes.

A knock at the door.

"Come in," I said.

Les walked in. He stood in front of my desk. His eyes were red and full of emotion.

"How do you feel?" I asked.

Les stared at a point above my head for a moment and then said, "Restless."

I understood.

"I'll be here," I said.

Les smiled at me but his focus was still distant. I don't think I ever saw him truly return from that place; he had left the hurting part there, I realise, where it was safe.

"Soon," he said. "Please."

"Of course," I said. I had found a purpose for my madness and I was as grateful to Les as he was to me.

"Well, then," he said.

"Well, then," I replied.

Les turned and walked out of my office.

LES RETURNED MANY times over the next few months and each time I sent him back to the time he was last at his happiest. He never told me what had happened after that, what had tried to destroy him but I could make guesses. Whoever awaited him there in that sunlit village, in that place of friendship and good company, had been taken from him and Les had felt responsible and broken by guilt.

And his contribution was his loyalty. In return for what I gave him, he and those he had chosen to share that place with him protected it from incursions. I didn't understand at the time what they were or why they came, but I do now, now I know it was real and not a delusion, that I had powers only time would enhance and reveal.

But something had been sent to intervene; something dark that fed on despair. The incursions grew; men were lost. Something was rising from the pit in the heart of that old, dead pub and its influence was reaching out beyond the Quay I had created.

As soon as it had begun, it seemed, my gift was gone.

*   *   *

TREVENA HAD LISTENED for over two hours. He was a good listener. It was starting to get light outside, just a quiet thinning of the night. He pressed his fingers against his eyelids.

"More coffee, Philip?" Elizabeth asked.

Trevena nodded. It was a tacit gesture for Daniel to go on with his story. Trevena wanted to hear it; he could guess some of what was coming. But he still needed to know where he fit in. "Why me?" he wanted to ask, but he waited, because he knew that was where this was all leading and he could be patient.

"They closed the hospital completely three months later," Daniel said. "And they moved what remained of us into flats out there." He pointed out of the small kitchen window; at the estate, at the town, at the whole world. "And they started the ECT and it all stopped. That was what led me to try and kill myself. Despair, Phil. Black, rotten despair. It's what it wants. That's why it's targeted you. Because you're good at what you do and you give hope where there should be none. The darkness that wants to destroy, to putrefy the dreams of desperate men, it hates people like you. Do you have faith?"

Trevena shrugged. "Not recently," he said.

Daniel said, "That's exactly what it wants to achieve. If it destroys your belief, even in yourself and what you set out to do, then it takes you out."

"A force, something elemental, is trying to knock me off?"

"Exactly," Daniel said.

"What are they?"

Daniel paused, looked down at his hands.

"They're Autoscopes," he said.

"Couple of slices of toast for you, Philip," said Elizabeth. "You must be hungry."

8

DANIEL STOOD ON the tracks as the line of light quivered in the air. It bisected the towering, blaring metal of the train as it thundered in temporary stasis.

Daniel squinted, tried to discern what lay beyond. He saw movement. Something was reaching out towards him. It was an invitation, he realised. An offer of escape.

Not knowing where it might lead, but hoping, truly *hoping* for the first time in years, Daniel went through the slot.

There were people there, gathered on a beach beneath a high sun. Daniel blinked. It was a bay they stood upon, a narrow cleft between two shelving outcrops of land. The tide was out and the sand was dark and spongy.

There were two other men, and a woman. The woman lay on the sand. She was bleeding from a wound in her side. She was pregnant. The others knelt by her and tended to her. She was alive, but barely.

Daniel looked up at the man who had pulled him through. He was tall, broad shouldered and blond. His age was difficult to ascertain. There was something ancient in his palpable strength, his presence.

"My name is Index," he said. "Welcome to the fold, Daniel."

Daniel looked at the men gathered around the woman. One of

them stroked her hair and wiped his eyes and nose and spoke softly to her. Another man, short and wiry wearing glasses soaked her wound with handfuls of seawater.

"There are more atoms in a handful of seawater than there are handfuls of water in the ocean," Index said.

Daniel nodded. He understood.

"Come over," Index said.

They crossed the sand and joined the group. The men looked up and said welcoming words, and then returned their attention to the woman. The younger of the two had rested both hands on her belly and was speaking, although Daniel couldn't make out what he was saying.

"In there," Index said, and pointed to the heavy bulge of the woman's stomach, "is a very special child."

Daniel said nothing, but continued watching their tender ministrations.

"We have lost a precious member of our group. A young man named Robin Knox. Something took him as we travelled through to this Quay. We can't lose another."

Daniel could smell the ocean as it flung itself against the shore; gusts of salty air blew like sobs amongst them.

"The baby?" he asked.

"Yes. Right now she has created a safe place for herself but time is short and she is in grave danger."

As if in response, the baby kicked in its mother's womb. The man scooping water over the woman gasped. "That was a good one," he said. "Come on, Chloe."

"If we teach you, if we show you what you really are, will you go back for her?" Index asked.

Daniel closed his eyes and breathed deeply of the sea air. He thought of his father, could see his face as clearly as he had as a child. He remembered his father's words, that day of his birthday. He remembered the warning, but also the hope.

"Of course," said Daniel. "Of course I will."

Index smiled and put a hand on Daniel's shoulder.

"Who am I? Who am I *really*?"

"You're the missing part of our team," Index said. "We can't proceed without you. Not with any hope of success."

Daniel looked into Index's intense blue eyes, saw the lines that ran from their corners; he knew what formed lines on a man's face. It was not always laughter. He waited, stilled.

"You're the *hypnopomp*, Daniel. You can control Dark Time."

"WHAT IS THE true purpose of dreams? I believe they were given to us when we were created as a fulfilment of God's ultimate gift of life. Were we created of matter to remain Earthbound, however perfect, however rich and varied that existence may have been? What if he wanted to give us even more, an experience beyond essential laws and mathematics? Here, have it all: here you can fly, run like a deer, create for yourselves beasts and vistas and wonders. Sleep, rest, go beyond and know what it is to be like gods yourselves.

"And that Dark Time, that flux above the linear, an even bigger reality for us to explore; truly limitless and eternal. A different substance of time flowing in all directions forever replenishing and infinite. A taste of Heaven before the re-creation of all things."

Trevena could appreciate this. His dreams had always been vivid, places of symbols and answers, but recently—recently they had become squalid and mystifying; dark, sensual reds and textures, a smell like sun-softened leather, brawls, hot bodies and open thighs. Perplexing sex from which he awoke at the moment of penetration, frustrated and trying to summon back images, trying to perpetuate the narrative. He'd put it down to age. Now he thought he knew different.

"Daniel," he said. "I've listened to all this, but can you prove any of it? I've heard so many things in my time, so much madness and delusion, and somewhere in it all there was always a germ of sense, something to maybe bring them back to. I always believed psychosis was a defence, a guard against total despair. But why Les? If he was your friend, if he believed everything you're telling me, why did he kill himself?" Trevena felt momentarily defiant. He didn't feel able to swallow everything Daniel was telling him without a fight, without challenging the story. How could he not, with his experience?

"Okay," Daniel said. He reached into his pocket and produced the matchbox.

Trevena sat back on his stool and raised his eyebrows. "Really?" he said.

Daniel slid open the drawer. "This is what I've been waiting for, Phil. You get to watch. Close your eyes."

Trevena shook his head in resignation. "I've come this far," he said, and closed his eyes.

AT A QUARTER to eleven that morning the nurse looked in on Les. Les was lying on his bed outstretched, his eyes closed. He opened an eye and smiled. *Nice girl, that Cherry*, he thought. *Not for her, this game, though. She looks terrified.* He waved and gave her a reassuring thumbs-up. Cherry reciprocated the gesture and asked if he wanted anything. Les shook his head. "I'm fine, love," he said.

Cherry withdrew, closing the door behind her.

Les sighed and rested back on his pillow. He closed his eyes again.

All morning he had been tormented by a coarse, critical, insistent voice coming from the en suite shower room. He had done his best to ignore it, using techniques he had been taught and listening to his MP3 player but it was almost too much to bear today. He knew what it was. It was the voice of the thing he had blocked up in his chimney. It was speaking down the pipes. It was reminding him how he had lost his family because he was a nutbag too self-obsessed to see the danger they had been in.

Les turned on his side, his back to the cubicle. He had closed the door and pushed a towel as far into the gap between the floor and the bottom of the door as it would go but still the voice raged, foul and interrogatory.

As Les lay there, his eyes shut tight and the voice hectoring him, a narrow line of light opened in the middle of the room. It broadened, to the width of a door and a man stepped through.

The man cocked his head. He turned and looked at the door to the shower cubicle. He took a single step towards the door and raised a hand, palm outwards.

He spoke. It was a rebuke, and a binding. The voice stopped. It choked and with it a hollow, tubular sound, like scaffolding poles collapsing.

The man turned and looked towards the bed.

"Hello, Daniel," Les said. "You're back at last."

"Seems like five minutes," Daniel said. "That's Dark Time for you."

"Indeed. So, one last favour, Dan?"

"If you think it's time," Daniel said.

Les sat up and opened his arms. Daniel stepped forward and embraced his old friend, his Paladin.

"I'd do anything for you," Les said. "I love you, Daniel. With all my heart."

Daniel nodded, the soft, dry skin of the old man's cheek against the flesh of his throat. He stepped back.

"Are you ready?"

"Yes." A simple, unadorned affirmation, almost a whisper.

Daniel closed his eyes.

"I can stay there now?"

Daniel smiled. "Yes. Forever."

Les put his head in his hands. He was weeping.

"That thing in the pipes," Daniel said. "It's gone back. It's enraged. It'll break through. Is there something you need to do?"

Les looked up. "I have to warn Phil."

"Okay. Close your eyes."

Les closed his eyes and sat on the edge of the bed, his hands clasped on his lap. They were trembling.

Daniel took the matchbox from his jacket pocket and slid it open. He closed his eyes, too.

"What about Phil?" asked Les.

"Call him from the pub," said the hermit crab in his seashore pink-orange voice, and they were gone.

AT FIVE TO eleven the door to the shower cubicle opened. It stuck against the towel wedged beneath it and then flew open as something applied its whole weight to it.

A man wearing a dirty parka coat stepped into the room. He stopped, breathing hard. He looked down at the figure sprawled on the bed. The shell of the old bastard. He'd missed him by fucking minutes.

Furious, the man stamped his feet and growled. He reached inside his coat and pulled out the remains of a broken long sword. He grasped its pommel in both hands, the foot-long ragged remnant of the blade trembling above the guts of the old man.

He paused and took a long, shuddering breath. He repositioned the sword in the belt of his jeans and closed his coat, toggling it with hands shaking with frustration and indecision. He looked around.

He saw the cup on the old man's bedside cabinet. Heavy National Health Service china. The man reached out and picked it up. He looked down at the old man.

"Gone to a better place, have you, you old fuck?" the man said.

He lashed out and smashed the cup against the wall.

With the shard that remained in his bleeding fist, the man in the parka made it look like suicide,

And when he was finished, he put the shard in the old man's hand and went back into the shower cubicle and closed the door.

"PHILIP? ARE YOU all right, Philip?"

Trevena opened his eyes. He started to sit up, disorientation causing him to panic. Elizabeth was squatting beside him. He was sprawled on the kitchen floor, both feet beneath the breakfast bar, head jammed against the cupboard under the sink. He groaned and let Elizabeth help him up. His legs were shaking.

"Fuck my life," he muttered.

Daniel hadn't moved. He was still standing on the other side of the breakfast bar. He was smiling.

Trevena staggered to his stool and sat down.

"Les didn't kill himself," he said. "He didn't kill himself."

"Of course he didn't," said Daniel.

"How was I supposed to know that?" Trevena barked, suddenly angry. And then he laughed, the anger dissipating as quickly as it had come. Relief replaced it and with it, a shedding of guilt. "So who's the bloke in the coat? Is he an Autoscope?"

"No. His name is Cade. He was human but now he's turned Toyceiver; he's become the monster within, a mockery. He's what you now might call a loose cannon. They used him once, because of his greed. He thinks they've betrayed him over power promised and never delivered. But now he's trying to buy back their *affections,* as it were. He's lashing out. If you want *real* madness, Phil, look no further than Cade. He's the real thing."

Trevena put his hand over his face and rubbed his brow, dragged his palm down over his eyes, mouth and ran it over the stubble of his throat. He blinked a couple of times and then looked at Daniel in expectation of more revelations.

He felt a lump rise in his throat. The silence in the kitchen and the expressions on Daniel's and Elizabeth's faces were explicit enough to tell him it wasn't going to be good news.

"What?" he said.

"It's Cade," Daniel said. There was no emotion in his voice, nothing alarming or histrionic. It was deliberately calm; kindly, Trevena thought. Daniel spoke with the gentleness and compassion of a specialist giving a catastrophic diagnosis.

"He's inside you," Daniel said.

"TELL ME THE last thing you dreamed about," Daniel said.

Trevena thought for a moment, trying to remember the heated dream he had been awakened from earlier that night. It had become recurrent; a walk along a sunlit boulevard and suddenly he was inside a red castle. All the walls, the floors, the fitments, everything was red, and studded with leather. It was mildly erotic and not unpleasant to begin with but as it progressed it became darker, more revealing of his intimate frustrations. He wasn't alone. There was a girl waiting for him in the bathroom. A young girl. *Too* young.

And as he walked through the castle, its impossible dimensions expanding around him, he could hear a voice. It was a hectoring voice, coming towards him over a great distance, but the person calling was already there, in the castle. Like a projection sent ahead, too agitated and impatient to travel the distance bodily, somehow powerful enough to reach into Trevena's head, his unconscious, and establish a presence.

Trevena described the dream to Daniel.

"That's Cade," Daniel said.

"I'm *possessed*?"

"Not yet," Daniel said. "I've been able to intervene. And Les helped, containing him with a psychotic ritual. It was too complex for Cade to fathom in the short term. It limited his movements. But now he's out. And he'll want you."

"For what?"

Daniel and Elizabeth exchanged glances. There was nothing sly about it, it was just a look of understanding between two old friends. Nevertheless, Trevena felt outside a certain, essential loop. He waited.

"If we don't act, in the near future, you'll do some things that are very bad, Phil. Or Cade will, through you."

Trevena swallowed. "I do?"

"But we can't let that happen. Too much at stake."

"Can you stop him? Stop Cade?"

"I think so. If you let me take you through. We can hunt the bastard down."

"What do you have to do?"

Elizabeth went over and took Daniel's hand.

"When Index sent me back, he gave me instructions. He told me to find Elizabeth, which is the first thing I did. It's no accident she's living here. While I was gone, she started seeing things again. Visions where her eye had been. Scaffolding and black wings spiralling up from the ground, like before, when she was a child. Elizabeth is a *prescient*. She has always been the link between my gift and the timing of my purpose. Her love is my fuel. I'm able to do what I do because she *facilitates* it. And that is what makes my gift so confounding. It's so weak and yet it's the most powerful thing we have. Its simplicity is its potency. Elizabeth never judged me."

"That I understand," Trevena said. "Okay, folks. You want to do this now?"

WHILE DANIEL PREPARED to take Trevena through the slot, Elizabeth busied herself making a bed up on the sofa in the lounge.

"You lie there, Philip, and let yourself drop off. You must be exhausted."

"You want me to go to sleep?"

"You have to be asleep. It's how Daniel works."

"What if I wake up?"

"You won't be able to," Elizabeth said, plumping some cushions against the floral arm of her sofa. "Lie down and make yourself comfy."

Passivity the greater force owing to exhaustion and perplexity, Trevena did as he was told. Elizabeth arranged a yellow blanket over his knees. Trevena kicked off his shoes and settled back against the cushions.

"Why?" Trevena asked, still determined to understand some of the process.

"Because Daniel is the Hypnopomp," she said. She didn't bother to wait for any more of Trevena's questions and continued: "It's his gift, his purpose. They all have gifts, which compliment each other. Daniel can stop time and bring people to the point of awakening but maintain the quanta of their dreams. They are at the point of being awake; yet still believe they are dreaming. You can show people a lot when they are in that state, and they don't suffer any of the trauma or stress. It's real, but their cognitive processes don't lay down the same deep-rooted pathways. No flashbacks, no dissociation, just the vague memories of a dream. Sometimes unpleasant but nowhere near as devastating if experienced consciously."

Trevena closed his eyes. From the kitchen he heard Daniel say, "I'm going to take us into Chloe's Quay, Phil. I don't know the environment so I don't know what to expect. I'll look after you but you'll still be thinking for yourself, so try and keep that in mind. See you in there."

"Righ—" said Trevena, and fell asleep.

The Night Clock's ticks are like the cooling of some infernal engine, something powered up from the beginning of time to run histories of our unlived and wasted potential. Its painted hands are at a quarter past three.

9

DR NATUS LIVES in a two-litre Kilner jar with a heavy glass lid held down with metal closing clips. The rubber-sealing band has rotted and clings to the lid like mould. Many years ago Daniel made sloe vodka in jars like these. Two months of shaking and that stuff was rocket fuel. Dr Natus floats in a blue fluid the colour of autumn sloes. In fact Daniel thinks he might have grown in the vodka left in an old jar he forgot about, and left for years in the back of a dark cupboard, in the kitchen of his flat. The flat is above a shop, on a side street, off the seafront.

He sits in the middle of a round table in the topmost room in the attic above the shop. The shop is called Elegant Lady and has a front still in the nineteen-fifties: green marble sills and porch columns and a heavy glass door with a large brass art deco handle and long brass hinges.

DR NATUS WAS removed from his mother's teratogenic womb on the sixteenth of February 1953.

He told Daniel this the night he found him in the back of the cupboard. He told Daniel his father was Berlyn Brixner, head photographer for the Trinity test, the first nuclear weapons test of an atomic bomb. Brixner had shown his mother a photograph of the first 0.016 seconds of the explosion, as the light bubble had inflated across the desert, and she had fallen immediately pregnant.

Daniel taps on the side of the jar, *tok tok tok,* and Dr Natus twitches in his thick blue fluid and drifts a little. His face drags up against the curved inner surface of the glass, smearing his cheek that scrunches his right eye and pushes his tiny cupid lips into even more of a pout. His useless little arms endeavour to push against the glass but they don't reach, they're like wren's legs. *His* legs, and long feet with their tiny, pearlescent toes, are more effective and with a kick he propels himself back from the glass and hangs in the fluid in the middle of the jar. His eyelids are as bulging and heavily veined as a dead baby bird's. They remain closed, as always, but Daniel can see the dark pinpricks of the pupils behind them. He floats blue above a disc of silt, a dead baby with the mind of a god.

HE TOLD DANIEL he was a god in the pantheon of ancient Greece. But then he'd told him he was Roman, Egyptian, Aztec and Babylonian too. He features everywhere, him and his friends. He tells Daniel they are the source of all myths. He tells him that Herod the Great had him killed during the Massacre of the Innocents, when he was searching for Christ, and he was reborn in his mother's womb in the immaculate light from the Trinity explosion. Herod, he says, was the most ruthless of all the Toyceivers. This is a word he has made up, Daniel is sure. A neologism dredged from the density of his floating dreams and undependable memories.

AT TEN PAST three they step out onto the road. Daniel carries Dr.Natus in his jar close to his chest. He swills about, tiny fingers flexing like cilia. Daniel can hear him thinking.

They step up onto the black-and-white tiled step beneath the porch over the Art Deco door to Elegant Lady and wait. At twenty past three Daniel hear footsteps.

The man is wearing a shoddy old parka with the hood up. He peers out at Daniel through a mane of matted fur.

Daniel invites him to step up onto the checkerboard tiles, which he does with a stumbling lurch.

Daniel can hear his breathing, and beneath that the constant wintry sound of the low calm waves moving up the shingle and lapping, with mild, feline caresses, around the legs of the pier.

The man is trembling. He is staring at Dr. Natus. The fluid is dark; there is only a little light reflected back off the wet pavement from a single streetlight on the corner and Dr. Natus is mostly obscured. Occasionally a fraction of him drifts or presses against the glass and he is glimpsed; a flutter of fingers or toes, a curve of belly, a wrinkled buttock. He is restless, excited. He loves this part.

Daniel lifts the jar in front of his face and starts to agitate it, gently at first, then with greater rhythm. The silt at the bottom of the jar lifts and spreads throughout the fluid and Dr. Natus is fully concealed.

"Close your eyes," Daniel says to the man. "Don't open them again until I tell you."

He closes his eyes. His lips pout and his nose wrinkles with the effort of compliance. He looks like a child awaiting a surprise present.

Daniel gives the jar one last shake and Dr. Natus takes them to the Quay.

10

CHLOE HAD NO recollection of arriving here. She had awakened, curled into a ball on her left side, at the mouth of a cave cut thirty feet up into the side of a hill of dark red rock. As her eyes had opened, the lowering late afternoon sun had cut through the treetops, turning the entire cave crimson around her. The rock seemed to pulse; Chloe closed her eyes.

She stayed like that for a while and when she opened her eyes again it was dark. Chloe was cold. Shivering, she sat and looked up at the craggy oval of moonlight shining in through the cave mouth. She stood, feeling unsteady.

Chloe looked through the treetops camouflaging the entrance to the cave and saw that she was at the edge of a forest. She had no way of gauging how big the forest was because the moonlight was insufficient to define depth or density, but she perceived the mass of it, pressing against the rock face both left and right of the cave and could hear the flat drumming of night air on the canopy, an outlying roar of shivering foliage like a drowsy tide.

Chloe turned and walked back through the cave. The floor was flat and smooth and she made her way to the back wall without obstacle. The cave was narrow; Chloe could reach out and touch both walls with her fingertips at the same time. The back wall was slightly rounded and to her left was an alcove big enough for her to stand in. If she stood on tiptoes she could just touch the ceiling.

On the floor at the back of the cave was a pile of rugs. Chloe nudged them with her foot. Nothing moved or scuttled out from under them. She knelt down. They were soft and fluffy. She curled up amongst them and stared out into the night. For a long time, before she fell asleep, Chloe lay there and wondered who she was.

HER HEAD HADN'T been empty, exactly. She knew the names of certain things, and how a lot of them worked, or could be adapted to work, although sometimes, when she looked at something, there was a sensation of blankness in her mind. She knew she was safe in the cave; something about the quality of the red rock—she knew the rock was *red*, and that it was *rock*—seemed to comfort her.

No, her head wasn't empty but there was a sense that it might once have been, and not so long ago, and that it had been filled at once with a massive amount of information and instructions. She had no memories beyond the cave; her mind just stalled, and teetered on the brink of some preceding, historical oblivion. It made her light-headed and fretful to consider this pale eternity behind her. How did she know—or at least *intuit*—this? She didn't know. Nor could she find out. In a town that appeared to be made up almost entirely of bookshops, Chloe was unable to find a single volume that could help her research *herself*. She could hold a book, a fragrant case of paper rectangles, and know it was a book, but that was all.

Chloe couldn't read.

This fact didn't frustrate her, because there was no learning either misunderstood or abstruse that had gone before to cause her to stumble, to *not* learn. It was, like trying to think back beyond awakening in the cave, something that had never been there in the first place.

She could speak. She knew her name was Chloe. She knew she was alone.

She just didn't know why.

* * *

CHLOE HAD DISCOVERED the town the next day after waking in the cave. She had wanted to explore her surroundings, make more connections, force more neural pathways in her brain; to stay in the cave was not an option. Chloe knew this, too. She wasn't to wait. She was to investigate.

Wearing the plain, loose-fitting clothes she had first awoken in, Chloe stood at the mouth of the cave and looked out across the forest in daylight. She looked down, to where the base of the cliff met the forest floor in a sloping, jagged contour of rocks. If she fell, she would die or be injured on those rocks. From white timelessness into an infinity of black hours. What would this bubble of existence have been, then? A singularity failed to inflate? Chloe shook her head. Numbers seemed to run behind her eyes like a ribbon of code. Numbers?

Chloe realised she could count.

She smiled, reached out for the branch of the nearest tree.

"One, two, three…" She jumped.

HAVING MARKED THE position of the cave in her memory in relation to the tree she had climbed down and those in its proximity, Chloe began to head into the forest. She tried to keep her course straight so that her return journey would be oriented as straightforwardly as possible. If she got lost she reckoned that as long as she found her way back to the cliff face she could edge along until she could see the cave, but she felt that now was not the best time to wander. She picked a path with caution, scuffing the virgin leaves to mark a darker trail, and snapped protruding twigs to act as flags along the way.

After some time the deep, cool light through which she walked began to dapple and shade up into a brighter, livelier green. Ahead, Chloe could see where the trees began to thin and beyond, a great burnished cauldron of blue pressing down on everything.

At the edge of the forest, Chloe stood, hands on hips, and grinned. She squinted in the wonderful broad, flat light of a clear day and, as her eyes adjusted, she could see across a long meadow, waist-high with feathery grasses, and in the distance, like a pile of someone's boxed-up belongings, the compact huddle of a town's buildings. They looked like crenellations against the horizon, flattened into two dimensions by distance and the quality of the light behind it, like a cog protruding from the vast workings of the earth.

Still smiling, Chloe strolled through the meadow and headed towards the town.

CHLOE WALKED THROUGH town. It was deserted and the bright morning sun lit the dewy cobbles of the high street and made them gleam like the bottom of a streambed. She took her time, strolling, her arms swinging, her eyes wide and taking it all in. The high street was narrow and lined with small, crooked buildings. At intervals alleyways and narrow lanes led off and she could see more buildings lining these.

Chloe stopped and peered through the window of one of the buildings. The room beyond was dark but she could make out shapes, rows of shelves filled with small faded box-shapes stacked together. She frowned as a picture formed in her mind, and a word came with it.

Books.

And then more, pulled into her head from some reservoir fathoms deep and stocked with bright shoals of information:

Books hop.

Chloe's focus pulled back, away from the interior and she regarded her own reflection. She wrinkled her nose. She smiled, her brow creased. She lifted her hand and waggled her fingers.

"Hi," she said. Then she laughed, and the bright sound of it rang down the street. And the word came again, and she spoke it aloud.

"*Bookshop!*"

She stepped up to the door and tried the handle. It was unlocked. Chloe opened the door and walked in.

*　　*　　*

CHLOE SPENT THE next hour perusing the shelves, lifting down books and gazing at them. She liked the smell of them, and the weight and substance of them. She blew dust from their pages and riffled them to liberate more of their aged, sour yet amiable fragrance. Chloe knew these were important things.

At the back of the shop, which was really only one small room with a set of dark, slender steps leading up to a trapdoor in the ceiling, she found a box full of larger books, stacked on top of each other. She lifted some out and sat on the floor cross-legged with them in her lap. They were heavy and she discovered when she opened them, they were full of pictures.

Chloe smiled. The words that filled the books on the shelves were as mysterious as code, but these... these she could comprehend. Her eyelids fluttered as the pages turned and the surface of that unfathomable reservoir inside her head began to churn with sparkles of light, as it began to boil with new words, new information.

And then she took up the last book remaining in the bottom of the box.

She sat down with it, head swimming, elated and bright-eyed, her lips moist and her heart thumping, and opened it, unable to read its title, of course, and flipped through a few pages, and immediately blacked out and lay inert on the floor of that book shop with *A Clock Mender's Handbook* open on her belly, her eyes moving with great rapidity behind their closed lids, her fingers twitching, and stayed like that for hours.

And only opened her eyes again after it had got dark.

AND WHILE SHE slept, something came to town, sent out from a benighted mind:

Find her kill her

She's here
Find her kill her

and things poured into the street, from alleyways and niches, and holes in the ground; from the fields they came, lifting from the dirt, shucking clods of filth as their legs unhinged and stretched out to propel them. They came with bodies and faces and eyes of glass, of ill flesh, of all metals that might soften and be worked; and with brains and hearts of silver gas and fire

Find her kill her

and scraped and scoured the high street and side roads and lots and yards and porches and rooftops and clattered and strutted on stick legs and scuttled on a dozen spider's legs apiece and stamped with limbs like tree trunks

Find her kill her she's here

and could not find her and could not see her though they pressed awful faces or flattened eyes or swarmed like vile molecules across the windows and could not smell her for the peppery dust from the books that were everywhere covering her scent and could not bear it for too long, or the thing with the voice could not, because it choked on the stink of the books and began to fade

Find her kill

and the things it had sent also faded, collapsed their many-jointed legs beneath their hollow bodies, their only organs things of weakening light that fluttered in lucent fibrillations and they dragged themselves away and hid, or died there on the cobbles and remained sprawled like ghosts of horrendous sculptures

* * *

CHLOE SAT UP. *A Clock Mender's Handbook* slid off her lap onto the floor. She blinked, startled by the sudden darkness and felt a wave of panic wash through her. She stood up and stared around trying to find something to *look* at to orient herself but all she could see was *nothing*. Chloe started gasping, and stepped forward, her arms raised, hands palm outwards with the fingers splayed. She stumbled, kicking something flat and heavy across the floor. It triggered a memory, breaking through the panic; pictures. *Book.*

She was in a *bookshop*. What had happened? Had she fallen asleep? No. The book. The book of *clocks* had done something to her. She felt her breathing slow, and now there was a watery quality to the darkness, a lessening of its totality. Chloe took another more careful step forward and emerged from between two high rows of shelves to find herself standing in front of the window. The glass was smeared and filthy. Chloe wiped a finger down the glass but her fingertip came away clean but for a silvery pad of dust. The filth was on the outside.

Chloe frowned. She turned and peered towards the rear of the shop. Her eyes were becoming accustomed to the poor light and so she moved back along the row of shelves and picked up the book she had kicked. On its wide rectangular cover was a picture of the workings of a clock—cogs, wheels, pendulums and hands—all arrayed on a velvet cloth.

Chloe put the book under her arm and left the shop.

OUTSIDE, A HIGH sea of clouds was lit in a patch to a sullen grey from above by the force of a gleaming but thwarted full moon. A strong wind was blowing along the high street funnelling in from the fields that surrounded it, and as Chloe stood there on the cobbles, book tucked against her ribs, the clouds broke and she had to squint as the moonlight bore down on the town through the rent, as sudden and diamond-white as a revelation, and then she shrieked, and stumbled back into the doorway of the shop because it really *was* a revelation; the light showed her the things that had died in the road.

Even in the pure, cleansing glare of the moonlight, the dead husks that they had become—oxidizing plates and wine-glass thin shells, of liquid meat and powdering bone—they were terrible. They were a nightmare installation set up in a deserted town by a troupe of artists obeying the compulsive, baying creativity of their disrupted and railing minds.

Chloe hugged the book to her chest, her chin against the slender spine, as if protecting her throat and heart. She looked along the length of the high street in both directions. The shapes of things gleamed in the moonlight, some piled up or craning over each other, some alone in gutters, drawn in on themselves and dissolving as she watched. She looked to her left and cringed back from the silhouette of something as tall as the gutters still clasping the wall even as it bowed towards her as it rotted.

Chloe turned and ducked back into the bookshop.

CHLOE SUFFERED A long night, but she felt safe there, tucked away in the back of that bookshop behind a battlement of shelves.

She passed time by going through the moonlit shop looking for more picture books (*A Clock Mender's Handbook* was wrapped in a sheet of soft cloth she had found in a drawer and was stashed in a nook beneath the window. She wasn't going to be perusing that particular tome again tonight. Not here, anyway) and she amused herself by learning about vehicles, and buildings, and animals and insects, and trees and flowers, and...

Food.

Cookbook.

Chloe sat staring down at the glossy photographs and felt her mouth fill up with saliva. A clear spot of dribble dropped from her bottom lip onto the page. She wiped it away with her thumb, lifted her thumb to her mouth and licked it. She tasted something. Another word rose up in her mind; she experienced it emerging as a sensation of warm blocks rising through a lavish medium, dark and swirling *chocolate*

and again her eyes rolled up and she slumped forward over the book in her lap.

But this time she fed.

Or, was fed by someone else.

AND WHILE CHLOE took sustenance, her body resting, her mind processing all the new things she had seen and learned, outside on the street all the dead frames rotted away.

When Chloe awoke the next morning refreshed, she gathered up a collection of books she liked best (*A Clock Mender's Handbook, Chocolates and Confections: Formula, Theory and Technique for the Artisan Confectioner, Little Garden People and What They Do*) and walked out into a chilly but cloudless day.

The street was empty now. Any evidence that it had been host to a horde of monsters the previous day had been erased.

Intrigue overtook the desire to run back to the cave. Chloe turned and walked further down the street, her books clutched to her breast. She stopped at intervals to peer through the dusty windows of the shops but all she could see were more rooms full of books. She continued exploring and as she did so she began to feel the weight and immensity of information these shops contained pressing out at her, rousing that fathomless ocean at the core of her being, forcing fissures and threatening a deluge where once there had been a stream; it was almost overwhelming, and she stopped, and closed her eyes, and willed it to abate.

When she opened her eyes again, the pressure dumped back to a manageable level (it was still there, though, in the background, a sense of standing with her back to something colossal, planetary, and trying to ignore its hideous attendance plucking at her periphery, as if turning to face it would, indeed, drop her dead) Chloe breathed deeply and turned to walk back to the cave. She felt exposed, and suddenly exhausted.

But as she turned she noticed something glittering in the window of a small store across the street. She walked over and realised it was sunlight glinting off metal.

Hardware

The word came as she looked at the objects in the display behind the glass.

Interesting.

Chloe tried the door. It opened.

ALMOST ABSENTLY, CHLOE wandered through the shop. Again, it was only tiny but crammed with shelves and counters full of stuff. At the back was a door, which she opened to discover an aisle splitting a long, low corrugated-roofed storeroom. She stepped back and pulled the door shut, her head pounding. She managed a weak smile but didn't open the door again. The storeroom was so rammed with stuff— with *words*—that she had experienced them as an almost physical mob, pouncing into her mind, trying to establish their existence with profuse, open-handed glee.

Chloe returned to the front of the shop where she had seen a display of large canvas bags. She took one and slipped the strap over her shoulder.

Bug-out bag.

She smiled at the words, liking the sound of them in her head but not really knowing their significance.

She slid her three books into the bag and then went through the shop taking items as she felt inspired. Finally, she walked out the proud owner of a Swiss Army knife bristling with attachments, a roll of pipe and flange protection tape, a hack saw, a pair of bright yellow neoprene industrial hazard gloves, a set of screwdrivers, an orange-handled claw hammer and a compartmentalised clear plastic box of nails of various sizes, a heavy duty LED lantern light (batteries included) with a strap *and* a handle, a red Zippo lighter, propane gas canister, a box of night lights, and, unable to resist, shiny hardback copies of *Remodelista: A Manual for the Remodelled Home, Renovating for Profit,* and *The Big Book of Weekend Woodworking.*

Smiling all the way, Chloe retraced her steps back to the cave.

BACK IN HER cave, Chloe unpacked her bag and sat cross-legged on her rugs, her things arrayed before her; if she'd known about Christmas, then it would have been Christmas she would have been thinking about. She picked everything up in turn and examined each one, trying them out. She sat for a while in her big chunky gloves, then pulled them off and unhinged all the attachments on her Army knife. She was particularly taken with the miniature scissors, the magnifying glass and the corkscrew. She hefted the hammer, liking its weight and balance. She put the hacksaw aside; she thought she would use this to take off the lower branches of the nearest tree to the cave, the one she had used earlier to climb down and then back up. She had an instinctive impression this would make her feel safer. Her mind was already considering options, and she was planning her next trip to the hardware store the following day and making a list of things to bring back, rope and ladders at the top.

She popped the Zippo lid and ran the ball of her thumb across the wheel. It sparked but did not light. She picked up the gas canister put it in her lap and slid the lighter out of its case. She was going on instinct again, but was not surprised that working knowledge came to her in this way. It was normal development for Chloe.

She pressed the canister's nozzle into the hole in the bottom of the lighter and pushed. Gas whooshed in a cold spray over her hand but she watched as the woolly filling darkened and once it was sufficiently saturated, she removed the nozzle and slid the lighter back into its case. She flipped the lid open and again struck the wheel.

Flame bloomed and ran down the case and across the back of her hand like liquid.

"*Shit*!" Chloe shouted, and hurled the lighter the length of the cave. The coating of gas on her hand burned off almost instantaneously, evaporating in a bluish wisp, but the lighter remained burning at the cave mouth like a tiny beacon. A little shaken, Chloe rose and retrieved it. She clicked the lid over the flame and extinguished it.

She returned to her rugs and sat down.

"Shit," she said. "Shit!" She grinned, wondering where *that* word had come from. A picture rose in her mind. It was similar in many ways to one she had had earlier, in the bookshop. Dark warm blocks rising through a thick, lustrous brown medium.

"Ew!" Chloe said. "Nasty."

THE NEXT DAY, Chloe went back to the town. This time she was more cautious, vigilant for those nightmare creatures, but saw none.

She went straight for the hardware store and gathered more gear. She helped herself to a padded body warmer and a pair of sturdy walking boots. Then she grabbed a loop of orange nylon rope and a set of ladders and went back outside. She was leaning the ladders against the side of the building when she heard something.

She ducked back inside the shop and peered through the window out onto the street.

The sound grew louder. It was choppy, metallic; Chloe could summon no mental image to identify it. She frowned and looked around. Hanging on a hook by the counter was a leather utility belt. She kept low and went over and unhooked it. She put it around her waist and buckled it beneath her body warmer. She took a large hatchet and a vicious-looking hunting knife from a shelf and pushed them through two of the belt's loops, one over each hip.

Thus tooled, Chloe went back to the window just in time to see the noisemaker rumble into town.

It was a lime-green split-screen Volkswagen campervan. It had white mudguards and was lidded with a striped green and white pop-top roof. Chloe smiled, despite the utter oddness of its appearance. She had seen similar vehicles in one of the books and had been rather taken by these cheerful-looking things with their pleasing lines and snug interiors.

This one was different, though. As it trundled up the high street, Chloe noticed that it was covered in antennae, glittering like quills, and on the roof above the windscreen sat a small metal dish.

The camper slowed and then stopped, idling at the kerb outside the hardware store. Chloe could hear the repetitive knock of some sort of mechanism. The driver turned his head, scanning the road ahead and the buildings on either side. Chloe ducked below the window ledge.

A moment later she heard the motor rev and she risked another peek.

The driver was looking directly at her.

Chloe gasped, but before she could react and take cover again, the driver cut the engine, climbed from his seat and disappeared into the back of the van. Chloe frowned. The mechanical knocking sound increased in volume and tempo, becoming a low thrum. And then, from gaps and alleyways between the buildings, and from over roofs and walls and gates, poured huge spiders in hundreds.

They converged on the van, their foul lobed abdomens suspended a foot above the ground between long, slender racks of racing legs. Chloe could see their eyes; each spider had a pair, like bulbs of black jelly.

They converged on the van and began to clamber over it, smothering it with their bodies, jabbing at the chassis with their legs. Chloe could hear the scraping sound of them as they jarred against the windows and doors.

She cringed as she heard movement on the roof of the shop. And then more spiders were pouring down the window, spilling across the path to join the others at the van. For a moment, Chloe was frozen with terror, and then she was reeling back against the shop counter as one of the spiders reared up and scrabbled at the window, its legs rattling like needle-sharp canes and putting long scratches in the glass. The glass began to crack and now others had joined it; Chloe was repulsed by the sight of their soft bodies flattening against the glass and the jagged mouthparts revealed like fistfuls of glass, and the vile articulations of their undersides, the churning of their their legs as they rose and fell, hard joints socketed in spongy cups of meat.

She reached for the hatchet in her belt and withdrew it.

And then, from the van, a shout, and a mighty *thump*, and all the spiders fell suddenly dead.

*　　*　　*

THE DOOR IN the side of the van slid open and the man stepped out. He was short and stocky and looked old and tired. His hair was white and thin and his face was tilled from decades of worry and concern. He trod through a drift of dead spiders, his boots kicking them aside. When he trod on one it snapped and broke into shards, its body already hardening and rotting away. He went around to the rear of the vehicle and opened a hatch. Chloe watched from inside the shop as he ducked down and worked on something. She heard him grunt and he emerged holding a metal cylinder, dull grey and heavy looking. The man straightened up and stretched, looking up at the sky and arching his back.

And then he closed the hatch with the heel of his boot and turned and walked over to the hardware store.

Chloe stumbled away from the window and raised the hatchet.

The man stopped outside and knocked once on the door.

The hatchet trembled in Chloe's fist.

"Chloe," the man said. "Chloe, my name is Babur. I'm coming in."

THE DOOR OPENED and the man stepped inside.

Chloe stayed where she was, backside pressed against the counter, hatchet raised. The man closed the door and turned to face her.

"I need you to do something for me, Chloe," he said.

Chloe stared. She realised her mouth was hanging open so she closed it, aware of how dry her lips had become.

The man held up the metal cylinder.

"This is an alternator. Look at it and say the word, please."

Chloe looked at the cylinder and then at the man's face. There was a tired patience etched there. And kindness, she discerned in the set of his features.

"Alternator," she said in a whisper.

"Excellent," he said. "Now, I'm going to walk past you and go into the store room behind the shop. You might want to cover your ears."

He smiled.

Chloe lowered the hatchet and stepped aside. She was smiling too now, suddenly at ease with this fellow—*Babur*—who edged past her and went to the door at the rear of the shop. He opened the door and Chloe was immediately assaulted with the inexhaustible delight of a million new things crowding her, trying to slip their meanings and their purposes into her mind. She put her hands over her ears and shut her eyes.

Babur went into the storeroom and shut the door. A moment later he was back in the shop, a brand new, shiny alternator clutched in his hand.

"Won't be long," he said, and he went outside and opened up the back of his van and got on with replacing the alternator while Chloe watched from the doorway.

When he had finished, Babur straightened up and wiped his hands on the legs of his trousers. He closed the hatch and strolled over to Chloe.

He held out a hand.

Chloe looked at it and raised her eyebrows.

Babur grinned and patted Chloe on the shoulder. Chloe experienced a sudden rush of emotion, intense and lovely, at the contact. She grabbed Babur and hugged him.

Babur stumbled out of her embrace, laughing. He held up his hands.

"Steady, girl. We've only just met," he said.

Chloe laughed, still trembling with the thrill of her first human contact.

"Are you okay?" Babur asked.

Chloe nodded, a little breathless. "*Shit!*" she said.

THEY SAT ON stools at the counter in the hardware store.

"That noise you heard earlier was a modified electro-magnetic pulse," Babur said. "It stops those things dead but it plays havoc with the alternator in my van. It's a machine designed and fitted by a young man named Robin Knox. He was a clever boy."

Chloe let the information settle. She was getting used to the process; the words went in, made connections, threw up images and impressions. She was learning at an exponential rate. For example: tenses.

"Was?" she said.

Babur nodded, his eyes suddenly bright with emotion. "He saved my life."

BABUR LIES BROKEN *in the doorway of a derelict shop in the plaza on the Invidisham-next-the-Sea estate. He watches as the transit van reverses into the rippling, golden Gantry split open in the air in the middle of the plaza and rams its back end into the tentacled beast emerging from within.*

The men have found the child, thank God. Now he is safe with his father in that horrible public house, The Macebearer, on the corner of the plaza, but these two, Mick and Frank, are warring with this thing, attempting to finish it off and close the Gantry.

Babur can feel the blood flowing from the wound in his side, a fatal gash dealt from a razored, lashing limb that has thrown him clear across the square. He groans. His vision is fading with each pulse of blood. He is laying in a pool of it, thick as fat. He can smell it even above the pestilential stink of the cockroaches and urine in the doorway of this dead shop.

There is an explosion. A great geyser of fire thunders up through the atrium, obliterating the Gantry and those monsters within. He sinks back into the drifted filth in the corner of the doorway and waits for death.

As the smoke clears he hears a new sound. It is the sound of an engine. He opens his eyes and through the entrance to the plaza comes a Volkswagen camper van. It is covered in antennae. It has its headlights on and they cast misty cones of luminescence across the plaza as it trundles beneath the archway. Babur squints as the light washes across the doorway.

The van stops and a man gets out. He is backlit by the headlights as he walks over so Babur cannot make out his features or ascertain his age.

The man kneels. Now Babur can see that it is a young man, no more than twenty-five.

"Can you get up?" the young man asks.

Babur wouldn't have thought so a moment ago, but he draws on a resource of strength and will that has served him well over the years—a dogged grit borne of experience, temperament and sheer cussedness—and grips the man's forearm and pulls himself into a sitting position. Blood begins to flow again and he shuts his eyes as white spots dance in his vision, drifting flakes of encroaching death he knows. Death is not blackness, but a sudden sweep of white, high-octane light, and you're away, gone. It's not so bad, he thinks. There's pain but there'll be an end to that with the great wave.

The young man is shaking him.

"Come on!" he says.

Babur struggles awake again. Now the boy—he really is no more than a boy—is pulling him to his feet.

Babur stands, leaning almost his entire weight against the other. His legs are bandy, wobbling.

The boy helps him over to the van and they climb up into the furnished interior. Babur groans again and sinks down onto a bed pulled out at the back of the vehicle.

"Son," he whispers. "What is your name?"

The boy is already climbing into the driver's seat. He looks back.

"Robin," he says. He sits down and starts the engine. As he swings the van around they pass the withering, smoking remains of the beast from the slot, and the grey, still burning shell of the transit van. The headlights pick out something lurching towards the front of the camper and Robin brakes sharply.

"Is it human?" Babur asks. He can see the head and shoulders of it approaching the front of the cab. It is indistinct, caped by swirling drifts of smoke.

"Not any more," Robin says and guns the engine.

"Then drive through it," Babur says and slumps back against

the pillows as Robin accelerates and ploughs into the thing in their path. It disappears beneath the front end of the van and they both feel the judder as the wheels pass over it.

They see more of the creatures as they drive through the estate. They look lost, aimless, drawn by the Gantry that had opened in the plaza, transformed by its power into grotesques, bestial phenotypes of their own inner corruption; now the Gantry is closed and the child taken, they are purposeless. As Babur watches, some fall where they stand and begin a rapid dissolution, melting or fracturing or rotting away.

They drive on, negotiating the thinning debris of fallen monsters until they leave the estate and turn onto the main road out of town.

When they have travelled about a mile Robin pulls into a layby so that he can tend Babur's wounds. He has dressings, antiseptic and bandages, which he applies with a field medic's skill, and a vial of oramorph that he makes Babur swallow. He withdraws a syringe and prepares a dose of antibiotic, which he injects into Babur's forearm. He hardly speaks as he works, just to ask compliance at intervals and explain what he is doing. Babur watches through a haze, the oramorph starting to kick in after about ten minutes.

When he has finished, Robin washes his hands at the tiny sink and puts a blanket over Babur.

"What now?" Babur asks.

"We go to Dartford," Robin says. "The others have left with the child and are on their way there. There's a safe house there. That thing that opened in the plaza? There are more coming. Bigger. They want to destroy us all. You'll be safe with us."

Robin climbs back into the cab and they drive off. On the way, Babur sleeps, and although it is good, healing sleep, he falls into it with reluctance. He had wanted to know more, a lot more.

"YAK ROZ DIDI dost, roze dega didi bradar."

"What?" said Chloe.

Babur focused on Chloe's face again. "Sorry," he said. "'The first day you see a friend, the next day you see a brother.' It's an Afghan proverb. I only knew Robin for a couple of days but he was very special." Babur smiled. "And now we know that your mother doesn't speak Afghan, which despite being an educated woman, I'm sure, is of no great surprise. But it proves something you might be interested in."

Chloe was giving Babur a strange look. Babur laughed.

"This place, all of it, the town, the mountains, these shops, you made them and your mother fills them. She can only fill it with what she knows, but it's enough for you to draw on." Chloe was nodding but she was feeling light-headed. Babur reached out and put a hand on her arm. Again, Chloe felt a warm rush of tenderness and the colour came back to her face.

"You haven't been born yet, Chloe. You're just a baby in your mother's womb. But you are very powerful and very precious. This place is your Quay and it's supposed to be safe but unfortunately it's not quite as safe as it should be. Something wants to hurt you and it wants to take what you have."

"Why?"

Babur sighed. "You're the Escape Wheel, Chloe. You're the most essential part of the Night Clock, and without you it cannot be wound."

Chloe's eyelids began to flutter and she swayed on her stool. Babur caught her in his arms as she fell.

"WHAT... IS... THE... what is the Night Clock?"

Chloe opened her eyes. Babur was kneeling by her side.

"You've been saying that for about five minutes," he said.

Chloe sat up. Babur helped her and together they sat with their backs against the counter.

"Robin told me things," Babur said. "So much in such a short while, while I was recovering. It terrifies me."

"I'm not scared," Chloe said.

Babur led his chin drop to his chest. He closed his eyes.

"The Night Clock is not an object. It is what happens when

enough of you come together. There are ten of you now and that is the smallest number possible for the Night Clock to function. Any fewer and it is lost to you, you forfeit certain celestial *rights*. If it is lost you lose control of Dark Time and there are no more dreams. Without dreams there is madness, chaos. You are a Firmament Surgeon. Others I met when I was recovering. There is a force that wants to destroy you so it can bring in an age of despair. They are Autoscopes and they were once like you. Imagine what dreams men had in early times. With so many of you in concert, Dark Time flowed like rivers. Now it is a trickle. Dreams are weak, *dreamers* are weak. The Night Clock is a *sundial* now, whereas once it was housed in a terrible tower swarming with wheels, thundering its hours out through the universe, its chimes winding galaxies.

"Each of you have remnants of the Night Clock in your Quays. Reminders, symbols, mechanisms. You have been scattered, killed, some reborn in time, others lost. The Autoscopes are strong now. So strong. You have all forgotten your highest calling, your first estate. It was Robin who put the theory back together and it was Jon Index who started calling you all. If he can start the Night Clock running again, he can destroy the Autoscopes."

"What do I do?" Chloe asked.

Babur took her hand. His felt warm and rough, and strong as she held it. "You keep yourself safe, girl. Stay off the roads at night. We will watch over you until it is time for you to be born."

"When?"

"Not long now," Babur said. "But you must know, your mother has been gravely hurt. She will survive, but she is weak."

"Where is she?"

"Index has taken her to one of the Quays. Your kind are gathering there, and your Paladins. He is preparing for the last winding of the Night Clock."

THEY SAT TOGETHER for another hour. Chloe rested her head against Babur's shoulder and let her mind drift. A part of her wanted to kick open that door in the back of the shop and run inside, revelling in the knowledge her mother could give her, but she was also aware that might be dangerous, too much of a distraction. What if she was overwhelmed? Or learned something terrible? Could her mother keep secrets from her or was it all fair game? Chloe considered that it was better to take what she needed rather than go blundering through her mother's mind and memory, greedy for information. Instead, she asked Babur to tell her about himself.

Babur shifted against her and reached into his inside jacket pocket. He took out a photograph. It was old, and faded and in black and white. There were creases that made white cracks across the picture. It showed four young men leaning against an army vehicle. They were in uniform and they were all smiling for the camera.

"That's me, second from the left," Babur said. "We've just appropriated that BMP-1 armoured personnel vehicle from the Russians during the Soviet War. I was a soldier, and when the war was over I came to England to start a better life."

"Was it better?"

"In some ways," Babur said. "In some ways, not. But here I am anyway, still fighting. And I like my new vehicle more."

"Was it Robin's?"

"He fitted it out with weapons and detectors. That modified EMP was something he designed to knock out the creatures the Autoscopes sent against us. Those antennae are calibrated to pick up their vibrations. He showed me how to use them but I really have no idea how they *work*. The Autoscopes take light from peoples' nightmares, *nihillumination* they call it, and use it as fuel for their monsters. It's foul and polluting and hurts the eyes. It lights up corners in minds that should remain in darkness. Before he left with the others to rescue your mother from the killer they sent for her, Robin opened a Gantry for me. He sent me through in the camper with instructions to find you and explain what you needed to know to keep you safe. But I think something went wrong. Or if not wrong, there was definitely trouble and I fear Robin was a casualty of the battle."

"How do you know?"

Babur put his photo back in his pocket. "I'll show you," he said, "Come on." He stood up and dusted his backside off. He held out a hand and helped Chloe to her feet.

They went outside and Babur took Chloe over to the camper. He slid open the door in its side and they stepped up. Chloe was immediately impressed with the decor. Plush purple carpet and curtains and a soft bench seat covered in silky red cushions. There was a sink and a cooker and a small fridge and lots of tiny cupboards. She noticed Babur was watching her, his eyebrows raised.

"I like it," she said. "Cozy."

Babur huffed. "This is my war machine," he said.

"I live in a cave," Chloe said.

"Point taken." Babur knelt and pulled a drawer from beneath the sink. It revealed a panel of glowing bulbs. Only ten were lit. He looked up at Chloe. She was biting her lip.

"A light for each of you who remain. I can track you through your Quays. When you're there, they flash. It's calibrated to the resonance of your Gantries. Look, that's Index's flashing. That's yours. You're home."

"Why are the others off?"

"It means they're gone." He pointed to one of the unlit bulbs. "That was Robin's."

"Gone where?"

Babur stood, stooped slightly beneath the low, curved roof of the camper. "When you're flesh and blood you can be killed. It depends on where you die. If you're killed in the waking world then you have a chance to be reborn or reside solely in the Quays. If you die in your Quay then it seems you go back to the ether. Job done. You're as eternal as any spirit but there is a limit to your power. You're not God."

Chloe was still looking at the panel. "Look at that," she said.

Babur glanced down.

Another light had started flashing.

"Who's that?"

For a moment, Babur looked stunned. He stood in silence with his brow furrowed. Then he said, "That, I believe, is Daniel."

Chloe felt a thrill of excitement, but then she noticed Babur's expression. "What is it?"

Babur looked into her eyes.

"Okay, Chloe, I need to go now."

Chloe's eyes widened. "Because of him?" She pointed at the newly lit bulb.

"Yes. According to Robin, Daniel has been missing for a long time, but Index has been looking for him. If he's in his Quay he might be disoriented. He might be open to deception. I have to go and find him and then bring him here. He'll be looking for you anyway."

"Can't I just come with you?"

"No," Babur said. "If I take you out of here, you'll die. You'll die in your mother's belly."

Chloe's eyes filled with tears. It was sudden and unpleasant and she rubbed her fingers against her closed eyelids.

"Babur—"

Babur held out his arms. This time when Chloe stepped into them he held onto her and they hugged.

"You'll be okay, girl. Look, we'll load some stuff in here and I'll take you as far as I can. You can lug it through the forest yourself though, I've got to get going. You have plenty of daylight. Come on."

Chloe shrugged against him.

"Come on, Chloe. Sooner I find him the sooner we can get back."

Chloe stepped from the embrace and ran her fingers through her hair, then pulled at the skin beneath her eyes with her fingertips. It pinched a bit but that horrid welling of emotion seemed to recede.

Without another word she turned and stepped out of the van.

Babur started to get out but Chloe held up a hand. "Go," she said. "I've got enough shit. I'll grab a few more bits and head back."

Babur looked relieved. "Good for you," he said. "Women, you know, I never know when they've got enough... shit."

Chloe laughed. "My mother has an awful lot of shit."

Babur began closing the door. Before it clunked shut completely, he said, "Say these words: *Junction Creature*."

"Junction Creature?"

"Excellent. It's a book. Your mother has already started buying books for you. It's one of her favourites. It'll be just inside the door. A lot of pictures. It might comfort you. It might give you some idea of what's coming and what we can do to defeat it."

Chloe nodded and watched Babur climb into the driver's seat. He turned a key and the engine racked into life. Babur turned and grinned and held his fist up, a thumb raised. Chloe copied the gesture and Babur laughed. Then he was off, bouncing the camper up the high street. Chloe watched until the road curved away behind the shops and he was gone. She listened for the engine, which continued to blat and rattle in the distance until that, too, had faded.

Chloe went back to the shop. Inside on the windowsill lay a book. It was a good-sized hardback with a glossy cover. There was a picture on the cover, an ink line drawing on a sepia background. In the picture a small boy was standing cowering at the bottom of a railway cutting at the entrance to a tunnel full of eyes. Chloe shuddered. Whatever was coming out of that tunnel was terrible.

"Junction Creature," Chloe said, and then thought: *comfort me*?

She put the book under her arm and made to leave the shop. As she was turning she heard a sound. She paused. An echoing, husky sound, full and deep. Once, twice: a good sound. She peered out and looked up the road. Overhead the sky was darkening as a low bolt of cloud rolled across it.

Something fell to the floor in the shop. She whirled around. Another book. Small and thin and delicate. She went over and picked it up. *A Ladybird Spotter Book of Dogs*. Chloe was frustrated that she still couldn't make out words, hadn't been able—or permitted, perhaps—to form the pathways necessary to decipher them. But a word did come:

Dogs.

She flicked through the pages. She thought these animals looked funny. And then she stopped and held the book up. An elegant hound peered out at her, its long snout raised, its brown eyes gentle and wise.

"Hello, handsome," she said.

And from outside, that deep, warm assent.

The Night Clock gathers its numbers to its own face.

11

TREVENA OPENS HIS eyes. The raggedy hood of the parka restricts his vision down to a dim oval. This coat stinks. He feels sweaty and stuffy and begrimed. Impatient with it, he rucks the hood back off his head and looks around. The night air is cool.

He is alone.

"Daniel?" he calls.

There is no reply. He looks around.

They are no longer on the street outside the shop. Instead he is standing on a broad promenade that stretches miles in both directions. The sea beats its black and foaming edge against a beach beneath him. He turns, and behind is nothing but darkness; it could be concealing anything but nothing he can discern. It's like the sky above has folded down to box in the promenade and he shudders at the enormity of it and fears he will lose his mind should the vast edge of a proximal planet begin to lift its arc above the horizon. He shudders and turns his back to it.

The sea at least is blunted in the distance by a starlit horizon, which gives Trevena a small but necessary focus. Something has a limit here.

He decides to move, to walk along the promenade and hope to

find Daniel. As he turns he sees that a red castle has appeared some way ahead, its rugged, curious bulk rising up from the sea like a beached and crumpled tanker thrown against the promenade and corroded scarlet by the salt, and its sudden materialisation—and its insolent familiarity—trigger an awful doldrums at Trevena's heart.

He slopes up the prom. He feels the tug of that drop into darkness to his right and concentrates his mind on the lashing hiss of the sea as he approaches the castle. And as he draws near it all changes again and he is standing outside an apartment block. The exterior of the castle is gone but as he looks up at the front of the apartment, Trevena has the sense that it has merely turned inwards and that its scale and internal dimensions are still contained behind the pink stone cladding of the facade.

Trevena walks up to the door. It is smoked glass and he can see the foyer beyond. It is sparse, marble-floored. There is a tiger curled up asleep in front of the lift. Its huge head lies on its front paws and its wild, flaming flanks ripple like a bonfire as it breathes. It has a long scar beneath its ribs, from a terrible wound. It has healed to a raw, pink curve.

Trevena pushes open the door. He approaches the tiger. He is aware of a great feeling of relief as the door closes on the black trench of space and the tremendous length of working sea. He stands in the silence of the foyer and listens to nothing but the air in the tiger's bronze throat.

A flight of stairs leads up to the right of the lift. Trevena walks across to the stairwell and starts up. He looks back and sees that the tiger is watching him. It yawns and stands, stretching low, its backside in the air and as high as Trevena's shoulder. Its tail curls like a crook and switches idly back and forth. Trevena continues upwards. There is a landing ahead and he reaches it and looks back and sees that the tiger is following him, padding up the stairs, its head swaying, grinning.

Trevena trots up the next flight. He can hear the click and clack of the tiger's claws against the marble steps. This is familiar, too, to Trevena, this lazy stalking, but it seems to hold no threat, as if there is an understanding between them, man and tiger. Trevena looks over his shoulder and the beast's head is coming around the corner, still grinning, looking up at him. Now Trevena begins to think that getting a door between them might be a good idea.

And perhaps the tiger knows what he is thinking, because it tenses there on the landing and springs, bounding up the steps in what looks to Trevena like a teleport because one moment it is down there, and the next it has its tawny face a foot away from his own. It is as broad and pointed as a shield reflecting the strewn fires of war, and Trevena is terribly afraid that if it roars he will be blown apart by it.

But it does not roar. It speaks:

"It would be a good idea to keep me close," the tiger says. Its eyes are almond-shaped, gentle. Its teeth, though, its jaws: like something lethal borne with enormous caution by a wise man, something that could explode and leave nothing behind but fluttering strips of flesh. The tiger smiles; it knows what it has.

Trevena recalls something he was once told, by his doctor, about his dreams: *everything in your dream represents a part of you.*

He has dreamed this tiger before.

But the tiger says, "This is not *your* dream, remember."

Trevena remembers and suddenly his knees weaken and he is galvanised by a barbaric terror and tries to turn and open the door in the wall of the landing but the tiger is on him before he can grasp the handle.

BABUR STOOD OVER Daniel's body and experienced a rush of deja vu. Or *something*-vu. He couldn't settle on a satisfying way to describe this unexpected, inverted scenario. *Inverter-vu?* This time it was he climbing out of the camper and approaching the prone body of a man. Babur realised his mind was struggling to accept the familiarity and, more significantly, the emotions it bore. The camper idled at the kerb. Babur knelt and shook Daniel's shoulder. Daniel opened his eyes.

"Dad?" he said.

"No, son," said Babur. "Come on, up you get."

He helped Daniel to stand.

"Oh, God, no," Daniel said. He was looking down at the pavement. His hands began shaking. His complexion was ashen.

Babur put a hand on Daniel's shoulder. "What is it?"

"Dr Natus," said Daniel. He fell to his knees and lifted a small, limp white object to his chest, rocking it with great tenderness. He wept. Babur noticed broken glass scattered around their feet, and a dark, drying puddle of gritty liquid.

"Oh, he's dead," Daniel said. "He's *dead*."

TREVENA FREEZES, PINNED against the door of the apartment. He can feel the tiger's opulent cheek, soft as ermine, against the side of his neck.

"Don't be afraid," the tiger says. Its breath is winter light radiating over the cold, exposed flesh of his throat.

"I'm afraid," Trevena says. "I am so *terribly* afraid."

"You're not afraid of me. You are afraid of what those rooms contain."

Trevena shakes his head. Tears run down his cheeks.

"We will go in together," the tiger says.

"No."

"*We will go in together*."

Trevena closes his eyes. Puts his hand on the door handle.

BABUR KNELT WITH Daniel. Daniel held the tiny creature in his cupped hands. He pressed the ball of his thumb into the palm of one of its hands making the fingers curl involuntarily around its tip like a pale anemone.

"Come on, Daniel, we have to go." Babur said.

Daniel stood up. He looked lost and Babur was unable to avoid thinking of the fathers he had seen during the Soviet war all those decades ago, broken men standing amongst rubble and fire holding the bodies of their children in their arms as the tanks rolled past.

He put a hand on Daniel's arm and guided him off the path and over to the camper van. Daniel was shaking his head.

They climbed up into the van and Daniel slumped down on the seat, still cradling Dr Natus.

"What happened?" Babur asked.

Daniel looked up, his expression distant. "He attacked me."

"Who did?"

"The man I brought through with me. I didn't know it was going to happen but I should have anticipated it when he came dressed in that coat. Cade got to him."

"Where is he?"

Daniel shrugged. "I don't know. Somewhere here. He has another controlling him. His name's Cade and he's a *very* angry entity."

Babur took off his jacket. "Here," he said, offering it to Daniel. "Wrap the child in this."

Daniel took the jacket and placed it beside him on the seat.

"He's not a child," he said in a quiet voice.

"No?"

"No. I don't know what he is. I don't even think he's real."

TREVENA AND THE tiger go into the apartment. Trevena moans and draws back as the door opens onto the first of a hundred red rooms, a glistening atrium studded with leather, walls, floor and soaring ceiling. To his right a balcony gives onto a sunken ballroom, it, too, surfaced with that carnal and immodest hide. Despite the size and inner dimensions of the building, the red leather makes Trevena feel *snug*, and suddenly capable of great acts against his will, acts of harm to flesh. The tiger nudges him. Trevena focuses on a door standing ajar at the end of a corridor that leads off ahead of them from the far side of the entrance hall.

They walk the length of the corridor and come to the door. Trevena feels a wild panic overwhelm him and he freezes, filled with a dread so paralysing he thinks he might be about to open a door that reveals all of God, and *God* is darkness and the weight of regret, and the Truth is this feeling, tremendous for all time.

"Open it," the tiger says. "I'm with you."

And Trevena thinks then that he could face an eternity of Hell with this tiger alongside him, and the dread recedes like a current, alternating in a quantum instant into courage, and he reaches out and grasps the handle and pulls the door open.

DANIEL WRAPPED DR Natus in Babur's jacket and covered his face with the lapels folded over, and then he sat back with his hands held limp in his lap. He blinked and looked around.

"I came to find a girl. Chloe," he said. "Can you help?"

"Yes," said Babur. "I know where she is."

Daniel's expression hardened, and Babur saw the strength of the man become apparent, the essence of who he really was emerge again, like a performer coming out of a gruelling role, and he was glad to see it. Glad to see the confusion and grief subsumed by a fierce and hard-earned will.

"What about the man you came with?"

"We'll have to leave him. He's a good man. He has his own conflict to overcome."

THERE SHE IS, the girl. Always the girl.

She has long red hair that lays straight and wet between her narrow shoulder blades. It glistens, enhanced by the light reflected from the leather that lines the walls of the bathroom. She is naked and has her back to him but she is not caught unawares because she is bent slightly over the sink and her legs are a little apart and Trevena can see the full, mature convexity of her cunt seamed with its tidy slit, and the indrawn pucker above it like a navel, a darker pink, and her head is turning revealing her prettily flushed profile, and Trevena knows that she is about to ask him to fuck her, and this time he will, despite the tiger, despite his repulsion, because he can feel the *other*, Cade, rising, and he is powerful and full of fury. And now he is fully here and he will make Trevena do the one thing that will destroy everything he believes in, everything he thinks he is.

There's an oval mirror above the basin, and Trevena can see his reflection. He watches himself shake his head. He watches himself take a step forward. The girl is smiling but her eyes are full of something else: uncertainty, confusion. Dread?

Her hand reaches around and it's soapy and she smears the palm between her thighs leaving herself pearled with a glaze of tiny bubbles.

Trevena groans. *Who are you?* he thinks, but he thinks he knows, and he can't bear it. He can't do this but his erection is monstrous, immeasurable, so big he feels that the lagged walls of the apartment itself want to contract and close around it.

A stranger is watching him from the mirror. The man is mad. He wears the parka coat but he is no longer human beneath it. He is misshapen as if the coat has been thrown over struts. Only the head with the mad, beaming face is something like human, although all that is fallen about it. The arms come up like a conductor's and the sleeves reveal wrists and fists of a beast that has been tearing at shit and guts.

"Lizzie," Trevena whispers.

"*Lizzie*," the man in the mirror hisses.

Trevena takes another step and can see more of the reflection, and he sees that the madman is standing in a much different room. It is an office with a view out onto an orchard. There is a desk, and a couch, and behind the desk a man lies dying, with a wound in his chest.

"No," Trevena says.

"Yes," says the man in the mirror, in the office. In Doctor Mocking's office. The man Trevena has been seeing for therapy for the last year, since his divorce, to stave off his mental collapse, his therapist, is dying. And what had Daniel said? *In the future you will do some very bad things, or Cade will, through you.*

Why the Doc?

The girl snarls. Trevena's attention is jolted away from the mirror for a moment. Her fingers are a V, her seam unpicked. The madman laughs.

"Fuck her, Phil. How you've *longed* to do it."

Trevena feels all that red throb in towards him, a warm cushion, tightening. He is sweating. He tears his eyes from the girl and looks through the glass, desperate.

The doctor, Trevena's kind and wise psychiatrist, has turned his head and is looking back at him. He looks tired, but he smiles. He lifts a hand an inch from the floor. His lips move.

This is not your dream.

Trevena stands still. He breathes out slowly and looks at the girl.

"*Fuck* her!"

"No," Trevena says. "Never."

"*FUCK HER!*"

Trevena stands aside and lets the tiger come through.

The madman gapes.

"Remember me?" the tiger says. And it leaps toward the dawning horror on the madman's face, and it must look to Cade like a furnace door has been flung wide beyond the mirror and a bolt of some righteous inferno has been launched at him, all broad white beautiful paws unsheathing their daggers. He staggers back, but the tiger hits the glass and passes straight through it.

Trevena goes to the girl. He has reached for a towel to cover her, but sees that he does not need it. This dream has changed again, and for the better.

It is not his daughter standing there, it never was. This girl is clothed, and small and dark and no more than eight.

Trevena squats down. "What's your name, sweetheart?" he asks.

The girl looks to be in shock. Her eyes are wide and she is pale, but otherwise she looks unharmed.

"Anna," she whispers.

"Let's get you out of here," says Trevena, and she goes willingly enough to him and he lifts her up and turns and walks out of the bathroom. He closes the door behind him so that Anna does not have to hear Cade's screams.

* * *

TREVENA STANDS ON the promenade and waits. The girl, Anna, is asleep in his arms. She is a good weight and his arms are tired, but Trevena doesn't mind. He looks out across the sea. The waters are still, all their temper spent, and the tide is out revealing a dark, drenched beach of level sand. He hears something. The sound of feet on the concrete to his right. Softly padding. He turns.

The tiger trots up to his side. There is blood beaded on its whiskers like eggs laid by some ghastly gore-fed louse.

"Is she unharmed?" the tiger asks. There is concern in the voice. Tenderness.

"She's fine," Trevena says. And as he speaks, the girl wakes. She sees the tiger and squeals. Trevena is startled and tries to comfort her, but she struggles and he has to put her down. "It's okay," he says, but need not have worried.

The girl runs to the tiger and throws her arms around it.

"*Bronze John*!" she says, her voice muffled in the fur at its throat. She pulls back and looks into its face. "Ugh," she says, and grabs a handful of her black jumper and wipes the blood from the tiger's mouth. The tiger grins, its teeth champed together like a lattice behind its manhandled chops.

Trevena laughs.

Then he stops, remembering the mirror and what it had shown. "The Doc?" he asks.

Bronze John nods his huge head. "He'll live," he says.

Trevena feels suddenly weak and bends his back, his hands on his knees. He breathes out long and slow. "Thank you," he says.

"Thank *you*," says Bronze John. "It was your choice."

Trevena shook his head. "No. It was no choice. Cade made me do that. He wanted to destroy me."

"Yes," said the tiger. "But he wanted more than just you. His sights were set high. If he could use you to kill Doctor Mocking then he thought he might regain the favour of the Autoscopes."

"The Doc? Why?"

"He is a Firmament Surgeon. And Anna is one of his daughters. Cade took her from her sister's Quay for *leverage*."

Trevena stands with his hands on his hips and puffs out his cheeks. He looks at the tiger, then at the girl.

"Are we winning?" he asks, eyebrows raised.

"Almost there," the tiger says. "Now take that coat off."

Trevena is surprised, and then realises he is still wearing the ratty old parka. His face screws up into an expression of disgust. "Oh, *mate*!" he says, mostly to himself, and uses his fingertips to un-toggle the coat. He drags it off his shoulders and bundles it up in his fists. He steps forward and throws it over the railings and onto the beach.

He wants to say something ripe, healthily off-colour, to purge him of any remaining feelings of revulsion, but he minds his language for Anna's sake, and only thinks it.

"What now?" he asks, but the tiger is ahead of him. Anna is sitting on his back and looks like a doll up there. The tiger is truly massive. A Siberian would look like a kitten next to him.

Trevena cocks his head. "Have you grown?"

Bronze John looks him in the eye.

"Climb on," he says. "We've got to get somewhere and fast."

Trevena shrugs and clambers onto the tiger's back. Anna turns and smiles at him. Trevena smiles back. "Hang on," she says, and Trevena's smile slips a bit.

Bronze John heads off up the promenade, and soon he is running, with Trevena hanging on, bunches of pelt gripped in white fingers, with tears of both terror and elation streaming from his eyes.

12

CHLOE STARTED BACK to the cave. She carried the ladder and the rope, which was arduous but she felt determined that day, vital. Her books were in her bag, slung over her shoulder and when she tired, she dragged the ladder behind, liking the rumble it made on the cobbles.

She reached the meadow and stopped to wipe her face with her hand. As she stood there, something caught her eye. It was movement, a glimpse of something fleet darting from the tree line at the edge of the forest. She squinted, her heart beating a little faster. Her hand dropped to her belt and she pulled out the hatchet.

Chloe knelt in the long grass at the edge of the meadow and waited. She was aware of how exposed she was. Despite the coolness of the air she felt perspiration spreading beneath her arms. She gripped the hatchet more tightly and tried not to imagine a horde of glass spiders crashing from the undergrowth and pouring across the meadow towards her. She glanced back, wondering what her chances would be of reaching the village at a run if she had to turn and flee.

But she need not have worried. What emerged from the forest was no monster.

It came running, its head visible above the grass, a long, feathery tail high and lively, wagging like a huge catkin in a breeze.

Chloe stood, waited, and watched the dog come to her.

THERE WAS A stream running through the meadow, its source somewhere high in the mountains ringing the town. Its course took it through a constructed stone gutter that ran through the town. Chloe had noticed it and thought it a pretty thing, bubbling shallow and clear. It was narrow enough to step over.

From the silt and pebbles at the bottom of the stream something lifted its head. A long body that ended in a tail equipped with a stinger like a cosh bristling with needle-sharp hooks rose from the dirt and used scaled, crocodile claws to paddle itself along the conduit. It swung jaws hinged like a swing bin, spewing water as its head came up, and the spikes that ran along the ridges of its spine, and the hooks on its lashing tail, filled with an electric blue poison like an array of syringes charging in preparation for a hundred lethal injections.

It lowered its head beneath the water and pushed on upstream.

THE DOG APPROACHED Chloe, its head up, panting. It stopped a few feet away and sat down. It barked, a soft, cautious woof and sat waiting, head tilted slightly to one side. Chloe smiled. She slid the hatchet back into her belt and held out her hand. The dog got up and came over and sniffed her fingers.

Chloe fussed it beneath the chin. The dog closed its eyes and wagged its tail.

"You want a hand with those?" it said.

Chloe startled. "You what?"

"Your stuff. I could carry the bag and the rope if you like. Get this done."

Not having an experience to the contrary, a talking dog didn't seem, to Chloe, a particularly odd thing. It felt special, though. A *connection*, like when she had first touched Babur.

"Ok," she said. "How do you want to do this?"

"Put the rope round my neck and strap the bag on my back and we're good to go. You'll have to lug those ladders, though, I don't want to overdo it."

"Right, that's good of you," Chloe said.

"I'm like that," said the dog.

Chloe hung the loop of rope over the dog's head and began strapping the bag onto its back. She buckled it under its narrow but powerful chest.

As she was working, Chloe felt the dog's posture change. It tensed and leaned forward. She patted its flank. "There," and she stood up.

The dog stood alert, its ears back, nose in the air.

"What is it?"

"There's something in the water. It's coming this way. We should go."

"In the stream?"

"Yes. I can smell it. It smells *off*."

Looking over her shoulder, Chloe gripped one end of the ladder. It was an aluminium extension ladder with steps rather than rungs, and quite light, but it was still unwieldy to drag and she hadn't expected to be doing this in a hurry.

"Shall I leave this?" she asked.

"Better not," the dog said. "We'll need it."

Chloe braced herself and yanked the ladder into the long grass. The dog trotted ahead, the rope swinging like a lasso and Chloe followed, walking backwards, dragging the ladder. The dog remained alert, sniffing the air.

They reached the tree line and entered the forest, and as the canopies closed over them something low and fast shot out from the grass to their right and clattered into the ladder, wrenching it from Chloe's grip and sending her over onto her side. She sprawled against a tree trunk and shouted with surprise.

She sat up and reached for the hatchet but it was gone from her belt. She looked around and saw it beneath some roots a few feet away. She started to crawl towards it but the thing that had come out of the grass was moving in the trees behind her. She held her breath. Where was the dog?

"*Dog!*" she hissed. "*Dog!*"

"My name's Bix," said the dog. He trotted out from behind a stand of trees, picked up the hatchet in his mouth and brought it over to Chloe. She took it and patted his head. She looked around.

"Bix. Right. Thanks. What was *that* thing?"

"Did you see it?" Bix asked.

"Not really. It was fast. I don't think it was a spider. It was sort of *flat*."

"Flat, you say," said Bix.

"Yes, you know, like a, like a...

surfboard

ironing board

crocodile

"And it had a tail, I think, like a...

scorpion

"I think it was a scorpodile," Chloe said, her face solemn with sudden conviction.

"Ah," said Bix. "I knew you'd get there in the end. So, we're looking for a scorpodile."

"I reckon," said Chloe. And then the undergrowth crashed off to their left and the scorpodile appeared.

"Shit," said Chloe.

"I was thinking the same thing," said Bix.

The scorpodile crawled towards them, its reptile claws digging clods from the moist earth. Its belly dragged on the ground, segmented and muscular, and its tail swung above its back, curled and loaded with poison. Its jaws opened and closed on bulbous joints beneath its eyes, which were located on the sides of its pointed head, and orbited in six deep sockets, three to each side, in a triangular formation, two below and one above.

Chloe hefted the hatchet. Bix lowered his head and shook off the loop of rope. Then he prowled forward, a low snarl in his throat.

The scorpodile rushed them. Its jaw swung open and Chloe saw it was filled with row upon row of jagged glass teeth. Its tail arched and the bolus of hooks hung over its head, incandescent with venom.

Chloe darted left and Bix skipped right. The scorpodile slithered between them, paddling crocodile claws through the mulch. Chloe raised the hatchet and swung it at the creature's back but the tail lashed and connected with the blade before it could complete its trajectory and bounced it out of the way. A number of barbs had snapped off from the cosh, and electric-blue poison was spitting in furious little arcs from the damaged hollow points.

Bix snapped and worried at the creature's head, ducking and bobbing his jaws at the thing's eyes. The scorpodile twisted and unhinged its mouth, scooping at the air where moments before Bix had been biting. It threw its stinger left and right but each time Chloe and Bix danced out of the way. Chloe was anxious for Bix; he was wary but seemed unconcerned for the proximity of that horrible stinger. He dashed in and bit, sprang back out of reach, and was in again. Chloe worked around carefully; she was much more likely to trip on a tree root or get caught up in brambles. The space between the trees was cramped and narrow and she dreaded falling and having that thing descend on her. She kept the hatchet tight in her fist and chopped and hacked, trying to do enough damage to perhaps see the thing off, if not destroy it. Could it be killed?

Bix was in again, and this time he was gnawing at the thing's eyes on the right side of its head. It made no sound, just the slap of its beaded feet and the rustle of its belly low in the earth as it thrashed but now, as Bix got purchase in the bony orbits, and shook his head like a terrier breaking some vermin's back, it shrieked, an unearthly sound of outrage, and black fluid jetted in a thick pulse across Bix's muzzle.

Bix leaped back, shaking his head, flinging ropes of ichor from his mouth. He paused on trembling limbs, wired from the brawl, and looked up at Chloe.

"Hit it," he said. "Take that bloody tail off."

Chloe had a moment to wonder, with a chill that sent a quiver along every nerve, what an infusion of that steaming toxin might do to her. How quickly would it burn her up? Lock her immobile in the dirt while it hollowed out her organs? Reduce her to a drizzle of fluid while she died staring at the sky?

Chloe measured her aim and dropped the hatchet onto the bludgeon with a sharp, precise downward hack. It shattered like a goblet, spraying flamboyant blue poison in a fan across the ground. It simmered in the mulch, bubbling down into the earth amongst the shards of the splintered cosh.

Enraged, it shuttled towards Bix, its ghastly rocking jaws sawing back and forth, and it caught the dog by surprise. Bix tried to jump back but was already pressed against the difficult, twined roots of a bush and he found himself trapped beneath the wide, rearing throat of the scorpodile. He snapped at the fibrous flesh beneath the swinging jaws, ducking his muzzle away each time they shovelled at him, but it was strong and determined with its pure impulse to kill, and it rose up and opened wide like a bunker full of jagged edges, and dropped its shark-load of teeth onto Bix's exposed chest.

Chloe screamed. It was an effort-filled sound of defiance, and before the scorpodile could fasten its jaws, the ladder crashed down onto its back and pinned it into the ground.

Bix kicked his legs and scrabbled out from beneath the scorpodile's thrashing torso. He circled away and watched as Chloe stepped up onto the ladder and walked along it, pressing the scorpodile further into the earth until she stood balanced above its writhing head. She raised the hatchet and brought it down onto the bony ridge between its eyes, once and then again, each time cutting deeper, hacking at where she hoped the brain of the thing was located. Black fluid sprayed from the deepening gash. She could hear Bix panting. She lifted the axe again and gripped its shaft with both hands and brought it down with a shout. The scorpodile's head split in two and its jaws dislocated with a wet tendinous pop. It stopped moving and lay beneath the ladder, venting the thick muck inside its head in a slow, mortal stream.

Chloe stepped from the ladder and stood on wobbling legs. She knelt, breathing deeply, watching the scorpodile for signs of life. She wiped the gory edge of the hatchet blade on the leaves beneath her feet and slid it back into her belt. Bix stood at her side.

"Nice work," he said. "I thought it had me there."

Chloe put an arm around the dog's neck.

"Not on my watch," she said. The dog laughed and licked her face.

"Really?" Chloe said, standing up, laughing herself and wiping her cheek.

Bix dipped his head. "It's what we do," he said.

"Well, you can pack it in," Chloe said.

"I *can't* promise," Bix said.

Chloe lifted the ladder from the back of the dead scorpodile and stood it against a tree. She hunted around for the rope and slung it over Bix's head. She straightened the bag on his back, which had slipped during the fight, and she tightened the strap beneath his belly.

"Good to go," she said. She took hold of the ladder and started dragging it through the forest towards the foot of the mountain. Bix followed.

THEY REACHED THE foot of the low mountain without encountering any further attacks. Bix trotted at Chloe's heel, vigilant and alert, as she dragged the ladder through the trees and over exposed roots.

Chloe pointed up through the trees to where the opening of the cave was just visible as a dark recess.

"Home," she said.

Bix sniffed the air. "We'll be safe here," he said. "I can smell the iron in the rocks. Those things don't like iron."

Iron

Lifeblood

"It's my mother, isn't it? The mountain?"

"Yep," said Bix. "Full of love."

"I can feel it," Chloe said.

She propped the ladder against the rock face and extended it out to its full length. It reached to about a foot below the opening.

"Can you climb those steps?"

"I reckon," Bix said. "Tie the rope around me and you go up first."

Chloe did as Bix suggested, cinching the rope beneath his chest behind his front legs. She climbed the ladder slowly letting the rope play out behind until she reached the mouth of the cave. She hoisted herself up and sat with her legs over the edge and her feet flat on the top step of the ladder to stabilise it. She wrapped the rope around her waist and held the end in both fists.

"Up you come," she said.

Bix put his front paws on the bottom step and allowed Chloe to take the slack. Then he climbed the rest of the ladder like he'd been shinning up and down them all his life. Chloe reeled the rope tight, laughing at the sight of the dog bounding up towards her.

Bix reached the top and Chloe stood and took a couple of steps back into the cave so that Bix could jump the last few feet.

"Easy," said the dog.

Chloe untied the rope and gathered it into a loop and dropped it on the floor. She knelt and undid the buckle of the bag and lifted it from Bix's back. Then she hugged him and kissed his head and ears.

"Really?" said Bix.

"It's what we do," Chloe said.

"Well don't stop," Bix said, tail wagging, and licked Chloe's cheek.

THEY SETTLED IN, and when the light started to fade, Chloe lit candles and stood them around the edge of the cave. They sat together on the rugs at the back of the cave and went through her bag.

Chloe showed Bix her books.

"Books are good things," Bix said. "Good choice."

Chloe picked up *Junction Creature*. The picture on the cover unsettled her, the dark thing bulging from the tunnel gleamed in the fluttering candlelight and seemed to swell closer to the boy cowering on the tracks. He looked full of dread and hopelessness.

"I know that book," Bix said.

Chloe looked sideways at him and raised her eyebrows.

"Read it, have you?"

Bix nosed at the cover. "Not yet, but I know all about *that* thing."

"What is it?"

"It's the *devil-in-dreams*," Bix said. "It's the darkness behind the Autoscopes. It's what wants to kill you."

"This was supposed to comfort me," Chloe said in a hushed voice. Her eyes pricked suddenly with tears. Was this a trick? Was Babur just another monster?

"It's knowledge, Chloe. Information. It was written so that you could know your enemy and learn how to fight it. A good man wrote this book for his own son for the same reasons."

Chloe nodded, still eyeing the cover with unease.

"Open it," Bix said. "And I'll read it to you."

Full of wonder—for this dog, for the book, for her *life*—and full of apprehension, Chloe opened the book to the first darkly illustrated page, and Bix began to read:

TOWARDS THE END of May, the surrounding fields become luminous. Beneath the wide, unsettled skies, the soil at the edge of the fens and beyond brings forth, for some dark spring days, brief, dazzling ingots of yellow, stinking rape. And then, almost overnight, the crop is harvested, the lights go out, and profusions of poppies emerge like beads of blood welling from the raw, grazed earth.

The countryside is flat, littered with machine parts and the shells of outbuildings, windmills, pump houses and neglected railway lines. There are plenty of working farms, stables, boat-builders, but it is the dereliction that seems to give the landscape an age. It leaves its history lying around like discarded rind.

Other abundant features are the water towers, great structures that bestride the fields and roadsides. The variety of their architecture is striking; some look like follies, with their turrets and fancy brickwork, others like alien war machines bristling with panels and aerials, others still look like colossal viruses, built from diagrammatic specifications in text books, their elevated reservoirs like stylised concrete capsids.

So this land, inert, dreary, interminable to some; an inspiration to artists, horsemen, travellers, preservers of Tudor architecture, bucolic, antique and primal, keeps secrets and legends tight in the dark back rooms of drowsy pubs, the fire-lit tiled parlours of isolated farmhouses and the intricate quarters of the tithe cottages lining the drives of the ubiquitous studs.

It is seldom fragrant. In fact it often stinks. The air carries the heavy odours of silage and ordure. Miles of churned manure; huge, slumbering pigs lethargic and deliberate outside their ranks of half-cylinder tin shelters; the scorched beetroot stench of the sugar factories and the miasma of hops fermenting in the breweries; that sudden, bright, dirty incandescence of rape.

And there are brutes at large in the fens, the fields, and the night-lone back streets of dark and secluded villages. Black Dogs and Big Cats, phantom beasts, elusive monsters. They have always been amongst us here, their burning eyes glimpsed across a yard, through dark windows, watching you from a remote horizon.

This is Old England and these are its legends, its Hob-footed thugs.

But now there is a new unease, a slow paranoia creeping through this old, measured shire. There is talk of a new beast.

And its name is *Junction Creature*.

A YOUNG BOY cycles to school on a cold spring morning. He has a new red sports bag slung over his shoulder. It's filled with books, trainers to change into at playtime and his lunch—chicken sandwiches with pickle, a Penguin biscuit and an apple, a bottle of water and a Hartley's lemon jelly (he tries to eat the jelly in secret because if the other boys see him with a *jelly*, he gets teased, but he loves them and he eats them in defiance of their opinions).

His name is Alex and he is ten years old. He lives on a farm with his uncle and aunt. It's not a working farm anymore. His uncle sold off most of the land and converted the barn so that he could concentrate on being a sculptor. Alex is fascinated by his uncle's work. He makes things from metal and glass, and they look alive as they arch, stretch and climb towards the timber roof of the barn. The light striking from his uncle's arc welder illuminates the barn with electric flashes long into the night.

Alex is just as fascinated by his uncle Sandy. Sandy is a large man, completely bald with an untamed black beard, and a moustache he teases out and waxes into two long, twitching stilettos of hair. His eyes are dark and his mood is often reflected likewise within them and beneath the intense crush of his brow. When he wears his welder's mask the top of his hairless, shining head rises like a dome above it and his beard and the tips of his moustache protrude from underneath it and from its sides like wild weeds struggling from beneath a cloche.

His aunt, however, is a different matter. She is beautiful. Like an actress, a *starlet*, his Uncle Sandy calls her. She has long, curling silvery blonde hair and a face that expresses an abundance of exciting knowledge and experience. She doesn't do much except lounge about the farmhouse drinking gin and looking gorgeous in her antique gowns and dresses, but she is kind, in a detached, mysterious way, full of her own enshrined passions which express themselves internally and are only occasionally evident in a rosy flush, or a deep, satisfied sigh. Sandy is devoted to her, is fiercely, overly protective and frustrates the life out of her with his constant fussing. For a big man, Uncle Sandy is gentle as a lamb. He adores his Jean.

Alex smiles, thinking of them both, and pushes down on his pedals and heads down the lane. He is looking forward to a brisk kick-about in the playground before the bell. They're about 26-12 up from yesterday's match. He can almost feel the tennis ball flying from the toe of his trainer with that satisfying and mildly painful hollow *crack* it makes when you catch it sweetly off your toes.

TODAY, THOUGH, ALEX doesn't make it to school.

A couple of monsters see to that.

AS HE CYCLED, from across the fields came a cry. He skidded the bike to a stop and stood with it tilted between his knees. He looked around. The sound continued, off to his left. He grimaced. It began as a low note and Alex felt it blanket his bones with a chill. It began to rise in pitch, gaining in volume and it was the most awful sound he had ever heard, a sound, he thought, that wanted to *hurt* you.

At once, all the birds for miles rose up out of the distant woods and filled the sky with wheeling black static. They flocked in great pulsing blotches against the low white cloud. Alex shielded his eyes with the palm of his hand and squinted through the low morning sunlight. He gasped.

The birds were flocking as one, regardless of species. They wheeled towards where he stood. Crows and doves, woodpigeons, starlings and magpies, all turned and shoaled together in total formation. It was as if the sky was folding and unfolding itself. They swarmed overhead and Alex saw nightjars and wrens, herons, ducks, kingfishers and owls all in profusion above him. But the thing that shook him, which made the whole spectacle upsetting rather than just bizarre—owls, flocking?—was how they all looked. They all appeared terrified, as if this whole thing was out of their control. Their beaks gaped and their little eyes bulged. And throughout it all, that screaming drove them, welling up out of the woods.

Alex turned his bike around and started to pedal home. He needed his Uncle Sandy to see this, to hear that cry.

As Alex reached the end of the lane and cut along a path worn into the earth at the outskirts of the farm, the weather changed. Snow began to fall. Great flakes swirled down from the darkening clouds. He rode through a dense and thickening blizzard, aware that the snow was settling quickly on the hard, churned earth and budding branches around him. Flakes drifted into his face and spattered against the back of his neck.

There had been snow here before in early spring, but the end of May? And this sudden? This *storm*? Alex skidded the bike onto the driveway leading up to the farmhouse. The wheels slipped on a thickening mat of snow. He reached the farmhouse. He climbed off his bike and kicked the stand down. He stopped for a moment and peered through the snow. The sky was white, the birds had gone. Whatever had terrified them could not keep them airborne in this blizzard. They had taken roost against it. The screaming had stopped, too. Alex breathed deeply, snowflakes landing on his head the size of moths.

He turned to go inside, but as he was about to push the door open he glimpsed something move in the field behind him. He paused and looked back down the path and as he did so two beasts charged out from the cover of the hedgerow and flew towards the farmhouse.

One of the beasts was low to the ground and scaly. It had a human face and outrageous curly blonde hair, as if someone had stuck a doll's head on a Gila monster. It walked on all fours, although all four limbs were arms with long fingered hands. It had spines like knitting needles in a ring around its neck.

The other creature had left the path and was circling; a cluster of eyes like a spider's high on its forehead glittered with malice as it stalked. It walked upright but with a stiff caution as if it had recently recovered from a near fatal accident. It had a face as round and pale as a pudding bowl, featureless apart from that handful of eyes. It wore a dark pinstriped suit, which was smothered in mud and blotchy with mould. For an awful moment of stillness it stopped and stood there, swaying slightly in the snowfall, and marked Alex. It reached out an arm and pointed at him. It made a gesture with its thumb and index finger like a pistol and mimed a shot at him. Alex felt a rush of air along his cheek and a small hole appeared in the doorframe behind his head.

Alex cried out and ducked. It only got off one shot.

From out of the farmhouse charged Uncle Sandy. He threw himself at the creature. It made to fire on him but didn't get a chance because uncle Sandy had seized its wrist and was wrenching at it like it was the leg of a stubborn Christmas turkey. The creature shrieked and made a desperate imploring gesture to its companion. Sandy punched it in the gut, collapsing it like a clothes airer. The doll-faced thing blubbered, rolled its haunting blue eyes and scuttled across the grass to assist. The three fought in the snow, Pinstripe on his back with uncle Sandy savaging its gun hand, the lizard-thing circling and slapping and whining. And all the time the snow continued to fall.

Then, from behind Alex: "*Sandy!*"

Aunt Jean put a hand on Alex's shoulder. She held a slender glass full of gin and tonic with ice and lemon in the other hand. The ice clinked as she leaned forward and yelled across the yard.

Sandy was up, his broad, muscular back heaving from the exertion as he stood over the injured brutes. His fists were clenched and he was trembling with fury. He booted the lizard-thing in the face and turned and stalked back to the farmhouse, barrel chest heaving.

The thing in the pinstripe suit lay on its back in the snow, arms and legs splayed out. It appeared dead. The other creature ran around it in circles, flakes of snow caught in its blond curls. Its hands were blue with the cold but it didn't seem to notice. Then, suddenly, pinstripe sat up. It fixed Sandy with its tiny cluster of beady eyes and something unzipped beneath its chin. Fluid dribbled down its tatty shirtfront and then two huge fangs like shards of porcelain slid out. It lifted its gun hand.

"Inside!" said Aunt Jean, and she shut the door behind them.

Alex was too shocked to say anything and went through to the sitting room. He went over to the window, which faced onto the yard and looked out.

There were no more shots though, only a shriek of fury. The creature was on its feet again and was holding its shattered wrist in its good hand. It flapped it and tried to point it at the cottage, but it was useless. Sandy, standing beside Alex, murmured something contented, and patted Alex's head. They watched as the two beasts turned and stalked away. They disappeared back into the hedgerow.

Sandy gave Alex a hug. He patted Alex's back and Alex could smell the good smell of paint and varnish on his clothes, from his work in the barn.

"I'm okay," he said. Sandy ruffled his hair and stepped over to the window. The snow was falling more thinly now and had yet to cover up the scuffed tracks in the grass where he had seen off the beasts.

"Who are they, Uncle Sandy?" Alex asked.

Sandy was silent for a moment. Behind them the fire roared. Alex could hear the clink of ice being added to the makings of another gin and tonic.

"Toyceivers," he said.

Alex didn't know what to make of the word, but before he could say anything else there was a sudden explosion of noise from outside. It sounded like a circus load of animals blundering around tearing up trees and bushes.

Sandy snarled. "Right," he said. "This is it. Let's get to the barn."

SANDY AND ALEX went through the cottage locking up and fixing shutters. Aunt Jean sprawled on the sofa in the living room with her drink. Sandy worried over her but she shooed him away and blew him a kiss saying she'd be fine.

Upstairs, Alex spared a moment to look out of the window but all he could see was the snow-covered yard, which appeared as smooth and mysterious as the wide white screen of the picture house he loved to visit in town.

And then, like grotesque images projected onto that screen, they began to come, edging onto the whiteness from the border of the farm.

Alex banged the shutters closed and locked them then returned to the top of the stairs. His heart was hammering in his chest.

He paused in the stairwell and looked down. Sandy was by the front door pulling on a pair of boots. He was speaking soothingly to Jean, who was telling him to stop it and get the boy to the barn.

Alex ran down the rest of the stairs and stood with Sandy by the door. Sandy reached for the handle, but before his fingers closed around it, something hit the front door with enough force to splinter the frame.

"Out the back," he said. His voice was calm and steady but there was a different look in his eyes now. Anger and regret together, and with that all-consuming protectiveness. It made him look stronger than ever.

Above, Alex could make out a sound. Something was on the roof, battering at the tiles.

Something crashed against the front door again, popping it open off its latch. Cold air blew in and something was out there on the porch craning in at them. It had a thick grey neck and a tiny head, all teeth, like a cricket ball studded with fangs. It made a sound unlike anything Alex had ever heard before, like paper endlessly tearing.

Outside came the sounds of growling and roaring, things slithering and purposeful. Something the size and shape of a marrow waddled across the yard carrying blades.

Sandy shouted and kicked at the thing jammed in the doorway. It swung its small, lethal head but missed and clocked itself on the doorframe. It slumped away from the opening and Sandy had to dodge as the thing beyond it slung a blade at him. It flew past his face as he leaped aside, and embedded itself in the banister rail.

Sandy shoved the door shut again and latched and double bolted it, top and bottom. Then he took off down the hall and through to the kitchen. Alex followed.

Uncle Sandy threw open the back door and checked outside. So far nothing had ventured around the back. The barn stood high and wide across the back yard, its large, heavy wooden doors ajar.

"Come on," he said, and they ran full tilt across the yard and into the barn. Sandy pulled the doors shut and secured them with more heavy bolts. They stood, breathless and wired, and Sandy immediately started looking around.

The barn was Sandy's workshop. In the middle of the floor was a huge workbench made of ancient pine. It was littered with bits of wood and metal, cogs and clockworks, oilcans, drill bits, engine parts and electronic circuits. There were tiny motors, resistors, amplifiers, canisters and beakers. Against the wall he had installed a lathe, a sanding belt and an angle grinder. The walls were hidden behind cabinets and shelves full of tools and equipment and the whole room was sweet with the smell of varnishes, linseed oil and paint. His welding equipment stood beside the bench, a spot welder and an arc welder, both with red steel housings and side ventilators like gills. The floor around them was scattered with welding tips that looked like a spill of bullet cases.

And everywhere else, arrayed around the barn and lurking back in the storage area, stood his sculptures.

Alex could hear the racket outside. Things barging around and battering at the farmhouse and the walls and doors of the barn.

"Uncle Sandy," he said. "What about Aunt Jean?"

Sandy was at the back of the barn amongst his sculptures. He was yanking leads and plugging them into sockets built into the floor.

Still working, he said, "She'll be fine, son. Nothing's going to harm your Aunty Jean."

Something battered against the barn door. It made a low drumming sound and then the tip of a tentacle pushed through the gap between the ground and the bottom of the door and probed about.

"How do you know?" Alex said, a little desperation creeping into his voice. The tentacle flattened beneath the door, leechlike, and tried to push further inside. Alex considered stamping on it but it looked clammy and repellent.

Sandy went over to the wall and pulled a switch. There was a flash and a crackle and Alex felt all the hairs on his head rise in an invisible caul of static. He looked around, his eyes wild.

Sandy was standing with his hands on his hips, looking up at his array of sculptures. Electricity was crawling across the floor in a rippling blue tide. Sandy was wearing rubber boots but Alex was still wearing his school shoes.

"Uncle Sandy!" he said, his expression stupefied, his arms out at his sides, hands spread wide.

"Oh, jump up on that bench, son. It's wood. It'll insulate you."

Alex climbed up onto Sandy's workbench, scattering tools and detritus.

The electricity had reached the sculptures and was climbing up their struts and along their spars like tinsel. Alex could see bulbs illuminated in their heads and within rib cages made from the hollow chassis of reclaimed cars and trucks.

Sandy was watching, eyes narrowed against the blazing currents. He took his welding mask off the bench and put it on. He glared at Alex from behind the green Perspex rectangle set in the face. He was probably grinning. He pointed at the monumental figures craning against the roof beams.

"I haven't just been making *art*, Alex!" he shouted. The noise outside had increased, as though most of the efforts of the creatures were now solely directed at the barn. The doors and the walls shuddered and dust sifted down from the roof. "I've been creating an *army*!"

Behind him, something moved. It made a grinding, groaning sound, like hollow cylinders of bronze being bent beneath a great weight. It was an unusually *antique* sound, but of something old filling with a very new life. Alex thought of a giant squid in a storybook squeezing the hull of an iron ship somewhere far out to sea, crimping its hull like a pipe cutter.

Alex squinted. Long bluish shadows rocked on the walls and against the roof beams. Sandy went over to the barn doors and undid the bolts.

And as Sandy pushed open the doors, revealing a scene of slush-churned riot, the creatures jostling in the yard to surround the barn, his sculptures lifted their craning bodies on their metal-glass limbs and marched, beneath their jagged, orchestrating shadows, out to meet the madness.

*   *   *

ALEX WATCHED IN wonder. He edged down from the bench and followed the energised creations as they ducked beneath the lintel above the thrown-wide barn doors and emerged onto the snow. Flecks still glanced through the air, blown on a light breeze. There were a dozen sculptures, all lit from within. Bladed arms flung out to greet the monsters, mouths that had been the grilles of cars, and the insides of presses and trashed machines, opened and bit at the air. They steamed, they glowed.

They attacked.

AND ALEX WATCHED a rout.

The sculptures advanced, limbs and jaws scything, scattering the monsters across the dirt-churned snow. From around the barn and from the roof they came, absurd, grotesque things, deformed by their malice, shrieking with wrath, to join their falling, gored, splintered collaborators, but they, too, fell, in as great a number, and as fast, beneath the sculptures' harmonized assault. They pincered, legs scissoring, blades flashing, impaling, chopping, until they had marshalled the monsters into a huddle off towards the entrance to the farm.

And then they dipped their steaming faces and slashed the remaining monsters to ribbons.

Alex stood, pale and shivering, just outside the barn door. Sandy stood beside him, a sledgehammer in his fists, his breath steaming from beneath the welding mask. His eyes glittered like the mean eyes of a pike glimpsed rising from the dark emerald water of a lake.

The sculptures returned to their hangar. Alex stood unmoving as they trooped past, ducking beneath the lintel, and re-took their places at the back of the barn.

Sandy pushed shut the doors. He turned and looked at Alex.

Alex felt the shock of the morning's events begin to do its cold work on him and he shuddered. Tears filled his eyes.

Sandy bent down and soothed him. "It's okay, son," he said. "It's okay."

How was this okay?

"Who... who are you, Uncle Sandy?" He asked, his voice muffled against his uncle's overalls. "Who *are* you?"

("THAT'S WHAT I'M thinking," Chloe said, breaking Bix's attention.

"Well, you'll find out," he said, the tip of his nose about an inch away from the print on the page of the book.

"Is Sandy a good guy?"

"Shall we find out?" Bix said.

"Stories," Chloe said, snuggling down in her rugs, the dog's warm flank pressed close, alive and lovely. "I like them. But they take too long. You read slowly."

"You're lucky I can read at all," Bix said.)

"COME ON," SANDY said. "I've got something to show you."

"I've seen plenty," Alex said. He was staring at the ground, at the gouges and impressions left in the dirt and slush. And the blood. And the *bits*.

"They're not human," Sandy said. "At least, not any more. Don't fret over them. Think of them like characters in a cartoon. Just, you know, a really nasty cartoon. *Anime*. That sort of thing." He leaned the sledgehammer against the side of the barn and walked off, towards the gate at the end of the drive. He pulled off his welding mask and dropped it in the mud.

Alex followed, stepping over lumps and chunks with his eyes half shut. He reached the gate where a vile heap lay steaming. He could see the bodies were already rotting.

"It *stinks*," he said.

"They don't last long once they're dispatched," Sandy said. "Won't be anything here in an hour. Just in time for Jean's late morning drinky. Come on."

Alex followed Sandy across the lane and they pushed through a hedge at the side of the facing field. Sandy led Alex across the field. It was fading yellow, a great sea of wilting rape. Alex wrinkled his nose. Everything smelt bad today. Off. The sky was white as a label. He looked around for the promise of poppies, but they remained discrete, bloodless.

They came to the bottom of the field and Sandy said, "This is the place."

Alex stood next to him and peered down. There was a cutting, and a railway line running through it, just a single narrow gauge.

"What now?" Alex asked.

"We wait for our ride," Sandy said. "And while we wait, I'll tell you more about Quay-Endula."

DURING SOME QUIET evenings, when they were sitting by the fire in the living room, or playing cards or board games at the kitchen table, Uncle Sandy would tell Alex stories about the glorious town of Quay-Endula.

Quay-Endula is a town spread throughout the steep hills surrounding a great blue bay. A place of turrets and spires and fabulous follies, rambling pavilions, markets full of billowing pastel tents and gazebos. Quay-Endula has fountains like cathedrals; it has plazas and parks, open-air theatres, carnivals, trams, funicular railways, cable cars strung between great glittering pylons and a pier like no other could compare.

The pier of Quay-Endula is a mile long, so they say, stretching out into the sea. It has its own fairground with a Ferris wheel the height of a skyscraper. It has helter-skelters and rocket ships that fly round on gleaming metal arms. It has arcades full of pinball machines and shooting galleries. All this built on a wooden raft held up on fragile, barnacle-brittle iron legs.

Alex really wanted to go to Quay-Endula.

It was a place you could go to in your dreams, Sandy told him. It was a safe place. There were people, he said, like angels, who looked after the Quays. There had once been countless numbers of Quays, all unique, all lovely. But something had wanted to destroy them. Something that hated their existence and the hope and love they gave.

The *devil-in-dreams*.

The devil-in-dreams was implacably opposed to the keepers of the Quays. The keepers were called Firmament Surgeons, and they had been created as engineers, to keep the mechanisms of Creation running against the entropy arising from the fall of man. It was a great task and one which would be superseded at the Re-Creation, but for now, while eternal events took their course, and wars raged on Earth and in Heaven, the Firmament Surgeons worked and fought and wove their Quays and upheld the dreams of man.

But having free will and being able to choose, over time the devil-in-dreams exerted his influence on the Firmament Surgeons as he had on man and angels before them, and many also fell. They became Autoscopes and they began their onslaught of the Quays and their struggle for command of Dark Time.

It is the *Autosomachy*, this war, and it is raging to an end.

"YOU WANT TO know who I am?" Sandy said as they sat together on the bank leading down to the tracks. "Well, I'm your Uncle Sandy. But I'm something else, too. Something I could only reveal to you when the time was right, and now it's come upon us early, but that's okay. I've been preparing for it, ever since you came to live with us. You were sent to me to be kept safe because you are a Firmament Surgeon and you're a very rare and important boy. I'm your Paladin, Alex. I've always looked out for you."

Sandy was watching Alex carefully. Alex hugged his knees and peered down at the rails.

"You've seen enough today to know I'm not making things up. I never was. Quay-Endula is real, as real as all this, but I wasn't being entirely honest with you when I told you it's a place you can only visit in dreams. Everyone dreams about it, everyone knows about it, somewhere in their subconscious. Firmament Surgeons can take people there and keep them safe, refresh them, give them hope. But there's another way in for people like you. It's called a Gantry and you can open one and we can go there."

Alex nodded, still staring off into the distance.

"You always said you'd love to go there," Sandy said, and nudged Alex with his elbow.

"That was different. Like wanting to go in a rocket to Mars. I didn't think it was *real*."

"It *is*! Isn't that great? Only thing is, the war's cranking up and Quay-Endula is now about to come under attack by everything the Autoscopes can throw at it. That will affect this world very badly. If they get in and they gain ground, then people will stop dreaming, and they'll stop caring. We have to help save the Quay and warn people here."

"You seem very confident, Uncle Sandy."

"Once we get there, you'll see things the same way, lad. You'll be in your element. Hah! I've been looking forward to this!"

Alex shook his head. He was about to say more, ask more questions, but then, coming from about a mile down the track, he heard something approaching.

He looked up at Sandy and saw that he was smiling.

("WHAT IS IT? What is it?" said Chloe.

"Shall we read on and find out?" Bix said, again.

Chloe nodded, and bit her lip.)

THE SOUND GREW closer, building and thrumming. They felt the ground beneath them tremble with its approach. Breathless, Alex waited. And saw it rumble into the cutting.

It drove a great caul of sparks before it, firefly debris from its shearing wheels. It was an iron bulk, a locomotive salvaged from a crusher. It was a square-backed, steam-driven thing of ancient industry. Driverless it thundered, following its route through the forest and the fields surrounding the farms. It had no lights, just the blazing cloak of molten swarf, which cooled and twinkled over its channelled flanks.

Railgrinder groaned past them, a dreadful, beautiful machine, and as it travelled, it reaped the rails of rust.

"Come, on," Sandy shouted over Railgrinder's noise. They slid down the cutting and onto the tracks, following the stately rocking of the locomotive's back end.

Sandy lifted Alex up and swung him into the open cab. He trotted along beside Railgrinder, grinning, and then grabbed a rail and jumped aboard.

They stood there, rocking and bathed in firebox heat, the whole world full of clangs and ferment and turbulent row. Everything stank of coal dust and old black oil, hot pistons and sparks.

Alex and Sandy laughed, at the noise, at the furious rocking of the machine, at the absurdity of it. Alex was filled with a strange, drifting relief. It was good. He hugged his uncle.

"Enjoy it, Alex," Sandy shouted over the noise. "This is yours. It's your *Instrument*."

"My what?" Alex yelled, still laughing.

"It's your Instrument. It takes you to the Quays. Only you can use it for that. It's engineered for you, for *now*."

Alex leaned out and looked up the line. Railgrinder swayed and ground its way with cumbersome utility.

"What do I do?"

"Wait. There's a tunnel up ahead. We can use it as an Ingress point."

As they came around a bend, Alex saw the tunnel mouth. It was cut into a low hill, a mouldering redbrick arch. Railgrinder took them in.

Alex looked up at his uncle. "You okay, Uncle Sandy?"

Sandy said nothing, his eyes fixed straight ahead. His fists were clenched and a sheen of sweat had broken out on his face. It beaded the dome of his bald head; he looked like he had been caught out in a light shower.

"Don't like tunnels much," he said through gritted teeth. "Never have."

Alex patted Sandy's arm. He hadn't ever considered his uncle to be the phobic type, but he looked like he was struggling now, really hanging on.

"We'll be out soon," Alex said, his voice bright and echoing in the tunnel above the rumble and clatter of the train. Railgrinder's sparks threw light around them like a cauldron of molten ore. Sandy's sweat gleamed golden.

"One way or another," Sandy said. And then: "There. Up ahead."

Alex looked through the porthole above the firebox.

Less than a hundred yards ahead, a circle of light hung suspended in the darkness. It looked no bigger than a wedding ring.

"Is that the end of the tunnel?"

"No," Sandy said. "There's more than a mile to go. That's your Gantry."

"It's tiny."

"Railgrinder's yours, remember. Here, take the throttle."

Alex slid past Sandy and took hold of the long, brass lever. He looked up at Sandy, who nodded, and then Alex pushed the lever forward. Smoke blew from its stack and rolled in a low, gritty storm above their heads. Railgrinder lurched forward and gathered speed. As they accelerated, so the circle of light began to grow. It expanded of its own volition, not merely owing to the decreasing distance between them. Its edges rippled outward and as Railgrinder approached, it spanned the tunnel with an opaque, luminous disc. Alex held tight to the throttle and closed his eyes.

Both he and Sandy bellowed with a thrill of terror as Railgrinder roared through the Gantry.

ALEX OPENED HIS eyes. He pulled back off the throttle and Railgrinder slowed to a crawl. Alex looked at Sandy. He was beaming, the weathered skin around his eyes, and his nose, were black with soot. His teeth looked very white. Alex rubbed a hand over his own face and the palm came away begrimed, smelling of cinders.

"I can't believe I'm finally here again," Sandy said. "Outside of a dream."

They had emerged from the Gantry into a different world. The sky was clear, unclouded, cooling to twilight blue. The tracks followed a ridge and beneath, on both sides, fields of purple flowers set off to the distance.

"Lavender," Sandy said. "Beautiful."

Beyond were mountains, a barricade of low, red rock against the sky. Further on, a stand of forest, and the tracks headed through it. Sandy breathed deeply.

Alex leaned against the side of the cab and looked out across the lavender fields. He could smell the dense, blessed perfume of it.

"It's later here," Sandy said. "Nightfall soon."

"Is this Quay-Endula?"

"No," Sandy shook his head. "This is your Quay. This is Quay Fomalhaut. We need to get to Quay-Endula as fast as possible."

"Are we safe here?"

"Not like we would have been once. There have been *incursions*, Alex. Parts of this Quay have been taken."

Alex watched the fields roll by, silent, breathing their scent. After a moment, he turned back to the Railgrinder's controls and thrust up on the throttle again. Their speed increased and they headed into the forest.

THEY TRAVELLED ON through the darkening stands of trees.

For a while, the track followed the curves of a stream and Alex watched the sparks from beneath the grinding wheels casting out in a continuous wave and alight in the shady water, brightening for the briefest of moments the gleaming pebbles just beneath the surface.

Soon the stream meandered away and he could see where it ran off into a channel built into the hillside. He could hear it frothing and chopping against the stonewalls at the channel mouth.

Sandy stood up and stretched. Railgrinder drove on, riding its endless flickering wave of embers. Ahead more obscurity beckoned.

"Can you hear the mines?" Sandy said. "The Fomalhaut mines are working again."

Alex stood still and listened. Above the continuous chafing of Railgrinder's plates and the incendiary crackle of its firebox, he could just make out the sound of something distant and industrial; it was like the clanging of dull iron bells and the muscular hiss of great plunging pistons. The more he attuned his ears, the clearer it became. They were approaching a place of heavy engineering.

"We'd better hide ourselves," Sandy said. He gestured for them to crouch down behind the low sides of the cab.

After a mile or so Railgrinder swept around a bend and they came into a clearing. They kept their heads down and Sandy peered over the side of the cab.

The noise was immense here, an endless clatter and thunder of machinery.

Alex peered past Sandy's shoulder and saw that they had entered an enormous yard. Railgrinder took a route around the outskirts and he could see that they were passing through a mining plant. There were pitheads and pylons, ranks of fat hoppers, rumbling conveyor belts and low, dark single storey factories. Flashes of cold, blue light illuminated the grimy windows, the spitting radiance of arc welders. Railgrinder rumbled over a set of points and Alex could see that more rails ran off towards the middle of the yard where rows of trucks full of coal waited in a siding. Everything was moonlit and coated in a thick, grey dust.

As Railgrinder took them behind a row of sheds, Sandy stood up and went to a lever by the firebox. He grasped the handle and wrenched it down. Railgrinder's wheels screeched and Alex staggered as it came to a halt.

"Don't worry," said Sandy. "Just going to make a bit of trouble here, then we're off."

He jumped down out of the cab.

"What are you doing?"

Sandy pointed to the closest pithead, a tall pylon supporting a drilling rig. It looked ancient, and it creaked and groaned as it worked.

"Sabotage," he said. "These mines have been abandoned for years. Now the Autoscopes have their Toyceivers working them again, drilling for materials for the war. I'm going to inconvenience them and buy us a little more time."

Sandy disappeared around the side of the shed. Alex climbed down and peered around the corner.

He watched Sandy walk over to a heap of large wooden reels. He crouched down and inspected them, then pushed one over onto its side. It was the size of a barrel and tightly wound with steel cable. He rolled it across the yard until he reached the pithead then took hold of the end of the cable and unravelled about ten feet of it. It looked heavy and very strong but somehow Sandy managed to loop it around the foot of one of the supporting stanchions. He reached into an overall pocket and took something out; it was one of the many tools he had designed and made to fashion his sculptures, and he began working on the end of the cable. The yard was lit by intermittent bursts of blue light from the arc welders and a conveyor belt tipped a load of ore into a hopper with a sound like a brief, localized landslide.

Alex kept watch while Sandy finished fashioning a hook onto the end of the cable and used it to fix the loop like a noose around the stanchion. He gave it a tug and it held firm.

Sandy pushed the reel back across the yard and up to the rear of Railgrinder. He unravelled the remaining cable and kicked the empty spool away. It rolled in an arc and came to rest against a heap of slate.

Sandy made another noose and hitched it to one of Railgrinder's buffers.

He returned to the cab and climbed in.

Sandy released Railgrinder's brake, and with a hiss and jolt, it started to pull away. They leaned over the back of the cab and watched as the cable grew taut. Railgrinder hauled against the weight of the pithead, steaming, its fire glowing white. The cable pulled tight against the corner of the first shed and bit into the wood. Railgrinder strained and began to gather momentum. Sparks gushed from beneath its boiler. The cable tore into the side of the shed and started to slice through it.

Wood splintered and the cable sang like piano wire. It carved through the planks, splinters flying and suddenly the entire structure collapsed. The cable dragged against the side of the next shed and sliced it in half as Railgrinder gathered speed. The third shed shattered in an explosion of decayed timber and now Railgrinder was pulling against the leg of the pithead. There was a moment of resistance when Railgrinder's fire seemed like a handful of tiny stars, blinding and tremendous, and Sandy and Alex had to cower against the heat, but then they heard the first screams of tortured wood and felt the sensation of something giving way.

The pithead buckled and the leg attached to the cable tore from the ground. The flywheel at the top of the mast flew off its axle and plunged down into the shaft trailing chains and a jangling constellation of cogs. The drill snapped like a stick of rock and flew into the air, ricocheting against the legs of the pylon, shattering them like driftwood. It soared up, arcing over the yard and harpooned the roof of one of the factories. There was an explosion and screams from the creatures working within. Gas cylinders blew in a succession of flat, punchy detonations and the entire building was engulfed in flames.

Railgrinder used its power to take down the entire structure. As they rode off into the forest, Sandy and Alex watched the pithead topple and crash down into the dry, rutted yard, flung to ruin in the grey earth.

Sandy reached over, lifted the coil of cable from Railgrinder's buffer and dropped it onto the rails.

Railgrinder took them away from the yard and the chaos, back into the trees, before their presence was ever noticed; its back end, its fire and steam, its crew, all gone rocking down the rails, cloaked by the forest.

Alex increased Railgrinder's speed and they made quite a pace. Sandy leaned against the side of the cab and squinted into the draught. Sparks landed in his beard and glowed like fireflies.

"Where does this line take us?" Alex asked.

"To the sea," Sandy said. "There's a line that runs the length of the Quays. It's been destroyed and the bridges are out east of here, but it should still be running to Quay-Endula. There are precautions in place."

Eventually they left the forest and Railgrinder crossed a dark moor. Immense, serrated tors rose from the earth, and bitter-smelling ferns grew in abundance, smothering the land. Visible in the moonlight, through a gap in the distant mountains, was a level horizon of ocean. The line where it met the sky appeared elevated owing to their altitude and it looked to Alex like a fractured dam, its pent waters about to inundate the moor.

But the waters held; the sea drew nearer, and soon they travelled a pass through the mountains and emerged, panting steam and throwing metal light, onto a sweeping line that took them down, and down, in graceful curves, to the edge of the sea. They passed a boarded, derelict town, and a castle, red as rust, rearing from the beach. Crimson lights shone in some of the windows and shadows flexed in the lines between the shutters. Alex shivered and felt a strange tingle in his belly, an excitement he had not experienced before, an anticipation of something inside him wanting to mature, to find expression.

"Is that a bad place?" he asked.

Sandy was also looking up at the castle. His eyes shone with those snug, crimson lines of light.

"It might turn out to be," he said. "There's a battle raging in there. It's another incursion."

"Should we help?"

"No. It needs to take its own course. We've got our own agenda, Alex."

The castle receded, and with it, so did Alex's sudden and powerful sense of longing. The light, though; those warm red gashes of light and the limber shadows that moved within them. They stayed with him for a little longer.

"Stop the train a hundred yards from here," Sandy said. "There's a siding and a shed. I want to show you something, but we have to go on foot."

As they neared the siding, Sandy jumped down and ran ahead, towards a set of points. He pulled a lever and Railgrinder clacked off the main line and onto the siding. Sandy jumped back into the cab.

The train shed was long and high with a curving corrugated metal roof. Alex engaged the brake and Railgrinder drew to a halt halfway along the length of the shed. He and Sandy climbed down onto the narrow platform.

"This way," Sandy said, and led them the remaining length of the shed and out onto the siding.

Once outside, and with Railgrinder's noise no longer dominant, Alex could hear a new sound. Again, hectic industry; clangs and thuds and squeals. It was coming from further along the beach.

They slid down a bank and onto a fractured concrete promenade.

"Keep close," Sandy said.

The high half-moon shone bright enough to throw shadows. They reached a row of storm-damaged beach huts and they crept along the promenade keeping to the cover beneath the awnings of the huts.

"There," said Sandy, and pointed down onto the beach.

The beach was teeming with activity. In the moonlight they could see hundreds of creatures dragging pieces of wood and metal across the pebbles. There were wrecks piled against the rocks, the remains of dozens of ships driven up onto the beach. The creatures were plundering them, ripping off planks and struts, sheets of steel, throwing huge chunks of machinery over the sides, burrowing into the engine rooms and tearing the mechanisms and instruments out. Alex watched as a group of three creatures tore a great, rusted propeller from the stern of a ship and sent it spinning up the beach like a wheel.

"What is this place?" he asked.

Sandy replied, "Contraption Beach. This is where the Toyceivers make their war engines, the Uproar Contraptions. When they're constructed, they'll be driven through the remaining Quays and used to destroy them."

"What can we do?"

"Nothing here," Sandy said. "We need to reach Quay-Endula. That's our purpose."

They continued to creep along the promenade, looking for some steps to take them back up to the rails. The beach huts were dismal looking things, more like garden sheds than cheerful cabins. Their wood was splintering and the roofs sagged. They each had a small, railed veranda, just big enough to sit on and some of them had no door. Inside they looked cramped and damp and unwelcoming. Alex could smell mildew.

As they passed one of the huts, Alex heard a sound from inside. It was a furtive scrape, like twigs being dragged across the plank floor. He turned and looked and as he did so, the door opened and he saw what was making the sound.

It was a dreadful looking thing. It had a small torso, like a child's, and a white, skeletal face. It wore an absurd crimson woolly hat, pulled tightly down over its bulging forehead. It had eight spiny, segmented legs, like a crab's, which ended in sharp points that scratched and scraped on the concrete. It hissed at Alex, and grinned.

Alex reached out and grabbed hold of one of the wooden railings running around a veranda. He pulled and it came away with a soft, splintery crunch. It was nearly rotten, but he held it up and brandished it as the creature strutted towards him.

Alex stepped forward and jabbed the railing at the creature's head. It darted to the side and rose up on four of its legs. It growled, its horrible pale eyes gleaming deep in their sockets. It fenced with its front legs, using them like four articulated spears. Alex clouted two of them out of the way and kicked it in the chest. It yelped and flipped over onto its back. It flailed its legs, the knee joints rattling against the concrete like hollow seashells. Alex ran towards Sandy.

Sandy looked pleased. "Well done, son," he said. "A good clean fight! If you can take care of Bom-Bertil, you can hold your own against others like him."

Alex looked back at the struggling creature. Its legs sounded like a teaspoon rattling in a china cup. Suddenly it sprang over onto its feet and spun around. It was glowering and furious. Its hat had come down over one of its eyes.

"Bom-Bertil?" Alex said. "You know him?"

"Oh, I know them all, Alex," Sandy said. "I've been dreaming about them since I was a child. Let's get back to Railgrinder, and I'll tell you more about it."

They went up the steps, leaving Bom-Bertil strutting in fury, but cowed into inaction, humiliated by the boy. They retraced the line back to the shed and climbed up onto Railgrinder. Sandy took over the controls, disengaged the brake and took them out in a grey tempest of steam and smoke.

"I'll tell you what happened, when I was a boy no older than you are now," he said.

On they went, to Quay-Endula.

I WAS OUT *playing with my best friend, David. It was getting on for evening and we were down on the railway tracks that ran past our village. It was summer and the day was long but we were getting tired and hungry. We were picking stuff up from amongst the pebbles alongside the line, examining them, pocketing the odd treasure. David was searching for pieces of jettisoned engine parts. We were making models in my dad's shed: robots, machines, gearboxes, spacecraft; all junk but good oily fun.*

I was feeling distracted. I had been having nightmares for weeks. Awful places that were like dimensions full of gloom and menace. I was being chased by something that wanted to take me up, absorb me and carry me inside it deep within these dimensions, forever.

David was a good lad. We had always been close, best mates for years, and he knew I was troubled. He was sensitive like that, gentle. I had told him all my secrets.

I used to be kind of small. Weedy. Vulnerable. David protected me from bullies, but he couldn't protect me from what happened that evening.

We were standing at the tunnel mouth and suddenly I experienced an effect on my mood so profound that I realised complete hopelessness and despair was all I would ever know and that this was my lot. My mind emptied of everything other than utter doom and I got one thought, like a black firework going off against a dying sky: It would be best to die.

I remember turning to David and seeing the expression on his face.

My heart broke, then, because I knew he had seen it, too. My future. No child should have such existential insight. Life stretches too far ahead to sustain it, an impossible slog towards nothingness.

But David was looking past me. At what was coming through the tunnel.

He stepped back, his hands raised and nearly fell. I stood, passive in the path of it, and felt the dark wind rush by as it pressed against the air. It stank of death. But it was a death that would always be alive.

David fled. He clambered up the bank and I watched him go. I understood. I reached out but he was gone. I was glad for him. I loved him and I was glad he was going to be safe.

I turned and watched as Junction Creature swelled from the tunnel and engulfed me in its black, eye-filled mouth.

I hung in the guts of Junction Creature as it roared back through the tunnel. It was vast, and the whole of its mass was filled with eyes. They drifted up to me in thousands and gazed at me, lidless and full of blood, but still seeing. Seeing forever. I felt Junction Creature's fury at being thwarted. I could hear its hideous, thundering mind as it raged. And all the time I could feel it, planting nightmares all over the world. Pieces of it constantly feeling, probing, budding out and using the dimensions of dreams to be everywhere, at all times. But it needed more. It had been after David, not me. I could sense it, calculating, fuming. To take away David's future and the good things he would do. The hope he would give people. And the son he'd have. I saw them, through Junction Creature's million stolen eyes, in a future place. I wanted to cry, to fight, but it was hopeless. It needed David, and others like him. Not feeble little boys like me. It wanted Firmament Surgeons, and it wanted the Dark Time they controlled. It wanted to be everywhere forever, not just constrained to doing this endless labour, this reaching. It was missing things. It knew it was limited and it loathed it.

And its limitations saved me.

I heard Junction Creature roar. We were no longer in a tunnel. It had emerged onto a plain of ruins. A bombsite pitted and populated with blown buildings and fragments of ancient machines. Junction

Creature slid through the wreckage. It was enormous. Junction Creature was supreme here.

And then it fixed its eyes on a building and swarmed towards it. It was a tower block, and as we drew closer, Junction Creature saw the man standing on a splintering parapet. I felt its hate grow immense, and with it, a determination to destroy this man. The building was collapsing. Junction Creature pressed against the block and it began to crumble. The man fell.

As he fell, I felt something. In my darkened mind, against the despair like a lamp held up by a distant guide, I felt a splinter of hope lodge there.

Junction Creature screamed, and I experienced a wave of pressure as its entire mass flexed against the awful irritation of my hope. It bucked away from the building and as it reeled, I felt myself moving through it, pushed to its rim. I drifted there, terrified.

And then the balloon rose alongside Junction Creature, buffeted by the air stirred by its rippling flanks.

A hot air balloon, piloted by a little girl. And the man was there. And a tiger. And I thought I must be dreaming again, of course, and I must wake up soon. And that hope was growing, and Junction Creature was enraged by it. And it ejected me like vomit.

The man caught me. He lifted me into the basket and the girl opened up the burner and we floated away. So serene. Junction Creature dropped away beneath us, flattening like a cumulus cloud full of all the storms left in the world to be spent.

They set me down, in an apple orchard by a stream. There was a house there. It was large, sprawling with an annexe with French windows that opened out onto the orchard. The man took my hand and led me through the orchard and into the annexe. It looked like a doctor's office. He told me to wait five minutes and then go out through the door facing the French windows. He told me his name was Doctor Mocking and that the girl was his daughter, Lesley. He told me that when I went through the door I would be different. I would have a new ability. He took something down from the wall and gave it to me. It was a long, slender tube. As soon as he gave it to me, I knew what it was. It was a pontil rod. A glassblower's blowing tube. I liked the feel of it immediately.

Doctor Mocking told me that I should hide it somewhere when I left because I wouldn't need it for a long time if I was lucky.

He also told me that I wouldn't see David again and that when I left this office time would be very different for me.

I understood. This man had saved me from an eternity in Hell and I accepted the new life he was freely offering me with gratitude and joy.

As Doctor Mocking turned to leave, he said, "You don't have to go through that door." He smiled and walked out into the orchard.

"I OPENED THE door and awoke, in my bed, in my house. Nothing was different. Lying across the foot of the bed was the glass blower's pipe. I sat up and held it, turning it in my hands. I could hear someone coming, so I rolled over and slid it beneath my mattress.

The door opened and my brother came in.

"Your breakfast's ready," he said.

I was delighted to see him, relieved, euphoric. I leaped out of bed and followed him downstairs. Mum and Dad were there. Nothing was different. I ate my breakfast and got dressed for school. I looked in my bag. Same books, same teachers' names on the covers.

I left the house and walked to the bus stop.

The bus came, number 5, nothing had changed. The children were the same. I went upstairs and looked around, my heart beating faster. The bullies were at the back, a tight-knit group of spiteful little faces.

"There's Sandicap!" one of them shouted the length of the bus. "Still seeing the doctor cos you wet the bed?"

I backed down the stairs and sat on a seat nearest the driver. I hugged my book bag to my chest and turned my face towards the tinted Perspex partition of the driver's cab. I could see my reflection, and the tears that ran down my face.

David wasn't on the bus. Everything was different.

*　　*　　*

"So I HAD to toughen up," Sandy said. "No option. Look at me now."

"You're a brute, Uncle Sandy."

"Heart of gold. Just don't get in my way."

"Does Aunty Jean know all this?"

"Of course. No secrets from my Jean."

Railgrinder clattered through an abandoned station, past a derelict kiosk and a waiting room hung with faded posters. Signal boxes filled with cobwebbed levers. A station clock hanging from an ornate iron bracket, its rusting hands frozen at ten past three.

They travelled in silence for a while and then Sandy said, "There she is."

Alex was unsure for a moment what Sandy was referring to. For a wild half-second he expected to see Aunty Jean standing at the side of the line, silver hair shining in the glamour of Railgrinder's shearing stardust.

But instead, he saw lights.

"Quay-Endula," said Sandy. We're home."

QUAY-ENDULA WAS everything Alex had imagined it to be. It sprawled around the bay like all the jewels ever mined poured in profligate adoration about the throat of the most indulged woman in the world. Even at night—or perhaps especially—it was magnificent. The esplanades and pavilions were lit with gleaming spotlights; cyclopean viaducts, cable car pylons, funicular railways bestrode the Quay and the parks glittered with delicate, twinkling installations, a million coloured bulbs strung through the night. And the pier, stretching to a point towards the horizon, white light blazing from the arcades and stalls all along its length, the spinning colours of its electrifying rides, the stately revolution of its immense wheel there at the end of the pier, the specks of tiny gondolas visible like a constellation rotating against the night sky. "Looks good to me," Sandy said.

"Are we stopping here?"

"No, we go on. There's a beach beyond that cliff. We're needed there."

"Who by?"

"The rest of us," Sandy said, and opened the throttle.

RAILGRINDER STOPPED UNDER the moon on a curve of track above a secluded cove. Sandy closed the firebox and dropped the iron latch. He reached down, beneath the furnace, and pulled something out. It was a long, narrow tube. It was his glass-blowing tube. He held it up, closed one eye and looked down its length. He put it to his lips and puffed. A gritty cloud of soot blew from the end. He wiped his mouth.

"Right. Ready?" he asked.

"Ready," Alex replied.

Together they climbed down from the cab and walked the short distance to the steps that led down to the bay.

There was a fire blazing halfway down the beach. Alex could make out silhouettes, a knot of figures moving in the firelight. He gripped Sandy's wrist.

"It's okay," Sandy said. "They're with us."

They crossed the dark, damp sand and walked towards the figures. One of them broke away from the huddle and approached them.

"Hello, old friend," he said. He was a huge man. Tall and blond and heavily muscled.

"Hello, Jon," Sandy said. The men embraced.

"Jon Index, this is Alex," Sandy said.

The big man reached out a hand. Alex took it and they shook. Alex was only able to grasp two of the man's fingers in his fist.

"Come over. She's close," Index said.

They went over to the others. The sea slid over the sand with a sound like secrets being given up in remorse.

They clustered around a woman. She was unconscious. She was breathing in shallow gasps. A young man knelt by her side and soothed her.

"Alex, this is Claire and her husband, Steve Iden. That man watching the horizon is Mick Reeks." Steve Iden looked up; his eyes were tired, red-rimmed in the firelight. "Hi, fella," he said.

Index took Sandy's arm and they walked off a few yards, into the shadows beyond the firelight. Alex looked down at the woman. She was pregnant, her belly rising and falling with her breathing.

Sandy and Index came back to the light after exchanging words.

The man who had been standing off towards the shore was also coming back. He was small and wiry, with glasses and short, curly hair.

"They're coming," he said.

All eyes turned towards the horizon.

They could hear them before they could see anything, a growing shriek of engines. And then dark smudges on the water and in the air. As they approached their weak lights broke through the darkness over the water.

"Toyceivers," Index said.

Sandy lifted his glass blowing tube, his jaw set. He walked towards the shoreline.

Alex watched. The woman moaned. Steve caressed her cheek, her brow. He put the palm of his hand on her belly.

"Come on, Claire," he whispered.

"Alex, I need you," Sandy called.

Alex followed his uncle and stood by his side.

"What do you need me to do?"

Sandy put the tube to his lips and bent his head towards the ground. He twisted his wrists and plunged the other end of the tube into the soaked, mildly wallowing sand.

"Put your hands on the back of my head. And don't be afraid."

Alex stood behind Sandy and raised his arms. His hands looked small and cold in the moonlight. Sandy bunched his shoulders and took an enormous breath.

"Now," he said.

Alex put his palms against the smooth dome of his uncle's head, and waited.

Bix stopped reading.

He looked at Chloe. She was asleep. Her eyes moved behind her trembling lids and her face was set in an expression of gentle peace. The walls of the cave were rippling in the candle light, contracting.

Bix stood up and stretched. It was dark outside. He could hear the sound of the wind in the treetops. It sounded like the ocean. Bix could smell the sea on the air.

He nuzzled the girl, licked her cheek.

"Good luck, kid," he said. Bix trotted the length of the cave and looked down. The ladder was still there. He jumped, hitting the top step with his front paws and let balance, momentum and a bit of trust in good things get him to the forest floor. He stood at the bottom of the ladder and breathed deeply. And then he set off, through the forest, across the meadow, following the scent of the sea.

13

THE TIGER-RIDE took Trevena and Anna through a ruined place.

They bounded through a bombsite, past blasted buildings and along wrenched and twisted roads. Factories leaned walls of disintegrating masonry across a road where the shell of a gasometer still burned behind them, its stanchions twisted and buckled, flutes of blue gas like the tails of a fleet of rocket ships blazing from its fractured pipelines.

At last they reached a district that was more or less intact. Bronze John took them through back streets lined with terraces and boarded-up corner shops. Trevena watched their reflection flash by in the unlit windows of the houses. The tiger was a racing orange fuse, burning through their vacant parlours.

They rounded a corner, and Trevena knew where he was.

There was the shop, with the pillars and the checkerboard step. He had run from here, a prisoner in his own body as Cade had emerged. He had left Daniel here after attacking him. Bronze John slowed to a walk. He stopped at the entrance to the shop, those big glass doors with their long brass handles.

Trevena got down and stood on shaking legs. He reached up and lifted Anna from the tiger's back. The three of them stood in the silence of the back street and waited.

They heard the sound of an engine.

Two cones of light splashed across the road.

They watched as a campervan followed its headlights around the corner and drove up the street towards them.

TREVENA FELT BOTH sheepish and vastly relieved when the campervan stopped and Daniel climbed out. The driver, a short, thickset man in his sixties, joined him at the kerb.

Trevena stepped forward. "Daniel, I'm so sorry, mate," he said.

Daniel held up a hand. "It's fine, Phil, really. I should have protected you better. It was my fault."

They shook hands.

Daniel introduced Babur and then paced in front of the shop while Trevena explained what had happened to him at the castle, about the death of Cade and the rescue of Anna. Anna stood by Bronze John, her hand stroking his neck.

"I'm happy he's gone," Daniel said, referring to Cade. "Filthy bastard."

The men conferred, agreeing that they should travel together and try to get back to Chloe. The immediate danger from Cade had passed, but the incursions were increasing and Daniel said he could sense the power of the Autoscopes growing.

They climbed into the campervan. Babur drove, Daniel next to him in the passenger seat. Anna and Trevena sat in the back on the rock and roll bench with Bronze John curled up, seeming smaller now, on the rugs spread over the floor at their feet. Trevena had noticed how Daniel and Babur were unfazed by the presence of the tiger. Maybe they had seen stranger things. And hadn't he accepted the attendance of Bronze John with the same unquestioning diffidence? It was that common experience of dreams, he concluded; a universal openness to quantum improbabilities. Time and familiarity took infinite liberties, he thought. He wondered idly whether there was an equation for it.

Trevena took in the strange arrays of switches and bulbs cobbled to the fittings in the back of the van. The screens and dials. It all looked very *retro* to Trevena, all form and no function, like a child's mock-up of a space lab. There was a touching innocence to it.

"What's all this gear do?" he asked. "You got a coffee maker in there?"

Babur started to explain about tracking systems, detectors and modified EMPs, with what, Trevena discerned, was a touch of mild defensiveness, but just as Trevena was starting to switch off, Daniel leaned forward in his seat and groaned. He clutched his head.

Babur stopped talking and pulled the van over. "What is it?" he asked.

"I can hear him," Daniel said.

"Who?"

"Les. My friend. There's trouble. Bad trouble. It's an incursion. A big one." He was gasping, the words coming staccato through his teeth.

"Tell me where to go," Babur said.

"I need Dr. Natus," Daniel said.

"No you don't," Babur said. "He was nothing but a projection. A totem. You created him out of your unconscious to give you faith, confidence. You don't need him anymore."

Babur swung the van back onto the road.

"Take us there," he said.

Daniel sat back against the seat, his eyes closed.

"Shut your eyes," he said. "All of you."

THE VAN ACCELERATED, and then it was drifting, as abruptly as if it had gone off a cliff. There was no sense of drop, just a loss of contact with a surface, but it was unsettling enough to make Trevena moan and squeeze his eyes shut against the urge to look at what was happening.

The sound of the van's engine was muffled, and through his eyelids Trevena perceived a rippling flow of light.

And then the van was back on solid ground. The tyres squealed and they were thrown forward in their seats. Trevena did open his eyes then, and saw that Anna was curled up on the floor against the curve of Bronze John's belly, her eyes squeezed shut.

He looked out of the window and could see they were on a street curving through a village. It was night here, too, and he could see lights blazing on a corner up ahead.

"Pull in on the left up there," Daniel said. He pointed through the windscreen at a parking area beside a large building.

Babur pulled the van in and switched off the engine. The three men got out and walked back to the road. Anna stayed in the camper with the tiger. Bronze John's eyes were narrow but alert. He quivered with energy, prepared to act if called upon.

Trevena could see that they were in a pub car park. The sign outside the building read, **THe Dog WitH itS EyeS SHut**. The door was open and he could hear voices raised inside.

Across the road a crowd was gathered. They stood on a vacant lot surrounding the collapsed shell of a building. Arc lights running from a generator were pointed down into the ruins. They made the rubble look like great ingots of silver. The group was comprised of men, all carrying weapons. Some were makeshift but Trevena could see shotguns and someone had a crossbow. They went across and joined the crowd.

One of the men came around from the side of the building and Trevena watched, mouth open, a feeling of wonder coursing through him.

Les waved.

Trevena stepped forward and met him. They shook hands, Trevena grinning, their profiles starkly lit by the arc lights. Daniel came over with Babur.

"How bad is it?" Daniel asked Les.

Les ran a hand across his face. He looked over towards the derelict building.

"It collapsed this morning," he said. "Just dropped away into a sinkhole. We've been guarding it since then. Something came out of it mid-afternoon but we beat the shit out of it. Since we've had the lights on all we can hear is movement and some voices but we've not seen anything else."

"Have you got the body?"

"No. It just rotted away. It had a lot of legs and a lot of teeth, though. A *lot*."

Babur pointed at a sign lying broken amidst the rubble and dirt. It had fallen from the wall when the building collapsed.

"The Night Clock," he said, his voice little more than a whisper.

Daniel nodded. "It was a big fucking clue and I wasn't even aware."

"Projections," said Babur, and clapped Daniel on the shoulder. "You knew, son. You were keeping people safe. You were doing your job."

Daniel shook his head.

"Have we lost anyone?" he asked.

"Not yet," Les said. "Couple of minor injuries but nothing serious."

Trevena looked back across the road. The door to the pub was shut now. He looked up at the night sky. It was clear, a crisp, inscrutable black, and without moon or stars. How could skies be so different? Trevena wondered, but then he had to factor that this was Daniel's Quay, or a dimension of it, and everything he knew about dreams from his training, from his psychotherapy, specified that it was all a projection of the dreamer's identity. The reddish light that limned the roofs of the pub and the cottages opposite intrigued Trevena though, and so he stepped away from the crowd and walked further down the road to see what was casting it. When he saw what was rising above the rooftops his flesh began to creep.

It was Mars.

The planet rose as he watched, and cast red shadows. It was huge, a muddy red arc lifting from behind the houses. Trevena stretched out his arms and tried to measure it. He closed one eye, to flatten the perspective. His fingertips were three feet apart and the planet hung between them. It was rising so fast that his arms rose with it.

He craned his neck and looked back at the crowd of men. Les was watching him.

"Mars," he said. "The God of War."

Trevena had time to look back up at the baleful face of the dead planet before the shouting started over at the face of the sinkhole and a great swarm of creatures blew up from its depths and set upon the men.

THE MEN FELL back and battle raged in the street. They were like birds, these things, but venomous. They had stings like needles unsheathed from their abdomen and they flew on noisy, throbbing wings. They had scissoring, serrated beaks and each one contained a wick of diffuse light that irritated the back of the eye like a scratch.

The men waded into them, swinging clubs and shovels. A shotgun fired and a swath of the stinging birds evaporated. They smashed them out of the air, grinding the fragile bodies beneath their boots.

Someone pressed a tyre-iron into Trevena's hands and he had time to swipe it blindly as something darted into his periphery. The iron connected with one of the birds and it burst mid-air, in a shower of brownish light and glass. Trevena waved the iron in front of him and saw Daniel, Les and Babur, each one now armed with similar improvised weapons, dashing birds to splinters at the edge of the ruins.

Trevena heard someone scream. A man was down, two of the birds beating at his face. Trevena ran across but it was too late. He winced as one of the birds curled its abdomen and jabbed its sting into the man's right eye. The man screamed again, but by an order of magnitude greater than before. His eye bulged as it filled with the blue toxin and he staggered back, clutching at his face. The second bird lanced the back of his hand and it immediately turned black and softened to a paste that he dragged, bubbling, down his face. He rolled on the ground, throat swollen, now unable to scream, as his eye ballooned from its socket.

"Someone help this man," Trevena shouted, but there was no one able to assist. Trevena knelt and put his hands flat on the writhing man's chest. He spoke to him, calming words, told him he wasn't alone, did his best to comfort him, but the man was already dead, his eye blown in a syrup down his cheek.

"Shit," Trevena muttered. He stood and raised the tyre-iron, horribly vigilant to the possibility of the same thing happening to him.

The shouts of battle continued around him but there were a lot less birds left to kill. They had been beaten out of the air by the fury and force of the crowd. Men roamed the road and the ground surrounding the sinkhole and took out the last of the birds with their tools and their guns.

For a moment there was silence. The whole street seemed to breathe as the chests of the men took in draughts of the night air, and all were watchful. Mars was above them, its canals visible on its surface like scars on a warrior's cheek.

And then, from the sinkhole, a clattering as something fast scaled it, and a piercing whine echoing up from its depths as engines fired and machines began to ascend.

Trevena and Les stood at the edge of the ruins and looked down. The arc lights scooped a deep, bright gutter out of the darkness. Trevena experienced a sharp crackle of vertigo in his belly and down the backs of his legs. He leaned against the parapet of sundered brickwork and closed his eyes.

He stood up and backed away, taking Les's arm. They retreated to the road where the others stood around, eyes wide and expressions set with grim purpose.

And then they were running again, scattering across the road and advancing on the sinkhole as a wave of spiders poured over its lip. They looked to Trevena like harvestmen, globular bodies on articulated stalks, each carrying a smeary torch of that repellent light in their vitreous cores. They were the size of ostrich eggs and they strutted across the ground to meet the men on their fast, rattling legs, incautious of the blows that met them, rupturing their bodies and splintering their legs in sheaves.

Again, they were repelled, many toppling back from the edge of the pit and spiralling like denuded umbrellas through the light and back into darkness.

Les stood alongside Trevena and Daniel and watched as the spiders were demolished. The men fought well and with sustained ferocity. Babur was in the midst of it, swinging a heavy towing chain, its links threaded with carriage bolts.

Trevena turned in time to see a cluster of spiders dart across the road and make for the campervan. He started to run towards them but he stopped when he saw Bronze John emerge from the side of the van and meet them head-on.

Maybe the spiders had little wits but the sight of the tiger affected them nonetheless. Almost comically, their legs slid on the concrete and pedalled backwards in an attempt to decelerate, but it was too late for them. Bronze John let them come and then he lashed out a paw and sent them all to smithereens. He licked his paw, turned and skulked back into the van.

Trevena turned back, sweating and breathless, the tyre-iron still clenched in his fist. The men had managed to destroy or throw down the horde and were now gathered again at the edge of the pit. The engine noises were louder now and with it came a wind, pushed up through the sinkhole, smelling of burnt oil, sulphur and something else more organic. Trevena put a hand over his nose. It smelled, he thought, like the dirt in the mouth of a month-old corpse.

Les turned and began pushing his men away. They backed off, faces pale and tired, eyes wide with apprehension.

Daniel came over to Trevena. Trevena wondered how the flesh of a face could bear to carry such anguish without falling slack against its bones in submission, declining for good to express any further form of raw emotion.

"What is it?" Trevena asked.

Daniel took a breath, a great hitching lungful of air.

"The Autoscopes are coming," he said.

THEY ROSE UP through the pit on heavy machines with armour and mighty weapons bolted to their rides. Their engines thundered and the sides of the sinkhole crumbled and dropped into the shaft until the entire remains of the building were gone. It ate up the ground and the arc lights fell and took with them the cables and the generator so that they all now stood in nothing but the red darkness.

Les waved the men away.

"Go home," he shouted. "Be with your families. You fought well. Don't be ashamed."

The men looked around, looked to each other in the hope of better options, but the air now stank and the sound of those machines was like the roar of a hellish turbine. They hung their heads. Some embraced, others shook hands. Someone grabbed Trevena's hand and pumped it, tears standing in his eyes.

They dispersed. Some went across the road and traipsed into the pub. Trevena, Daniel and Les stood at the kerb and waited.

Daniel said, "Where's Babur?"

THEY DIDN'T HEAR the campervan engine start over the noise coming up from the pit, but when they were lit up by its headlights, they turned to see it bumping across the road. It stopped, idling for a moment, and they could see, in the red backwash from the brake lights, Bronze John and Anna standing in the shadows of the car park. Bronze John's head was down and Anna was holding onto him, whispering into his ear. She was crying.

Trevena stepped forward, intending to get up into the van, but before he could reach the door, Babur stood on the accelerator and the van lunged towards the pit. Trevena could see his face, strained but serene. Their eyes met for a moment, and Babur smiled.

And then he drove the van over the lip of the pit.

THE THREE MEN stood and waited. No one spoke.

The rim of the sinkhole darkened again as the lights from the van fell away.

The turbine noise rose in pitch. The men could hear rotors chopping the vile air. Trevena held his breath.

Then: a deafening, punching *thump,* and the ground shook beneath them. Cracks jagged out from the edge of the pit, buckling the road. The turbines and the rotors fell silent.

The machines had stopped.

Trevena strained his ears, and then the screaming started.

A scream of rage and a scream of metal. Trevena held his head, his knees weakening. He clenched his teeth. He imagined the drop through darkness, Babur seeing those frightful heads turned up towards him, great angel-eyes burning in the plummeting headlights, claws and frills of spines glittering, the black metal of their machines gleaming, before he activated the EMP for a final time. A full charge, loaded, discharging at the last minute, knocking out those ascending engines.

There was a moment when the whole world was filled with the chaos of their plunge. It sounded like an avalanche calving out the side of an iron mountain. There were more earth-shaking explosions and the rim of the pit flickered orange from the flames.

The three men were on their knees. Trevena thought he might be screaming. He looked up and saw, through vision blurred by tears and the shaking of the earth, that the planet was setting. Mars was going down behind the hills, taking its bloody traces with it.

Trevena lay on the road and closed his eyes. He felt the sharpness of grit against the backs of his hands. Silence returned to the village. He heard voices. Daniel and Les talking. Others. People venturing from the pub, conferring in tones of wonder, caution, speculation. Somewhere, a dog barking.

Someone was standing over him. He opened his eyes and saw it was Daniel. He let the man help him to his feet. They looked around. There was no sound from the pit. Trevena brushed dirt from his clothes and examined himself. He had a shallow graze on his cheek from a fragment of flying glass. Daniel appeared unharmed and a look of composure had returned to his face.

"Are you okay, Phil?"

"Yes," Trevena said and felt surprised saying it. "I'm fine."

"That was a remarkable sacrifice," Daniel said.

Trevena nodded. "We need to take this thing out. What now?"

"We still need to find Chloe. Babur told me where he'd found her. He said she'd be safe for now. I want to get to her. We need transport."

Bronze John and Anna joined them at the side of the road. Anna was pale.

"How you doing, love?" Trevena asked.

Anna shrugged. "'Kay," she said. The tiger stood close, watching her.

"Nice job with the spiders," Trevena said to him.

Bronze John lifted a lip revealing a sardonic picket of teeth.

And then Bronze John's ears pricked up and he swung his head to look down the road. He padded off, his tail switching in anticipation.

The dog barked again, closer now.

"I know that bark," Daniel said, and his face lit up.

The dog emerged from the darkness at the end of the street. He bounded up to them, tail thrashing. He was greeted first by the tiger, letting the dog jump up at his face and lick him, and then he approached the others.

"Hello, Bix," Daniel said and knelt down to fuss him. Anna was intrigued and Bix enjoyed her attentions, too.

"What do you know, fella?" Daniel said.

"I know Tashkent is the capital of Uzbekistan," he said. "Chloe's mother is quite an educated young woman. She doesn't speak Afghan, but she has a working geographical knowledge of the region. I also know it's too late to get to Chloe in her Quay."

Daniel's face registered shock, but Bix said, "She's safe. I just left her. But she's being born, and where her mother is, they're in danger. We have to get to Quay-Endula."

"Have we got time?" Trevena said.

Daniel turned and looked at him.

"Time's what we do here," he said.

LES COMMANDEERED A truck from one of the men in the village, a high-sided flatbed of indeterminate make and model. It was old, diesel, and rumbled up the road on its big, worn tyres. A column of off-white smoke rose from its exhaust.

"She'll do," Daniel said. "You drive, Phil."

Trevena pulled the door open and looked into the cab. He wrinkled his nose at the sour smell that wafted into his face. He seated himself behind the no-frills dashboard and wound the window down. It dropped an inch and stuck. He put his foot on the clutch and rattled the gear stick around until he thought he'd found first, and stalled it.

"Bollocks."

Daniel lifted Anna in through the passenger side and climbed in. He patted his lap and Bix jumped up and settled himself between them. "Roll your window down, Dan," he said. He looked excited. Daniel did so, getting his window to lower all the way. Trevena raised his eyebrows.

"I like the wind in my ears," Bix said to him.

"So do I," Trevena said.

There was a sudden jolt and the front of the truck lifted a foot off the ground for a moment. Trevena glanced in the rear-view mirror.

"There's a tiger in the back," he said. "So you know."

Daniel smiled. "Let's go," he said, and pointed up the road. Trevena reached for the ignition and turned the key. The truck roared and Trevena lifted his foot off the accelerator before he flooded it. He found first and, holding his breath, pulled them away. Les watched from outside the pub. He raised a hand and blew Anna a kiss. She waved back and then sat with an arm around Bix while Trevena trundled the truck up the road, crunching into second.

"Can you go a bit faster?" Bix said. His tongue was hanging out and there was a daft look in his eyes. *Talking bloody dog, he was still a bloody dog*, thought Trevena, and waited until the speedometer read thirty before he boldly negotiated third. The gear stick felt like it might snap off in his fist. Bix leaned across Daniel's lap and stuck his nose out of the window.

"You know the drill," Daniel said as Trevena careered the truck up a lane so narrow the bushes either side whacked against the wing mirrors.

"You're kidding," Trevena said.

"Nope. Shut your eyes."

Trevena swallowed, knuckles white on the steering wheel, and shut his eyes.

ONCE MORE, THAT sense of drift, and ribbons of light across his eyelids. Trevena could feel the curve of the wheel clenched in his hands, cool and tacky with grime. He was moaning again. He didn't care. This time *he* was driving.

He jolted forward in his seat as the truck came back into contact with the road. His eyes flew open and he wrestled with the wheel, steering the truck up onto a verge at the side of a railway line. The truck stalled. Trevena didn't swear this time, just sat slumped in his seat breathing deeply.

They got down from the cab and stood looking out onto a moonlit cove. Beyond the cliffs to their right could be seen the lights of a city sprawling around the perimeter of a much larger, sweeping bay.

"Is that a *pier*?" Trevena said, but the others were already halfway down towards the beach and nobody heard him.

Trevena shrugged and followed them onto the sand.

There was a fire burning on the beach, and the movement of people around it. As they covered the distance between them, a figure moved off towards the shore. Trevena looked in the direction of the horizon and felt a familiar dread settle over his spirits.

Something was coming over the water. He could recognise the sound now and felt the backs of his eyes prickle as their light evolved from the darkness.

Daniel was running towards the people around the fire. He shouted. Bronze John and Bix covered the distance quickly, with Anna scampering behind. Trevena decided he'd better get over there and began to run, too.

Three men met them at the fire. A giant with blond hair, a much smaller man, slight and edgy with curly black hair and glasses, and a young chap with long hair tied back in a pony tail. Trevena could see they were standing guard around a woman. She was in labour and clearly struggling. She cried out and the young man went to her side, smoothing the sweat damp hair on her brow and over her ears. He kissed her and held her hand. The curly haired man knelt also, tending them both.

Daniel and the tall man embraced. When they separated, Trevena could see the tall man was weeping. "Incredible bravery," he said, and Trevena realised he was talking about Babur. He stepped forward and held out his hand.

"Phil Trevena," he said.

"Jon Index. Good to meet you, my friend. Thank you for all you've done."

Index cupped Anna's cheek in his huge hand. She smiled up at him. "And hello, my sweet," he said. "It's good to finally meet you. Your sister will be relieved to see you, I think. And your father, thanks to this man."

Trevena watched Anna turn and run off up the beach with Bix and Bronze John in tow and he wondered if this was what salvation felt like.

"Come with me," Index said.

They walked down to the shoreline. As they approached, Trevena could see that what he'd thought was just a single large figure standing silhouetted in the moonlight was, in fact, two people. A young boy was standing in the shadow of the man and he was reaching up to grip the sides of the man's head in his hands.

Index took Trevena's arm while they were still a way off and stopped. Daniel continued down to the shore

"That's Alex and his Uncle Sandy," Index said. "Sandy is the Glassblower and Alex is his facilitator. You know what those things are out there? Uproar Contraptions driven by Toyceivers and their vitreophim creations. We can't fight them all and hope to save Claire and the baby. Sandy and Alex will lay down cover for us and then we must get Claire away from here."

"What do you want me to do?" Trevena asked. Index's eyes were very cold and very blue in the moonlight. If he'd asked Trevena to wade into the sea and fight the oncoming horde on his own while the others escaped, he would have agreed without hesitation.

But Index said, "Can you drive that truck down here?"

Trevena had a moment to appreciate the mundanity of the request and smiled. He was amongst gods here after all. The least he could be was their designated driver.

"I should think so, if I get a good run-up down the slope. But I don't think she'll be going anywhere once she gets into this wet sand."

"Just get her down here, Phil. If you can."

Trevena headed back up the beach to the truck at the top of the slope. He climbed into the cab and started the engine. He switched the headlights on and swung the truck in a half circle away from the verge so that the beams shone down onto the beach. He gunned the engine and took his foot off the clutch. The front wheels of the truck left the road and dropped onto the packed sand at the top of the dune.

"Here we go," Trevena said. He wished the truck had a radio. He would have liked to do this to a bit of rock. Maybe Whitesnake. The only soundtrack he had was the whine and clatter of the approaching Uproar Contraptions, rising on the wind blowing in through the passenger side window.

"*Trouble always comin' my waaaay,*" Trevena sang, dropping an octave to his best Coverdale blues moan, and popped the clutch.

THE NIGHT CLOCK is calling its numbers to its face and a man whose name is metal knelt and held the body of his friend in his arms. The Gantry had closed with Cade inside. He had ambushed them, running from an alleyway, his broken sword swinging in furious arcs as the Gantry was closing.

The man, whose name was Bismuth, and his friend, Plummer, both large men, formidable, had elected to remain behind to confront the Autoscopes that had come to London through their own colossal ingress Gantries.

Plummer had stepped forward to cut Cade off from the children and the pregnant girl, and Cade had thrust his shattered sword through Plummer's side.

Bismuth moved as fast as he could, feeling the restrictions of his size, and the long, heavy coat he wore, and the weight of his damned boots, but could only reach Plummer as he fell, and that was too late, because Cade had thrown himself through the Gantry and it had closed behind him.

Bismuth caught the falling man and held him and lowered him to the ground.

Blood bubbled from Plummer's mouth. He was trying to speak. Bismuth put his head an inch away from the scarred and weathered face of his Paladin.

"Tell me..." Plummer whispered. "Tell me..." His eyes rolled and his head moved, agitated, in the crook of Bismuth's arm. Blood was pouring from the wound in his side, pooling in the gutter.

Bismuth looked up at the London skyline.

The Gantries were gone and with them the Autoscopes that had poured from them.

"They're gone," Bismuth said. "Maybe they were never there."

"Cade... *fucked* them..." Plummer's chest heaved and he sprayed a fan of blood from his mouth as he laughed. He reached up and patted Bismuth's bearded cheek. Bismuth looked down at his friend and smiled. Something had happened beyond the Gantry that Index had opened to take the children and the woman to safety. Cade's presence there had either thrown Dark Time out or someone had done something in the Quays to prevent the incursions.

Bismuth closed his eyes and waited.

He heard nothing, no message from the Quays, saw no visions, but he smelt something.

"I can smell an ocean," he said, but he spoke it to himself.

Plummer had died.

*   *   *

Bismuth placed the body of his friend in the back of Cade's car. It was a convertible Saab, lowered to look louche and powerful. The keys were still in it. Bismuth switched on the ignition and operated the roof, letting it unfold and ride up over the interior. He took hold of Plummer's right hand and kissed it. He closed his eyes and gave thanks for this man and his years of devotion.

Then he straightened up and reached into the pocket of his coat and took out his Compass and Levers, his Instruments. He opened the Compass and watched as the needle settled on Northeast. He would go there, to where they were all gathering.

There was a square of dry earth in the concrete by the side of the road, and a slender tree growing from it. He lifted his Egress Lever and plunged it into the dirt and compressed the handle.

A line of light, like a slot in the air, opened, and he went through it.

Trevena stopped singing the moment the truck started careering down the dune. He gritted his teeth and held onto the wheel with all his strength, the muscles in his forearms standing out like cords, as the bonnet rose and fell, the truck bouncing on its large tyres, sliding and kicking up clouds of sand. The offside headlight blew and something beneath the chassis came loose, battering against the sand until it dropped off completely. Trevena hoped it was part of the exhaust and not the drive shaft.

The remaining headlight lit up the beach as it flew towards him and he braced himself as the front of the truck hit the level sand and the wheels tried to bite, bald tyres spinning like belts. Momentum carried it down the beach and Trevena coaxed the accelerator, trying not to over rev, trying not to stall the bastard, allowing the weight of the truck and the paddling tyres to do the work for him.

The truck got as far as the campfire and slid to a halt, wheels turning without any traction, sinking lower into the damp sand. The engine whined and Trevena switched it off.

The Toyceivers were clearly visible now, their Uproar Contraptions aglow, putting a sick glaze of reflected light onto the water that looked like blooms of contaminated algae adrift just beneath the surface.

Index waved to Trevena to stay in the cab. Then he and Daniel, Steve and Mick, lifted Claire with great tenderness and carried her around to the back of the truck and lifted her onto the flatbed. Index whistled and Anna, Bronze John and Bix raced down the beach and climbed up with them. Index secured the back of the truck and walked around to the passenger door. The single beam of the remaining headlight shone a diffuse cone of light against the sand.

"Full beam, Phil," Index said.

Trevena fumbled with the steering column and clicked a lever. The windscreen wipers scraped an arc across the glass sweeping two thick bars of sand into the gutter at the side of the bonnet.

"Sorry." He tried a lever on the other side and engaged full beam.

Alex and Sandy were spotlit on the shoreline.

THE NIGHT CLOCK is calling its numbers to its face and a man and his son stand together on the stony earth in the middle of a disused and abandoned reclamation yard. They have come here before, in happy times and in troubled times. They won time for themselves on this very spot not so long ago.

Earlier that night they had both had the same dream and had met, in comical disarray, on the upstairs landing outside their bedrooms, knowing it was the hour.

They had taken a few moments to dress and had left the farmhouse to go to the reclamation yard, their dream vivid in their still-sleepy heads.

It was cold and they were glad of their boots and coats. The man stood with his arm about his son's shoulder. They were looking towards the fields and the forest that lay beyond them.

"*There*," said the boy, pointing over the turned earth.

His father looked and saw it too.

There was a light rising out of the forest. It fluttered and abruptly brightened. It glowed a sparkling green and then settled to a hard blue flame. Even from where they stood, they could hear the burner roar.

They waited in nervous anticipation as the hot air balloon drifted over the fields towards them.

Eliot and his father, David, waved.

Doctor Mocking waved back.

The Toyceivers brought a cold wind with them.

Alex was shivering. His hands looked small and white like rarefied orchids as they pressed against the sides of his uncle's head.

"Are you ready, Alex?" Sandy said, his words muffled around the end of the pipe.

"Yes," Alex said, trusting his uncle.

"Don't let go, whatever happens."

Suddenly their shadows sharpened and raced away from them. The truck was aiming its headlights down the beach. It lit the water's edge and the things that were advancing towards it.

Sandy took an enormous breath, his shoulders bunching, set his mouth around the pipe, twisted it so that it dug further into the sand, and blew.

His cheeks bulged. Alex felt the strain go through his uncle's body, the muscles in his neck and across the flesh of his head. Alex gripped hard, his own young muscles tensing in concord with his uncle's.

Sandy's cheeks began to glow.

Alex felt the heat through his palms and nearly let go in reflex but he held on as his uncle's face lit up and shone like a bulb. The pipe glowed, too, a blazing filament connecting the man with the earth, the Glassblower and his medium.

The sand around the end of the pipe began to heat up and the heat radiated out from it. The sand bubbled and softened and the entire beach along the shore began to incorporate the energy Sandy was imparting, rippling along its width, growing supple, turning to glass. It steamed like magma as the slow waves slid over it.

Sandy was shaking. Alex dared not speak, but clung on, his ability operational through his uncle, letting Sandy work his glass.

Shapes formed along the shore. They lifted huge sagging heads and elastic limbs from the vitreous swamp. They grew quickly into vast, translucent sauropods. As the air hit them and the waves foamed over their extruding bodies, they hardened. They wrenched themselves from the lava and waded into the sea. Their eyes were dark, unformed. Their mouths hung open and their throats blazed, funnels of radiant heat where they remained pliant and blistering.

Sandy collapsed and fell backwards. Alex dodged out of the way as his uncle keeled over. Sandy lay on his back staring at the sky. The skin around his mouth and the tip of his nose was red as sunburn and his lips were blistered and split, but he was grinning. He propped himself up on his elbows and looked down the beach. He watched his vitreosaurs ploughing through the waves. Their necks swung and lashed at the first wave of flying machines, baking mouths crushing them like insects. Wings and rotors shattered and burned as they dropped from the sky onto the machines beneath them. The vitreosaurs trod through a churning mass of wreckage.

The glass was hardening, and as the first Contraptions struggled from the waves, their frames and wheels sank into the solidifying mire and became stuck, and smouldered. Those that baled out fell victim to the same fate; they sank, screaming, their limbs blackening. The lucky ones fell face-first.

Alex helped Sandy to his feet and they backed away, still enrapt by the carnage at the shore. A flying Contraption had lowered chains and was attempting to snare and drag over one of the vitreosaurs. Three smaller Contraptions bobbed in the water between its stamping legs. They fired serrated harpoons from racks of cannons bolted to their sides. The harpoons hit the belly of the beast and it shattered, great panes of thick, blackened glass falling from beneath it like windows from a burning cathedral. The vitreosaur butted the Contraption out of the air with a blow from its massive head; it span out of control, its rotors buckled, and scored a smoking arc through the air. It hit the beach and rolled like a car wreck. A deluge of molten glass poured from the hole in the vitreosaur's belly and smothered the Contraptions paddling beneath it. They disappeared under the water beneath the boiling blanket of glass. The vitreosaur sank to its knees and slid below the oily, steaming sea.

Alex and Sandy ran towards the truck. Index waved them on, pointing to the flatbed. They climbed up and Index joined them in the back of the truck. He banged on the roof of the cab.

"Engine on, Phil," he said.

Trevena was numb. His eyes were wide and his mouth hung open. He was watching a battle waging between glass dinosaurs and steaming machines less than a hundred yards away through a windscreen. Part of his mind hoped that maybe he was at the pictures watching a Guillermo del Toro blockbuster.

He reached out slowly and found the keys beneath the steering column. He started the engine, still staring straight ahead. A herd of vitreosaurs had separated from the rest and were treading through the water towards Quay-Endula. Trevena could see more lights on the horizon further across the bay. A second wave of Toyceivers. Maybe when this was over what glass dinosaurs remained would stand in the parks and gardens of Quay-Endula as a permanent installation commemorating this conflict. Trevena liked the idea, and the image of those proud, craning beasts pearlescent in the glare of spotlights.

He heard Index say, "Daniel, take us out of here."

Trevena took one last look at the scene on the beach, following the passage of Sandy's super-sculptures as they rounded the headland.

Then he closed his eyes.

14

TREVENA AWOKE IN the middle of a house party. He sat bolt upright, all effects of sleep gone, and looked around. One hot afternoon, halfway through his divorce, he had fallen asleep in a ward round somewhere, when he was drinking too much and not sleeping, and he'd snorted himself awake to find the whole room sitting quietly, watching him. The consultant, a cocky young locum in a linen suit, had regarded him with the contempt usually reserved for a cleaner trying to have a chat with him about darts. Trevena had wondered whether he'd broken wind.

But nobody was looking at him now. He relaxed and rubbed his eyes. He was sitting on Elizabeth's sofa and the sun was up. Trevena looked at his watch. It was seven o'clock. He had been asleep for about half an hour.

He recalled the events in the Quays with the same surreal elation one experiences on waking from a particularly vivid and exciting dream. He remembered what Elizabeth had said before he'd gone to sleep on her sofa, about the intensity of emotions being tempered by the unconscious. He felt no mental trauma despite what he had seen, no overload. In fact he felt more refreshed than he had in ages.

Index came and sat next to him. He had a cup of tea. The fine china looked like something from a child's tea set in his hand.

"How are you doing, Phil?"

"Good. Yourself?"

Index had a sip of tea. "Well, we made it back. Claire's upstairs with Elizabeth and Steve. She's doing better now she's getting some proper attention. She'll give birth soon."

Trevena listened. He could hear movement upstairs and an occasional cry of pain that he assumed were contractions.

Alex was sitting at the dining table playing cards with his Uncle Sandy and Mick Reeks. Anna was sitting on the floor by the gas fire playing with a small toy tiger made of plastic.

"Is that...?"

"That's how he is in the waking world," Index said.

"Wow," Trevena said. He noticed a collection of dolls on the sideboard and a number of stuffed toys: a teddy bear, a leopard that looked like it had been a free gift from the World Wildlife Fund, and a fluffy dog. Trevena blinked.

"Oh no, is that...?"

Index nodded, his face serious.

And then Trevena heard a bark and turned to see Bix come trotting out of the kitchen. He came over and Trevena grabbed him and gave him a fuss.

"You little bugger," he said, and felt closer to tears than he had at any other time throughout this entire ordeal.

Bix licked his face.

"You can't talk can you?" Trevena said.

Bix put his head on one side, tongue lolling.

"Never mind," Trevena said, laughing. He wiped his eyes. "At least you're real."

"I wouldn't let Bronze John hear you say that," Index said. He was smiling. He put a hand on Trevena's shoulder. Anna was holding the toy tiger and waggling it in Trevena's direction. Its painted grin looked like it could take a finger off.

"My apologies, big fella," Trevena said.

Then he said, "Where's Daniel?"

DANIEL HAD STAYED behind. He watched the truck disappear into the Gantry and then turned and trudged back up the beach. Behind him the great glass beasts had destroyed the first wave of Toyceivers and were wading through the smoking wreckage to meet the second wave that were on their way to Quay-Endula.

At the top of the dunes was a railway line. Daniel stopped. He looked at the lines for a moment. He measured his breathing, and then he stepped onto the line between the rails. His boots crunched on the gravel between the sleepers. He closed his eyes for a moment, remembering that day he had gone to the seaside intending to die.

And when he opened his eyes again, he saw the back end of the locomotive, Railgrinder, still and patient a hundred yards up the line. Daniel frowned, recognition dawning on him. He took slow steps along the line until he reached the engine.

He went around it and stood looking up at its blunt, swarf-scarred grille. He reached out and touched it, stroked his fingers down the iron.

"It was you," he said in a hushed voice. He remembered the smell, and the noise, that overwhelming chthonic roar he had heard in his nightmares as a child and which had terrified him. Somehow he had personified it into the image of his mother, and her wails of need. But it had been Railgrinder, rumbling on its Dark Time loop, always coming to save him, and Daniel stood on the rails there beneath the moon over Quay-Endula, and wept.

THERE WAS A signal post telephone at the side of the line. It was housed in a weatherproof box with a circle painted on it and a number inside the circle. The number was 10. When it rang, Daniel went over and answered it.

"Is she safe?" Les asked. His voice was faint and the line crackled and hissed.

"Yes," Daniel said. "They all are."

"Are you coming home?"

"Yes."

"We need you, Daniel. It's on its way. Can you hear it?"

Daniel closed his eyes and listened. Out there, on its way to the village, a wave of pressure was forcing a screaming wind towards them. The devil-in-dreams was casting out death and despair one final time as it fought for control of the Night Clock.

"I'm coming," he said.

"Daniel."

"Yes."

"Are the others ready?"

"Yes."

Daniel replaced the phone and walked over to Railgrinder. He climbed into the cab and opened the firebox. Heat baked out at him. He closed the iron door and released the brake. Railgrinder shuddered and jolted. Daniel put the engine in reverse and, leaning an elbow on the back of the cab, he used the throttle to take Railgrinder on its final journey.

He reached into his coat pocket and took out a matchbox. He opened it with his thumb and looked at the tiny hermit crab on its bed of cotton wool. He remembered the man who had given it to him. Gordon. A good man. He had known what Daniel was. Some people just did. His father had, too, but his dread, and the devil-in-dreams, had broken him and had used that calamity to break Daniel in turn. Daniel replaced the threadbare cardboard drawer, put the matchbox back in his pocket. He sighed. Melancholy and joy sluiced through him. It was a rare combination, like an alloy trying to form out of antagonistic elements, never able to settle into anything stable, but it was oddly sweet. Daniel had suffered a lot worse.

He closed his eyes and took Railgrinder through the slot for the final time.

* * *

TREVENA STOOD UP. Everyone had stopped what they were doing and were looking towards the foot of the stairs, even Anna, who was sitting cross-legged on the rug holding Bronze John loosely in her lap. Her eyes were wide and expectant.

They had heard a sound from upstairs. An unmistakeable sound.

A cry.

A baby's first almighty lungful of air.

"We go now," Index said. He was heading for the front door. Mick was close behind. Alex and Sandy stood more warily but followed, their eyes still on the stairs. Anna came over to the sofa and put out her hand. Trevena took it. She smiled up at him.

"You don't have to come," she said. She put Bronze John in Trevena's hand.

Trevena shook his head and pressed the tiger back into Anna's hand.

"We've done our business together," he said. "He's yours. I'm coming with you."

Anna nodded, suddenly grave.

"Thank you," she said and walked out of the lounge. Trevena stood for a moment looking around.

"Thank *you*," he said.

AT THE BOTTOM of the stairs Index shouted up, "How is she?"

Steve appeared on the landing. His eyes were red and he stood on unsteady legs.

"She's beautiful," he said.

"And Claire?"

"Sleeping," said Steve. "Peaceful now."

"Congratulations, Steve," he said.

"Thanks, man."

"Take care of them."

Steve lifted a hand, made the peace sign.

Index opened the front door and they went out.

*   *   *

TREVENA WAS SURPRISED to see the old truck there, parked at the side of the road. It looked like it had just crossed a desert.

"We're going to Lakenheath," Index said.

Trevena nodded. "It's not too far. It's right at the edge of my patch as it happens. I've got a patient out there."

"I know," Index said.

"That sounds ominous," Trevena said with a watery laugh.

"Will you drive?" Index asked.

"It's the least I can do," Trevena said.

He got in the driver's side and Index lifted Anna in between them. Bix jumped up beside Index and was squashed against the door when he slammed it shut. Mick got up onto the flatbed with Sandy and Alex.

Trevena switched on the ignition and the old truck fired into life. It blatted like a novice's drum solo beneath the chassis where most of the exhaust had fallen off but it pulled away in first without conking out and Trevena accelerated it gently through the gears until they were barrelling along the main drag through the estate heading for the A10.

Trevena glanced over at Bix. The dog had a daft expression on its face.

"Open the window a bit, Jon," he said. "Bix likes to feel the wind in his ears, you know."

Index wound the window down and Bix slid his nose out and shut his eyes. His ears looked like scarves, blowing in the wind.

They drove for half an hour and Index said, "Turn off left here, Phil."

Trevena said, "It's alright, Jon. I know where I'm going."

THE DEVIL-IN-DREAMS can feel the Firmament Surgeons gathering. That part of it able to ride the Dark Time flux—ride it, like a tanker steering through the swell of an infinite sea but no more able to control it than the fish that swim in it—is still able to plot a course. It identifies its target and pours out its filth, budding and blackening inside the man's head, distorting his dreams and drawing him into the conflict. His name is Barry Cook and he is a sick man. He is hiding the vilest of thoughts in his head and the devil-in-dreams will use its power to increase the torment. The devil-in-dreams has detected one of the Ten and will use this *Cook*, use his sickness, to exterminate him in his Quay. One more kill and the Night Clock will belong to the Autoscopes for eternity.

Daniel.

The devil-in-dreams is blinded by its hatred of this one. More overpowering than anything he feels towards the others. He has put more effort into this one's suffering, and yet he still stands. Still he fights. And it is this resilience that the devil-in-dreams abhors.

Because it is so very frightening.

RAILGRINDER SLID FROM the Gantry, its iron wheels screaming and sparking on the surface of the road. Its momentum carried it on a slanting course towards the sinkhole. Daniel slammed on the brake. The wheels locked, biting like blades, fracturing the potholed tarmac, gouging grooves in the loose grit beneath it.

Daniel jammed the throttle into its forward position but the wheels wouldn't turn. Daniel had reached the limits to his skill as an engine driver and he prepared to bail out of the cab. Railgrinder was slowing, though, and when its back end slid as far as the edge of the road, its wheels hit the kerbstones and shattered them like teeth. The engine bucked, throwing Daniel to the footplate, and came to rest a yard from the lip of the pit.

Daniel stood and wiped coal dust from his hands onto his coat. He took a last look around Railgrinder's cab, at the gauges and valves, feeling the last warmth from the ebbing firebox. There was a whistle chain hanging from a lever above the firebox. Daniel reached out and took hold of it. He pulled it gently and listened to the forlorn, wavering chord.

Daniel turned and jumped down from the cab.

He went over to the pub and opened the door.

One man sat on a stool at the bar. Otherwise the pub was empty. Les smiled when Daniel walked it.

"What's the plan, Dan?" he said.

Daniel pulled a stool out and sat down. He rested his elbows on the bar and put his chin on his clasped fingers. He stared into the flecked mirror below the optics.

"It knows I'm here," he said.

Les nodded. "The whistle."

"Yes. A challenge. *A summoning.*"

"That'll piss it off," Les said.

"That," said Daniel, "essentially *is* the plan."

Les was silent for a moment, and then he said, "You have to go back, don't you?"

Daniel nodded, still watching his reflection in the mirror.

"I have to do my *thing*," he said.

"Will I see you again?"

Daniel stood up. "I don't know," he said.

Les held out a hand and Daniel took it.

"I love you, Dan," Les said.

Daniel took the matchbox from his pocket and put it on the bar.

Les picked it up and slid open the little drawer.

"Hey, Bert," he said. He looked up at Daniel, his eyes shining.

"Take him," Daniel said. "I don't need him anymore. Not for what I have to do. Listen, though. Listen to what he says."

Les put the matchbox back on the bar, the tiny hermit crab cushioned on its grubby ball of wool.

"Goodbye, Dan."

Daniel turned and walked out.

DANIEL STOOD AT the lip of the pit. The wave of pressure was pulsing from the depths. He could feel it moving the air around him. The smell was awful, that shallow-burial stink. A memory came to him and for a moment he teetered on the edge of the sinkhole. It took him off-guard, ambushing him.

He was attending his father's funeral and, disoriented by the unreality he felt, and the unremitting absence of his father, and the rain that fell in a fine sheet across the cemetery, he stumbled away from the small group he was with and found himself standing in a small lot surrounded by a grove of trees at the edge of the graveyard. He was only lost for a few moments, but as he looked around he saw the most incongruous thing and it made him stop, his eyes wide, a hand plastered to his mouth.

There were toys here. They were soiled with age, rusty and untended, the effort of placing them there so terrible it was as if they had been fled from, never to be revisited. There was a tin windmill on a plastic stick. It rattled round on its tarnished pin in the sheeting rain. Sodden, ragged dolls and teddy bears slumped in the understanding of their empty comfort. And photos in frames, of children, when they had been briefly alive and smiling without knowledge of the ground. How could they know?

Daniel had sobbed, looking around at the children's graves. He had never imagined a place like this, set apart like a sanatorium, away from those that had lived fuller lives. He felt suddenly terribly exposed. It was like he had walked unwittingly into a minefield and could now see the detonators everywhere, poking from the ground. The graves, and the toys that consoled them, corralled him in the misty rain. He wondered – and wished he hadn't – whether cold, decaying little fingers reached through the earth during the night to touch these old beloveds, to play and spin the corroded tops, to listen to their dead hum as they turned in the dark.

Daniel stumbled from the lip of the pit, much as he had stumbled away from the graves as a child. But now there was no mother to catch him, to fret over him in the projection of her own guilt and grief. And he was glad of it. He wiped his brow and glared at the pit.

"You *bastard*," he said.

He made fists and stuck them in the pockets of his coat. He closed his eyes. He locked himself onto the flux of Dark Time he could feel rushing up through the sinkhole. He could feel its corruption, its rage. He concentrated, waiting.

The dream came to him, and the identity of the dreamer.

The devil-in-dreams was in there, as Daniel had hoped, its entirety whipping up the filth it found there. It was using this man as its final push to eliminate him but it was distracted by its hatred.

"Come on," Daniel said through his teeth. "Make it personal."

He allowed the pressure wave to take him out of the Quay and he entered Dark Time.

15

TREVENA FOLLOWED A dirt road up to the farm. He knew it well,
knew where the ruts and potholes were deepest. He had driven it
many times before.

Barry Cook was one of the most unpleasant patients on his
caseload. He cropped up with dispiriting regularity complaining
of depression. Trevena's ethical code strained almost audibly
at the necessity to offer this man a service, but it was all non-
judgemental, this job. Like fuck. He nursed this young man with
a cold heart.

"He's a sex-offender," Trevena said. "A proper fiddler."

Index said nothing, just stared ahead through the windscreen.

"On the register. He reckons he's reformed but I'd like to have
a look at what he's got on his hard drive. Well, *I* wouldn't, but I'd
like someone else to. Someone with the authority to put the little
shit away forever. It's part of his conditions that he doesn't use a
computer but his family's collusive. They can't believe their little
Baz could be capable of that kind of thing. There's computers all
over the house and I bet they're not password protected."

Trevena stopped rambling. He was nervous. He was frightened.
What did they want with Barry Cook?

*   *   *

AT EXACTLY TWENTY past three the previous night—about the same time Graham Knott was undergoing radical amputation—Barry Cook had jolted awake. He had been fighting sleep paralysis, coming up from the nightmare but unable to completely wake up. He sat up and looked around, a searing panic crushing his chest like a heart attack. He was sweating and his right arm was completely dead. The dream was vivid still. He had been doing those terrible, unforgivable things again. His urge was back, raging like an unslaked addiction. He knew the signs of old, the creeping obsessions that built to a point where it was impossible for him to resist them, but this was new, an irresistible clawing inside his mind. He swung his feet off the bed and put them on the cold floor. He froze.

There was someone in his room.

Barry cowered, his right arm flopping, and whispered, "Dad?"

Daniel stepped from the shadows by Barry's desk. A laptop blinked a small blue light as it charged.

"Who... who are you?" Barry said.

"I am the Hypnopomp," Daniel said. "You're dreaming."

Barry's expression glazed over.

Daniel moved some books and magazines around on Barry's desk with the tips of his fingers. He found a spiral bound notebook.

"Come here," Daniel said.

Barry stood up and walked to the desk.

"Write what I tell you," Daniel said.

Barry picked up a pen and leaned over the desk.

"Are you right or left handed?"

"Left," said Barry.

"Aren't you lucky."

Barry smiled, sly and collusive. "Always," he said.

Daniel told Barry what to put in the note.

*   *   *

BARRY FOLLOWED DANIEL through the house and down to the front door. At one point a man stepped out from a bedroom and stood in the hallway watching them. He stood aside as they approached. No surprise registered on the man's face. In fact he smiled as they passed and then continued on down the hall and went into the bathroom.

Barry was mute, his arm lolling at his side. If he tried to lift it, it flew out at an angle, unresponsive to his brain's attempts to direct it. He tried to keep it by his side. In the end he held it there with his left hand.

They walked across the yard to a barn. Daniel led Barry over to one of the machines. It was a hay-baler, attached to the back of a tractor.

"Make it work," Daniel said.

Barry walked over to the machine and pushed a button. He reached up into the tractor's cab and switched it on. The tractor rumbled and came to life. Barry looked at Daniel. "It needs to be running," he said. "For the PTO shaft to turn."

"Get in," Daniel said.

Barry got up into the cab and put the tractor in gear. He pulled away, aiming the tractor's nose at the open barn doors. The baler began to turn, its tines and augurs rotating within the unguarded pickup.

Daniel walked over to the side of the tractor and stepped onto a footplate beneath the door to the cab. He opened the door. He put his foot next to Barry's on the throttle and then kicked it away, replacing it with his own.

"Get out," he said.

Barry climbed past Daniel and jumped to the floor of the barn.

"Follow the baler," Daniel said. The tractor trundled through the barn. Daniel kept his foot on the throttle but ensured the tractor was crawling at the slowest speed possible without stalling.

Barry walked alongside, his right arm clasped to his side. He looked pale but was looking up at Daniel as he walked.

Daniel watched Barry in the long wing mirror.

The barn doors were wide and the tractor trundled out into the night. It headed towards a high whitewashed wall encompassing a cowshed.

"Now," said Daniel, "put your arm in the baler. *Make it look like suicide*."

Barry looked down at the baler and let go of his right arm. Seemingly of its own accord, it shot sideways and plunged into the pickup.

Barry watched as his arm was mangled. He hopped along beside the baler, the flesh tearing from his arm, muscle from bone, bone from socket. Daniel heard the pop and crack as the arm tore from Barry's shoulder and he took his foot from the throttle and jumped down from the cab.

He was confident of his plan, at least in regards to its execution. The denouement was new territory, though, hard to predict. Perhaps impossible. He went to where Barry stood, arterial blood jetting from his stump.

"Sit down," he said. Barry sat cross-legged in the dirt of the yard and watched with disinterest as the tractor ploughed into the wall and stalled. Daniel tore a strip of material from his shirt and made a tourniquet that he used to tie around Barry's shoulder. It wasn't intended to save, merely prolong. He looked at his watch. Four o'clock. He was unsure how long the others would be, so he sat with Barry in the dirt and waited.

He cast out his power as far as he was able, keeping people who would be coming awake soon in a dream-state, hoping it would be enough.

He sensed something, a presence behind and above him, and he craned around to look.

A purple hot air balloon was drifting above the farm house.

Trevena parked the truck and they all piled out. He had stopped in front of the farm house and as they gathered, a man opened the front door dressed in overalls and headed over towards them. He stopped.

"Morning," he said. Then he turned and walked off around the side of the house.

Trevena and Index exchanged glances.

"Daniel's here," Index said. "Come on."

Together, they followed the man around the farmhouse. They watched him trudge across the yard in his filthy boots and head towards the barn. He walked past three people standing in the middle of the yard and seemed to pay no attention whatsoever to the hot air balloon moored on his land. He went straight past them and collected a stainless steel bucket from inside the barn and returned the way he had come. He didn't seem to notice the tractor, either, buried nose-first in the cowshed. Trevena could hear the lowing of agitated beasts.

Trevena was amazed to see his psychiatrist standing with Daniel and a mutilated Barry Cook. Truly amazed. He felt light-headed and bent forward, his hands on his knees.

"Steady, Phil," Index said. Trevena knew what he meant. This was real. No unconscious protection now. What he saw from here on in would stay with him for the rest of his life; hard facts, laid down in his brain. He breathed deeply and stood up.

Doctor Mocking came over to him. He put a hand on Trevena's arm.

"Hello, Phil," he said. "How are you feeling?"

Trevena laughed.

"You tell me, Doc," he said.

Doctor Mocking smiled. Then his eyes lit up and he said, "Excuse me, Phil," and stepped into their midst and scooped Anna up and hugged her to him. Anna was crying.

Trevena went over to Daniel. He looked exhausted, strained to a point Trevena couldn't even begin to estimate. He gazed at the raw stump where Barry Cook's right arm used to be.

"Bet that stings a bit," he said.

Barry regarded him from beneath half-closed eyelids.

"Anything I can do?" Trevena asked.

Daniel managed a weak smile. "Hold me up?"

"If you need me to," Trevena said, and put a hand out to steady him.

"How long have you been here?"

Daniel shrugged. "Three, three and a half hours."

Trevena's head swam. "How could you have?"

"I'm using Dark Time," he said. "It's not linear."

"Right," said Trevena.

Index, Mick and Sandy were talking with Doctor Mocking. Alex and Anna were playing with Bix, throwing an old plastic ball they'd found for him. He pranced dutifully through the muck but wouldn't pick the ball up in his mouth. He nosed it back towards the children with a look of suffering on his chops.

Then his ears pricked up and he started to bark. He was looking towards the entrance to the farm.

Cars were coming up the lane.

AN OLD WHITE Hillman Minx arrived first, followed by a crappy looking Ford Cortina. There was a sticker on the front bumper of the Cortina. It read, *Colin Dack's Caravan Courses*. It swung around and Trevena saw another similar sticker on the rear bumper, this one defaced with the additional words, *for cocks,* scrawled in marker pen, or biro, which lacklustre scrubbing had failed to erase.

The Minx stopped and a young man got out followed by a girl of about ten years old. She stopped, her hands raised to her chest, and then hurled herself at Doctor Mocking. She cried, "*Daddy*!" and then she saw Anna and burst into tears. Anna was scooped up again and the three of them held each other and the doctor rocked his girls and kissed them. His eyes were closed tightly with delight.

The young man knelt on the ground and Bix barrelled into him, knocking him over. "Oh, Bix, you made it. You *good* boy! *Good* boy! Well done, my *good* boy!"

Trevena was still holding onto Daniel's arm.

"Who's that?" he asked.

"That's John Stainwright," Daniel said. "One of us. And that's Lesley."

The Cortina wheezed to a halt and the occupants got out. An elderly man in Bermuda shorts got out of the passenger side and stretched. He had a long, thinning grey ponytail and bandaged hands. He saw Bix and grinned.

"Hey, Bixter!" he shouted. Bix bounded over and got some more love from the man. "Glad you made it, my friend," he said. He waved to John Stainwright, who had regained his feet. "He made it, John!"

John nodded, gave him a thumbs up.

The driver was a man in his late thirties with short dark hair turning grey at the temples. He looked tired. He opened the back door for the huge figure hulking in the back. The man that emerged was bigger than Index. He had a wild beard and a huge mass of tangled, dreadlocked hair. His long coat reached almost down to his heavy, worn boots.

"Met him walking up the road," the old man said. "Knew he was one of you lot as soon as I saw him. Name's Bismuth. He doesn't say much."

Bismuth made for Doctor Mocking. They stood looking at each other for a moment, and then they embraced.

Index seemed to be counting heads. "Where's the boy?" he said.

Doctor Mocking pointed to the balloon.

Index went to the balloon. Its basket was tethered to the ground, the burner puttering, putting enough hot air into it to keep the balloon from wilting. Inside a boy of about twelve and a man were asleep, curled up together.

Doctor Mocking came over and whispered something. The sleepers awoke and stretched, and climbed out of the basket. They blinked and looked around.

Index said, "Eliot, welcome. And welcome, David. David, there's someone I want you to meet."

He stood aside.

Sandy was trembling, tears running down his face.

"David," he said. "Oh, Dave. I've missed you so much, mate."

The man said, "Is that you, Sandy?"

"Yes. Yes it is. It is!" He stumbled over to his friend and grabbed him in a bear hug.

"I'm sorry I ran, Sandy. I truly am."

"I'm glad," Sandy said. "It's all worked out. Doctor Mocking kept us safe." Sandy blinked and wiped at his eyes. "And this is your boy!"

"Eliot."

"Eliot! Great to see you, son!"

Eliot was looking to his father, his face serious. A solemn boy, Trevena thought. Close to his father. His father nodded.

Eliot beamed. He had a great smile.

Trevena watched all this knowing it was a moment of immense significance. A gathering part reunion, part introduction. These people had been lost, scattered and isolated, and something had been trying to destroy them. Now they were all together, Trevena could feel the power, the *intent,* resonating in their midst.

The driver of the Cortina looked a little out of his comfort zone, Trevena thought. He was standing by the back of the car looking at his fingernails.

"Hey," Trevena said, "You okay, fella?"

The man looked up. He skirted the group and came over.

"Phil Trevena," Trevena said and put his hand out.

"Eddie. Eddie D'Andrea," the man said, and they shook.

Now all that remained were here together.

"Take the tourniquet off," Index said. "Let him die."

Daniel pulled the strip of sodden material from Barry Cook's shoulder. Blood welled from the tattered vessels and pattered to the ground. Barry's knees went from under him and he slumped onto the bloody earth, his face slack.

The Firmament Surgeons stood around him in a circle. Index, Bismuth, Doctor Mocking, Daniel, John Stainwright, Alex, Lesley, Anna and Eliot. Their friends, their relatives, their *Paladins* – those that remained – stood outside the circle, Trevena included, as directed by Index.

Those that had their Instruments displayed them; Bismuth had his Levers, Lesley and Anna had Bronze John, Doctor Mocking had a small brass detonator cap. John Stainwright had Bix. The dog sat at his master's side, his eyes clear and bright.

Barry Cook bled out. His face drained of colour and his eyes rolled up into his head and he fell forward and died.

As he hit the ground, his last breath about to leave him, Daniel reached down and touched him. Put a fingertip on the nape of his neck.

"Now," he said.

THE FIRMAMENT SURGEONS made their connection.

Upstairs in Elizabeth's bedroom, Chloe went quiet in her father's arms. Steve looked at Elizabeth, eyes wide with wonder.

"Is this it?" he said.

Elizabeth nodded. She was sitting on the bed, her breathing laboured. Her head ached and if she closed her good eye she could see crow's feathers swirling upwards from the ground, encaged within a scaffold frame.

"Are you okay?"

"Yes, dear," Elizabeth said. She lay back on the bed and closed her eyes.

BARRY COOK'S BODY convulsed. He scrambled to his feet and stood switching his head about in hellish panic. He was dead. His brain was dead, but in a deep, unfiring space inside his mind, amidst the stillness of those billion darkened cells, Daniel had opened his Quay.

Together, the last of the Firmament Surgeons stepped into Dark Time and ran the Night Clock again.

LES HEARD THE door handle rattle but didn't look up. He was playing clock patience on the bar. He had already turned up three kings, which wasn't so good this early on in the game. He had only revealed all the tens so far. He sucked on his bottom lip. Of course he had. He felt satisfied at this and stopped and turned around as the door opened and the devil-in-dreams walked in.

Les stood to meet it.

It was not as he'd imagined.

It was a man, dressed in pyjama bottoms and a dirty red tee shirt. Red from the blood.

The man stood, swaying on unsteady legs. He had a faceful of eyes, which rolled and peered in all directions. He opened his mouth and there were eyes inside him, too.

Les looked at the man, at the torn stump at his shoulder. *He looks confused*, thought Les, and stepped towards it.

The eyes blinked and rolled. They were all of different colours and different sizes. They had been stolen, those eyes, and had seen too much, for too long. The man sagged a little and put out his left arm and leaned against the bar.

He tried to speak, but his mouth was too jammed with eyes and he uttered a wet hiss.

"Oh," said Les. "Are you looking for this?"

He held out the matchbox and thumbed open the drawer.

When those eyes swivelled to see nothing but a dead hermit crab, speaking softly in Daniel's voice, he did manage to scream, despite the eyes stuck in his craw.

TREVENA SAW THEM change.

For a moment the air around them turned to a haze and the circle of figures became indistinct. When they solidified again, they were different. They were bigger and they shone. He could see wheels of light turning amongst them, attached by filaments to their bodies, linking them all, making a mechanism of them.

He felt himself going over, and put out his hands to break his fall. He pressed his face into the ground in awe but before he closed his eyes he saw the others outside the circle had done the same. Eddie and Sandy, Mick and the old guy, Colin Dack, and David, were all likewise prostrate. Colin was laughing, and mumbling something that sounded like an elated prayer.

Suddenly, Barry broke through the circle and made a run for it.

Trevena lifted his head in time to see Barry staggering off down the yard. He reached the edge of a field and barged through the hedge. He ran across the field, bare feet tripping over the blocky, turned earth, and made for a small house at the bottom of the field and across a lane.

Trevena stood up and went over to the barn. He found what he wanted and followed Barry across the field towards the house.

He trod more carefully, the pitchfork held in front of his body in both hands, like a tightrope walker's pole, and hoped Daniel's hypnopompic influence was wide enough to persuade the woman and her little boy watching from the kitchen window that they were still asleep and dreaming.

THE DEVIL-IN-DREAMS reeled away from the man holding the matchbox. He could hear the voice of the one he hated, an incessant taunt. It tried to cast out for its Autoscopes but there was nothing but dead pressure, a spatial lagging that went out in all directions forever. There was nothing beyond this place, no memories or emotions to use. It was cut off from the Dark Time flux. It was inside death.

It swivelled its stolen eyes and glared at the man with the matchbox.

TREVENA HELD BARRY vertical on the end of the pitchfork. His arms were tired and his muscles trembled with the effort. But he hung on.

Mick and Colin had met him halfway across the field. They both carried cans of fuel. Eddie, David and Sandy waited with the Night Clock, three resolute sentinels.

"It's inside there," Colin said, and tapped a bony finger on the centre of Barry's forehead. "Trapped in a dead dream." He shuddered and the corners of his mouth turned down. "An appropriate Compartment of Hell for the bastard. A corpse's mind."

Barry flailed at Colin with his left arm. He uttered a rasping, desperate screech. Colin stepped away. He picked up his can of fuel. It made a heavy wallowing sound. He hitched it up beneath his arm and unscrewed the cap. Mick did likewise, and then they emptied their cans over Barry's head.

Trevena placed the end of the pitchfork in the mud and let Barry sink to his knees. Mick and Colin placed their cans a distance away and Mick came back carrying a Zippo lighter. He put a cigarette in his mouth. He offered the pack to Trevena, who shook his head.

Mick lit his cigarette and inhaled.

Then he lit Barry.

THE DEVIL-IN-DREAMS howled at the blistering agony that consumed it.

The man with the matchbox had backed away, circling towards the door. There was an old Bakelite phone fixed to the wall. It rang. The man picked it up.

"Yes," he said. "It's here."

The devil-in-dreams felt its eyes melt. Its face ran with their sizzling humours. Its throat filled with thick, boiling fluid as they burst in his mouth. They were throughout, and as they burned and ruptured the devil-in-dreams cried out and reached for the man, blinded, its body subject to a thousand searing brands. It tried to break free of the corpse it inhabited but it could not draw power from anything; there was only nothingness.

The man opened the door and backed out.

The door closed, and non-existence pressed against the walls.

The devil-in-dreams sank sightless to the floor, ablaze, time without end.

TREVENA LOOKED DOWN at the charred corpse. The handle of the pitchfork had burnt to charcoal. His nostrils were clogged with the stink of burnt meat. He coughed into his hand and spat on the mud.

The others were coming. Doctor Mocking carried Anna, treading carefully over the broken earth. Eliot was holding his father's hand. Daniel arrived first.

"Has it worked?" Trevena asked.

Daniel nodded. "It'll hold for as long as it needs to."

"What is it?"

"A trap. A quarantine. A small loop of Dark Time. I'll be honest, we didn't know if it would work. I had to rely on Les."

"Where is he? If you've cut off your Quay?"

"It's just a part of it. A blind spot. A dream within a dream."

"What about this?" Trevena jabbed the toe of his shoe at the corpse.

"Leave it," Daniel said. "He left a note. You're familiar with his history? His family won't want an investigation. I'll be betting they'll be secretly relieved Barry's gone. The shame, you know?" He smiled at Trevena, but Trevena noticed his teeth were clenched.

"Violent and demonstrable," Trevena said.

"Exactly," Daniel said.

"The pitchfork might raise a few eyebrows," Trevena said.

Daniel shrugged. "Fuck it."

Trevena had to agree.

DANIEL LOOKED LESS strained now he no longer had to sustain the dream-state. He seemed to just let it go as the truck drove away from the farm.

"Like letting go of a kite," he confided to Trevena.

They had left Doctor Mocking and his girls with David and Eliot. As they drove away Trevena watched the balloon lift from the yard.

About half a mile down the road Trevena saw the Cortina flashing its headlights. He pulled over. Colin got out and came up to his window.

"We'll see you," he said. "We're going back to the caravan park. Got a lot of work to do. Big fella wants dropping off, too."

Trevena assumed he was talking about Bismuth.

"Says he's got a child to find. Poor mite. Got himself trapped in a refrigerator on a tip somewhere. Bismuth's possessed with finding him. He says there's an Autoscope there with him, perpetuating the loop. Job's never done, is it? Well, it's his calling. Nothing but grief and dying for him. Shows on his face, don't it?" Colin grinned revealing a mouth naive of molars. "Well, that's his next adventure. Cheers, Phil." He patted the door panel and went back to the car. He swung it onto the road and gave the horn a toot as they went past. The Minx, driven by John Stainwright, followed. John waved. Trevena waved back. Bix, sitting on the Minx's passenger side, squinting in the breeze, tongue hanging out like pennant, barked once, and then they were gone.

Trevena pulled the truck back onto the road.

STEVE WAS STANDING at the door when they arrived back at Elizabeth's. He held Chloe in his arms, wrapped in a pink blanket. Everyone made a great fuss of her.

"Elizabeth's asleep," Steve said.

Daniel turned to Trevena.

"I'm going to go and sit with her," he said. "Thanks for all you've done, Phil."

"It's fine," he said. "You've done more for me."

They shook, and Daniel went upstairs to sit with his friend. He held onto the banister all the way up.

What now? Trevena wanted to ask. He was still waiting for shock to kick in, or some species of it to set him trembling and weepy, but he felt *good*. Strong. Now they were back in Elizabeth's cosy little ladylike lounge everything felt as it should be. He had always meant to be here.

Index spoke to him.

"Huh?"

"How you feeling, Phil?"

"Good," said Trevena.

Index put a huge hand on his shoulder. "Daniel said it already, but thank you, Phil. From all of us."

Sandy, Alex and Mick were watching him.

Trevena nodded. He smiled as the implication dawned on him. He didn't feel bad at all.

"I can go now?" he said. "You don't need me anymore, do you?"

"It's not a question of need, Phil. There are still Autoscopes out there. Dark Time's awash with them. They'll be easier to track now the devil-in-dreams is contained. We just have to get on with the job."

"I understand," Trevena said. "About the job."

He made a show of looking at his watch.

"I'm on a late shift myself."

He turned and walked down the short hall to the door and let himself out.

He fished in his pocket for his keys and walked to his car.

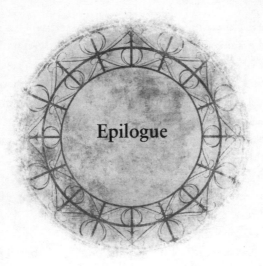

Epilogue

Trevena stood outside the office and knocked on the door.

"Come in, Phil."

Trevena opened the door and went into the office. He sat on the wicker chair opposite the desk.

"Welcome, Phil," said Doctor Mocking.

"Hi, doc."

"How are things with you?"

Trevena took a moment to think. This was his first appointment with the doc since they had all been together. He had phoned for an appointment last week, feeling the need for closure. He had been putting it off, though. He understood the workings of denial. He looked past the doctor through the French windows that gave onto the orchard. It was early July.

"Good," he said. "All good."

Doctor Mocking smiled. "That's great, Phil. This is going to be our last session, as we discussed on the phone. Are you happy with that?"

"Yeah. Discharge me, doc, I'm fixed."

"How's work?"

"Better. Stibbs got moved on. He did his damage. Now he's

wreaking havoc on some other team. The Assertive Outreach Team have needed a shake up for a while." He grinned. "That's just how the system works now. I've accepted it. I can retire in seven years so I'm just keeping my head down. Doing what I'm good at and keeping it simple. Had some good news. Rob Litchin's been dry for a month now. I got him an old computer from a charity and he's working on a website business. Moved back in with his mum. It's not ideal but at least he gets three meals a day and his clothes washed."

"And how's Lizzie?"

Trevena spread his hands. "She's moving to France with her mum and Clive. It'll be good for her. She seems happier."

"How do you feel about it?"

"Okay," Trevena said. "I'll miss her but I'll see her for holidays, and there's Facetime."

They filled the hour reflecting on Trevena's progress and talked of endings and closure. Before the session ended, Doctor Mocking asked about his dreams.

Trevena laughed. "They're good. They've improved. Is it like that for everyone?"

Doctor Mocking shook his head. "Not everyone. It'll never be a perfect world, this one. The Night Clock is running and the containment is holding. For now. We watch."

The session ended and Trevena stood up. He reached over the desk and shook the doctor's hand. "How's Daniel?" he asked. "Are he and Elizabeth, you know...?"

Doctor Mocking smiled.

"They're fine, Phil. Never been happier."

Trevena shook his head. "Happy endings, eh?"

"Absolutely. Happy endings. It's why we do this, isn't it?"

"We live in hope," Trevena said. He pulled on his jacket and turned to leave.

"You know where I am, Phil," Doctor Mocking said. He was silhouetted in the sunlight slanting in through the French windows. Trevena couldn't see his face. "Any time."

Trevena left the office and went to work.